BLUE

A NOVEL

by
Kayce Stevens Hughlett

BQB

Georgia

Published in the United States by BQB
(Boutique of Quality Books Publishing Company)
www.bqbpublishing.com

Printed in the United States of America

ISBN 978-1-939371-72-0 (p)
ISBN 978-1-939371-73-7 (e)

Library of Congress Control Number: 2015904507

Book design by Robin Krauss, www.bookformatters.com
Cover illustration by Debbie Patrk Vinyard

Also by Kayce Stevens Hughlett

As I Lay Pondering: daily invitations to live a transformed life, 2012

Blue is the only color which maintains its own character in all its tones . . . it will always stay blue.

Raoul Dufy
French artist (1877–1953)

PART ONE

PART
ONE

DAISY

Blue. Everywhere. As the dawn light began to flicker through her sable-tinted lashes, all Daisy could see or sense was the color blue. Faint shadows distinguished themselves, and as her eyes adjusted, she began to notice shades of green moving toward black with strands of deep violet woven within. Aqua. Amethyst. Navy almost turned to black. The colors enveloped her vision. The primary variation in hue was between multiple shades of sapphire. No white or distinct light. It was like her corneas were covered in some outrageous version of that awful plastic wrap that came in different colors and made your food look anything but appealing.

Slowly, she turned her head from side to side, hoping for a different view. Nada. Nothing. Zip. Only the changing shades of blue appeared in her vision. It was mildly disconcerting and slightly alarming. She wondered what could possibly have happened since she'd last opened her eyes.

Twilight shone ever so slightly as her eyes adjusted to the new sight. Her senses expanded until she felt a light touch she could only describe as more blue. It whispered to her heart. Her olfactory sense began to twitch with a hint of an aviary-like scent. Her nose crinkled and her thoughts ran rampant. *What's happening here? It feels like a dream, but I can smell it. And taste it and hear it. Weird!* The beating of her heart thrummed in response.

Daisy imagined rubbing her taste buds against the scene that enveloped her: this object of blue with shadings of violet, green, and black. Brown, too, she noticed on another round of observation. Her mouth watered and her tongue thrust outward, struggling for momentum toward any point of contact. Something tacky brushed against it and stuck to the sparse moisture. *Eww. What is that?*

She bristled at the gummy touch, but her instincts were tinged with an element of excitement and extreme curiosity. Somehow, she knew this wasn't a tragic event. Nevertheless, the ability to experience only shades of blue was not how she'd ever imagined her day unfolding.

"Hmmm. Whaddya do when you can only see blue?" she mumbled aloud.

What if the sky has fallen and this is the result? What if I had a brain aneurysm and my vision is messed up? What if I stay like this forever? Would that be so bad? I do like the color blue. Except it's only the color—nothing else. Only that weird hint of something, I don't know what. Maybe this is what blind looks like?

So it went for a while: the wondering and musing, approaching panic and calming down again, as Daisy vacillated between amusement and concern. Finally, exhausted from her mental gymnastics, she closed her eyes and drifted back to sleep.

MONICA

"Does Your Name Fit?" Monica read the headline aloud. *Yes. No. I don't know.* She sighed, wagging her head from side to side. *Does it even really matter?*

She sat alone at her kitchen table reading a survey in *Ladies Home Journal*, the kind she usually skimmed over because they were too personal or ridiculous to give merit. Moving her gaze away from the magazine, she examined the teacup in her hand as if it might hold the answer to the question. *Does Your Name Fit?*

The first syllable of her name was *"mon,"* the French masculine possessive. *Masculine possessive? Ha.* She shuddered at the thought.

"I" was the fourth letter of her name. "I lost myself a long time ago, didn't I?" This time she spoke to the slice of toast between her fingers. She observed the bread like a scientist, thought about how "I" united with a masculine possessive, and then took a voracious bite out of her crusty confidante.

Munching away, she considered the last two letters, "CA." California? No. She'd never been south of Portland. Cats Anonymous? It sounded like a support group for octogenarian women with feline-infested homes. At this particular moment, she was grateful for the allergies that would save her from becoming a pledging member of the CA society she'd just envisioned.

Ça? There, or that? Again, she was thinking in French. She wondered if she would ever make that journey across the ocean.

Monica tucked her bobbed auburn hair behind her ear, pushed her heavy-framed glasses up on her nose, and turned her attention back to the survey.

Question #1: *If you could name yourself at this moment, what would your name be?*

Pathetic, forty-three-year-old spinster. It wasn't the first time this self-flagellating image had popped into her mind. Her shoulders slumped and her spine curled inward as she dropped the magazine onto the table.

Rename Yourself, beckoned the glossy image on the page. *Be Who You Are Destined to Be.*

"Oh, please," she groaned. "I tried reinventing myself once, didn't I? Look where that got me."

Does Your Name Fit? The magazine was relentless.

M.O.N.I.C.A. She sounded out each letter inside her mind. *Possessed by a man. I am that. Evidently, it does fit.* She sighed as her thoughts drifted back to another place and the time of her so-called reinvention.

IZABEL

"Puuuussshhhh, Shannon. Come on, honey. You can do this. One more good one and you'll be holding that beautiful baby girl in your arms."

"Tired, Izzy. Can't."

"Come on, sweet woman. You know we talked about this. It's always hardest before the beauty arrives." Izabel squeezed Shannon's hand and leaned in with her best "doula" tone.

"Oh, cut the crap! Put yourself in my place and then tell me 'It's beauty.' It feels like Farmer Ryan's calf is trying to push its way out!"

"Now, Shannon honey, you know Farmer Ryan has the sweetest calves on the island," Izabel purred. "Give us one more strong push, okay?" She stroked the laboring mother's forehead, then bent over, wincing, as a rogue contraction gripped her own belly.

"No way! Grrrrrr . . . oowwwwwww . . . eeeeeeeeee . . . "

"I see the head, Shannon," announced the midwife, Jaylene.

"Push, sweetie," Izabel offered through her own shortened breath.

"Yoooowwwwwww . . . eeeeeeeee . . . ooooooohhhhh!"

"Here's the shoulders. You're doing great. Keep it up."

"Hooooooooly cooowwwwww!"

"And here's our girl!" Jaylene announced.

"Way to go, Shannon. Oh, honey, this little angel looks just like her beautiful mama. Come on, Jaylene, hand the baby over to Shannon."

"Hold your horses, Izzy. Give me a minute to clean the mucus out of her nose and cut the cord. Hey, Papa Roy, you want to do the honors?"

Roy, the only man in the room, blinked as if he were the one who'd just emerged from the birth canal.

"Are you okay, Roy? Do you need to sit down?" Izabel looked at him with concern.

"Um. I think maybe I just need a bowl of cereal." Roy turned his glazed eyes away from the women and staggered toward the kitchen.

"Cereal?" Jaylene and Izabel lifted their eyebrows and spoke in unison, but Roy was long gone.

"He always eats cereal when he's stressed out," Shannon murmured, as she reached toward the infant Jaylene had swaddled in a cotton blanket. "It's a miracle we have any left in the house after the labor I've had."

"Hey, I heard that," Roy said as he reentered the room, holding a soupspoon and a large mixing bowl filled with Cheerios.

Izabel patted him on the shoulder. "No offense, but your wife did a bang-up job with the delivery. My hunch is she could use a few Cheerios herself."

Roy hung his head sheepishly, perched on the edge of the bed next to his wife, and offered her his cereal-filled spoon.

"My hero," the contented mom said, beaming.

Izabel and Jaylene moved about the room, tidying up extra blankets and pillows, storing Jaylene's medical instruments in her tapestry satchel, and changing the sheets of the bed while the new family cuddled on the living room sofa.

"So, are you all set now, Shannon?" Izabel asked.

The new mother nodded, focusing her dreamy gaze on the tiny infant nuzzled against her chest.

"Think you've got a handle on breastfeeding and your man Roy can stay upright for a while?"

"Oh, she's an angel, Izzy, and Roy's more helpful than he looks. I'm pretty sure we'll all be okay, especially since you're close by."

"I'm just a phone call away if you need me. Now you three snuggle up and get some rest. It's hard work getting born."

"Thanks for everything, Iz. You're the best doula on Orcas Island."

"Thanks, honey. I'll take that as a compliment, even though you know I'm the *only* doula on this island, unless you count Farmer Ryan's wife," Izabel replied, with a twinkle in her eye. "I'm going to take off now. You call me if that little angel gives you any trouble. I'll check back with you in a day or two unless I hear otherwise. Love you guys!"

"We love you, too, Izzy. And thanks again!"

— — —

It had been a long night helping the Andersons birth their baby girl. Any other person would have been exhausted and ready to sleep for hours, but not Izabel. She was always exhilarated after assisting with a birth, although today she felt a twinge of melancholy that she didn't understand. Shaking it off, she exited the shake-shingled cottage and went to the side of the house, where she'd left Rosie, her bicycle, leaning against the clapboard shingles.

Her strawberry blonde hair fell in soft ringlets to her narrow waist. Her white embroidered peasant top flowed over the camisole she wore beneath it. Last night, she'd foregone her usual African print skirt for narrow capris that skimmed her slim yet curved hips. Her features tended more toward quirky than classic, but overall she was a striking presence. Men adored her, and in the normal scheme of things, women would have despised her, but her ethereal spirit and genuine love of others could not be ignored. Everyone on the island seemed to like Izabel Nivel: doula, artist, yogini, and cyclist.

"Hello Rosie." She smiled and her eyes brightened as she greeted her two-wheeled companion.

Rosie, the current love of Izabel's life, was an extravagant gift from a grateful client: two wheels of streamlined grace and beauty. The color of a clear and unclouded sky, her official hue was called azure, a word that made Izabel's heart purr whenever she said it out loud. The three-speed wonder shifted gears automatically on the rolling hills of Orcas Island and left its rider feeling like she was sailing atop cotton puffs in the sky.

"What's it going to be, Rosie? A ride through the countryside or coffee at Brooke's before we head home?" Izabel's stomach rumbled and she put her hand on it, a brief flash of concern crossing her face. Shaking her head as if to clear it, she returned her attention to Rosie. "Coffee, you think? Me too. Brooke's it is."

With that decision, Izabel and Rosie exited the Andersons's front yard and headed west toward Deer Harbor.

MONICA

Breathe, Monica thought as she closed the door to her unoccupied office behind her. Releasing her typically erect posture, she slumped into the cheap, padded chair and wheeled herself to face the metal and faux-wood desk. Reaching to straighten the plaque near the front of her workspace, she impulsively turned it around to read: *Assistant Director of Patient Affairs.*

What the heck does that even mean? She shook her head and closed her eyes in disgust. *It sounds like the patients need help directing their illicit and nonexistent love lives.*

Pushing her heavy-framed glasses higher up her upturned nose and tucking a stray strand of hair behind her ear, she freed a deep sigh from her chest. The only "affairs" she'd been directing today were the persistent complaints from a visiting daughter-in-law. The brash woman from Orcas Island had asserted that her mother-in-law's closet was filled with indistinguishable KMart clothes instead of the designer tracksuits she'd provided for her mentally deteriorating in-law.

Monica had pasted a look of compassion on her face and explained for the nth time about one resident's penchant for "shopping" in other patients' closets. But the woman had been more concerned that her mother-in-law was dressed shabbily rather than the potentially serious issue of one resident's stealing other people's possessions.

Shortly after breakfast, the cockatiel had escaped from its cage in the game room. This had caused a ruckus only Monica could quell, by tossing her sweater over the quivering bird and returning it to its safe haven. During the commotion, patients had watched from wheelchairs and wrung their hands, while others had shouted encouragement in rasping voices. Moments later, as she'd continued her rounds, she'd heard the hullabaloo rise again, announcing that the bird was once more flying free.

Monica had also wasted a serious chunk of time trying to convince Mrs. Johnson, another resident, that she wasn't her daughter Ethel. Monica berated herself for the uncharacteristic need to argue the moot point. She knew from years of experience that there was no derailing Alzheimer's patients' train of thought once they had the track programmed for a destination.

Monica had tried everything she knew to defuse the situation: nodding in agreement, evasion tactics, pretending she didn't hear the conversation, and (the least helpful) explaining that Ethel had actually died several years before. This strategy had set Mrs. Johnson weeping until one of the nurses was able to console her.

Monica had continued on her rounds and altered her customary path throughout the Center, hoping to steer clear of Mrs. Johnson's unyielding pursuit, but it was as if Monica had been tagged with a homing device and Mrs. Johnson held the control. Instead of a woman with deteriorating mental capacities, the patient had taken on the persona of a diabolical tracker. If Monica had had a bounty on her head, Mrs. Johnson would certainly have collected the prize. *If she tells me one more time I'm the spitting image of her dear daughter Ethel, I'll scream bloody murder!* Monica thought.

Monica's patent reserved manner and painstaking attention to detail normally fit with the tasks required of her at Stratford Estates Memory Care Facility. Today, however, she found herself muttering under her breath, exasperated with the tidy office she called her sanctuary, and wanting to pummel sweet old Mrs. Johnson for initiating an elaborate game of hide and seek for the past few hours.

How had this come to be her life? Listening to moderately functioning Alzheimer's patients loop their ingrained stories through an auto-rewind every fifteen minutes, trapping elusive cockatiels, and wanting to dive under her perfectly ordered desk when anyone approached the door?

A flash of her days at Briar Cliff College rose in her mind. She smiled as she remembered her English Lit studies. What would her favorite heroine do in this situation? Monica found slight comfort in imagining herself at the center of an Elizabethan tragedy, instead of a modern-day woman stuck in a soul-sucking job and lonely existence.

I'm only forty-three. There could still be time for me. I'm supposed to be somewhere, anywhere else, doing anything but being a pitiful director of patient affairs. Oh hell, not even director, just a lame-o assistant director. Oh God, help me!

KNOCK. KNOCK.

Monica jumped as she heard the sharp tapping on the door. Reflexively, she smoothed her freshly cut hair and waited for someone to enter, until she remembered that she'd locked the door when she slipped behind it moments ago.

"Monica? Monica, honey? Are you in there?" Mrs. Johnson cooed from the other side of the door.

"Breathe," Monica whispered to herself, before responding. "Yes, Mrs. Johnson. How may I help you?"

"Someone let the birdie out of its cage and it's making horrible noises."

Again. "Okay. I'll be right there," she said, as breezily as she could manage.

Like a soldier preparing for battle, Monica adorned her face with the armor of a good girl smile, straightened her weary shoulders, and opened the door of her refuge. Mrs. Johnson stood like a sentry guarding the passage. A helmet of salon-teased bluish hair topped her head, and turned-up crimson lips punctuated her lined face.

"Ethel? Is that you?" she whispered, tender hope in her voice.

"No, ma'am. It's me. Monica."

"Monica? Oh, yes." Mrs. Johnson shook her head as if waking from a dream. "Have I ever told you that you're the spitting image of my daughter Ethel?"

Monica thought: *Dear Lord, I'm living in the morning that won't end.*

— — —

As she drove south on Greenwood Avenue after leaving Stratford Estates for the night, Monica heard her stomach rumble. She knew she should stop by Northwest Hospital and check in, but today had been interminable with the escaping birds, ranting daughters, and erratic patients. She couldn't face seeing the night nurse on call, who would only shake her head with downcast eyes and say, "No change."

No change. It seemed as though they were all stuck in the same endless loop. Monica thought about her own perpetual days of drudgery and boredom. Her days were so regimented it wasn't even funny. She was up at six each morning, followed by a quick shower and twenty minutes of yoga, if there was time. Special K, a banana, and skim milk for breakfast. An autopilot drive to Stratford Estates, where she filled the mornings with staff meetings, mounds of paperwork, and the same conversations dozens of times over with the clients.

Lunch consisted of Caesar salad with skinless chicken breast, if she managed to stop for lunch at all. More of the morning's blandness continued throughout the afternoon. Her norm was working past dinnertime until she decided to move the monotony from one space to the next.

The most hopeless hours of her day came when she stopped by the hospital and sat in silence next to the unresponsive figure until she could cope no longer. Then she'd make the autopilot drive home to her empty duplex near Holman Road.

That night, after arriving home bleary-eyed at 9 p.m., Monica turned on the television, put a Lean Cuisine in the microwave, and poured a glass of Two Buck Chuck wine from Trader Joe's. Tonight she felt like she could use a little indulgence. Instead of setting her place at the table, she took her food and wine and climbed into bed with the remote control.

She considered that she really was no different from Mrs. Johnson. The main difference between the two of them was that Mrs. Johnson seemed to be enjoying her life, or was at least oblivious to the dull repetitiveness of it all, whereas Monica was becoming acutely more aware of her own mortality with each passing day. She tried to put the depressing thought out of her head, flipped through a dozen channels, and watched mindlessly until she fell asleep during *The Daily Show*.

— — —

The next morning, as Monica headed toward her car with slumped shoulders and her gaze focused on the sidewalk, she cringed at the sudden sound of her neighbor's voice.

"Hey, Monica! Hey, how are ya?"

Oh no, Monica silently swore under her breath. *Please go away.*

"I hate to be the bearer of bad news, but something got ahold of one of

those wild cats from the park and left it on your driveway. It's dead, ya know?"
The woman scrunched her mustached upper lip to her nose and shook her
head. "I would've had Matt take care of it, but he's gone off huntin' this week."

Monica turned her deadpan face toward her well-meaning neighbor, Jenny.
The woman had thinning hair plastered to her head and a strange rosacea-like
rash sprinkled across her left cheek. She couldn't have been more than thirty-
five, based on all the little kids running around her yard, but her weathered
skin and stooped form spoke of someone who'd lived a harder life than many
of the patients at Stratford Estates.

Monica stepped closer to where Jenny pointed. A lifeless creature sprawled,
limbs askew, on the cracked concrete path less than ten feet from her front
door. Just this past weekend she'd meticulously replanted her flowerpots in an
effort to brighten the appearance of the sixties-style duplex. The animal's once-
gray fur was plastered to its skin by blood from a gaping wound in its throat.
Its body was contorted, with feet splayed out as if there were no bones inside,
and bright red entrails poured from a hole in its stomach.

Monica lifted her hand to cover her mouth and nose, and swallowed hard
as her gag reflex jerked like a caged animal. *A cat's rage is beautiful, burning
with pure cat flame . . . William S. Burroughs.*

"No. No. *No.* I can't take this! Why does everything die?" The words poured
out from behind her hand.

Jenny shifted from foot to foot, questioning furrows forming on her brow.
"Like I said, sorry to be the bearer of bad news. You want me to go fetch a
shovel from my storage shed?"

Jenny's earnest, twanging voice made Monica cringe. She was starting to
feel ungrateful, because Jenny was only trying to help. But the thoughts came
anyway: *If she'd wanted to be really helpful, she could have taken care of the cat
when she found it instead of leaving it for me to deal with.*

Monica turned toward Jenny, squaring her shoulders in an attempt to gain
her composure. Behind her fixed façade, her mind went wild. *What do you do
with a dead cat in the middle of the city, for Christ's sake? Call Animal Control?
Toss it in the garbage bin? Is that even legal? Bury it? Maybe set up a bonfire and
have a private cremation? Offer a royal ceremony for the dead? Oh geez, I'm
losing my grip. Hold on, Monica. It's going to be okay.*

Monica believed that if you just did the right thing, everything would be fine. She couldn't fall asleep at night if there were dirty dishes in the sink, and she wanted to send apology notes to the city hall if she accidentally ran a red light. At work she filed her reports on time and kept her desk neat and orderly. Her home was the picture of perfection, even if it was a little shabby around the edges. A place for everything and everything in its place. There was no place for a dead cat in her tidy world. This was messy, disgusting, and more than a little disturbing. Not orderly at all.

On the outside, Monica was the picture of a professional woman heading to work: tidy auburn hair, black button-down shirtdress, sensible one-inch pumps. Inside, however, she felt like the cat raging in her last moments before death: fur flying, teeth barred, and insides tumbling out. A persistent gnawing in her gut murmured that this was *not* about the cat.

"Shovel? You want me to fetch it now?" Jenny offered again.

DAISY

Daisy began to stir groggily, remembering the weird dream she'd experienced earlier. Whether hours or days had passed, she couldn't tell. She smiled at the ridiculous notion that the sky had fallen and the whole world had been wrapped in blue. As she stretched her arms, feeling the warmth of waking up, she pretended she was in high school gym class, getting ready for the next exercise.

With blood flowing through her youthful body, she purred like a sanguine and content cat, until the moment she opened her eyes. Blue. Everywhere blue. Her vision was still sheathed in blue-tinted plastic wrap.

She jerked up to a seated position, her alarm intensifying as her senses kicked into overdrive. Vision was a bust. She still couldn't see anything but blue. She strained her ears and thought she detected something that sounded like a pigeon cooing. The rapid pounding was, no doubt, her own heart. It felt like it might try to escape from the center of her chest.

Her olfactory sense again noticed something slightly bird-like. It was strange and foreign. Mystified, she began to stretch her arms and legs, and wiggle her fingers to see if there was anything she could touch or feel. Smoothness. *Nice.* Something soft. *Ouch!* Something pinpricked her finger. Since her tongue had offered the most tangible clue before—the tacky thing—Daisy decided to try that again.

Gingerly her tongue peeked out from its hiding place inside her mouth. At first, it met only air. Then, there it was again, the thing that made her want to rub her tongue against her teeth and pucker her lips and spit. *What the heck is going on? Is this for real? Clearly, I'm not dreaming.*

Her tongue was attached to something plume-like and she couldn't shake it loose. Her mind flew in a hundred different directions, none of them making sense, until finally reality came into focus. She was stuck to what appeared to be a feather, and not just any feather, but a resplendent peacock feather of brilliant cobalt.

"Pffft. Pffft," she sputtered as she tried to disengage herself from the cottony surface. She shook loose and broke free only to discover herself eye to eye with the bird in question: a royal peacock of grand stature.

Holding her gaze with his crystal-clear eyes, the peacock kept Daisy immobile with a mere twinkle. As her own vision came more clearly into focus, she began to distinguish other shades of color she hadn't been able to see when she'd been buried inside the nest of his feathers.

Blue turned to green that moved toward black and back again. There were two parallel lines of ivory feathers on either side of the glistening eye, and they folded seamlessly into the pointed beak that punctuated the graceful head. Daisy found herself in a state of spellbound fascination. She was so caught up in the beauty and grandeur of this elegant creature that she forgot to be either confused or frightened. Relaxing slightly, she continued staring at this glorious phenomenon that she was suspended upon.

"Hello." The fabulous beast spoke with elegance and a voice of kind authority. Astounded by that single word, Daisy tumbled from her perch near the base of his neck (it must have been at least five feet long) and landed with a thud on the earth.

"Goodness gracious, my dear. Are you all right?" the peacock queried.

"What's happening to me?"

"Well, it appears that you've taken a fall. I'll ask again, are you all right?"

"*All right?* Are you kidding me? I'm talking to a giant peacock! How could I possibly be all right? I'm obviously going crazy, and you're not helping!" Daisy flapped her arms like an awkward baby bird, and her bottom burrowed into the mossy blue ground beneath her.

"Well then, please let me know how I might be of assistance and I'll do my best to comply."

"Stop talking!" Daisy closed her eyes tightly and shook her head, golden hair flying, before sneaking another peek at the animal. "You're still here? I thought you were a dream or something. What is going on?"

"May I please speak now?"

"What?"

"Well, when I asked how I could be of assistance, you told me to stop talking. You must realize, however, that it's impossible for me to answer your questions if I can't speak. My goal is to help you in the best way possible, so do you want me to talk or not?" The bird tilted his head toward the girl.

"Oh geez. Clearly you're able to talk whether I want you to or not, but I appreciate you being so considerate. I'm sorry for yelling, please go on. I really need to know what's going on here. Let's start with, where the heck am I?"

IZABEL

As Izabel and Rosie made their way along the winding roads between the Andersons's place and Deer Harbor, Izabel tried to let the exhaustion of the previous day and night drift away. She tried to use her visualization techniques to imagine that her melancholy thoughts were like the passing scenery, here one moment and gone the next, but the method was only a stark reminder of the rattling sensation she was trying to loosen.

Cruising along the two-lane road, wavy hair flying behind her and strong legs maintaining a steady rhythm both uphill and downhill, she looked like a modern-day storybook character: Little Red Riding Hood without the cape, perhaps, or Snow White floating through the forest in capris and Keds. One almost expected birds to land on her shoulder or deer to rise up and wave good morning as she passed by.

Izabel was known throughout the island for her calm presence and bold artistic flair. In many ways, she'd become an urban legend (even though Orcas Island could scarcely be called "urban") since she'd arrived out of the blue nearly twenty years earlier. Tourists visiting the island had been known to inquire at local establishments about the ethereal creature they'd seen pedaling through the rolling countryside and on deserted beach roads.

While Rosie was a new acquisition, Izabel had used a bicycle as her primary form of transportation for as long as she'd lived on the island. Even though the local doctor and sheriff often reminded her of the dangers of riding helmet-free, she couldn't bring herself to strap on one of those confining contraptions. She loved the way the breeze blew through her hair and tickled the tips of her ears. It might have been only in her imagination, but she was quite certain that her thoughts flowed more freely when they weren't trapped inside a hard plastic dome. *So why aren't they flowing today?* she wondered.

Since becoming a doula nearly fifteen years ago, she had helped deliver more than a hundred babies, and nothing like this morning had ever happened to her. During those final minutes of labor when Shannon shouted, "Put yourself in my place and then tell me it's beauty!", Izabel had felt as though she had switched bodies with Shannon and become the one giving birth.

Even though she was childless, she'd felt her womb tighten along with Shannon's, experiencing a mirrored urge to grimace and growl like a banshee. For a brief moment, *push* had been the only thing she could think and feel. The impulse lasted less than a second, so briefly, in fact, that she hadn't remembered it until she'd climbed onto Rosie twenty minutes ago and started up the hill.

Weird, she thought. *I must be starting to over-identify with my birthing mothers.*

HOOOOOONNNNNNKKKKKKKK!!

Izabel realized, too late, that she had moved off the shoulder of the road and drifted near the yellow dotted line in the center of the thoroughfare.

"Geez, Izzy. Are you trying to get yourself killed?" yelled Hank, the island handyman, as he pulled his old beater truck to the side of the road.

"Sorry, Hank. I must've drifted off."

"You gotta watch it around here, Iz. I know to keep an eye out for cyclists and deer and stuff, but if I'd been a rubber-neckin' tourist coming 'round that corner, you'd've been a goner for sure."

"I know. I know, Hank. I'll be more careful. I guess it was a longer night than I thought. Hey, did you know the Andersons have a new baby girl? She's a real beauty."

"Another girl? This island's gettin' overrun with those little beauties you keep deliverin'. Where ya headed now?"

"Oh, I was going to Deer Harbor for some coffee, but maybe I'll just head home and get some sleep instead."

"Let's put Rosie in the back and I'll take ya home. Not sure it's safe to keep you on the road this morning." Hank winked.

Too weary and shaken to pedal all the way home, Izabel nodded and let Hank toss her bike in the back of his dilapidated Ford.

"Be careful with Rosie now, Hank. She's not much for lying on her side," she teased him, with a wilted smile.

MONICA

It was Monica's turn to monitor the Saturday evening shift. She was grateful for the justification to be busy on what most unattached people of a certain age considered "date night." With the excuse of work, she'd be off the hook for making up any explanation about what she'd done during her off time.

Monica hated weekends. When it came right down to it, Monica pretty much detested life in general these days. What did she have to look forward to? Frozen TV dinners and *Late Night with Jon Stewart*? Monotonous shifts with memory care patients? Somewhere along the way, her life had taken a sharp turn from dull to dead end, and she had no idea how she was going to back herself out of it. At times like this, she wasn't sure if she had the energy to even try.

— — —

In the Stratford Estates's community center, things were ramping up. It was the twilight hour, perhaps better described as the twilight zone. During the late afternoon, until dinner was served, the residents often went through major personality swings, and the staff stood on high alert for extreme behaviors. Monica's job tonight was to make sure nothing untoward happened, like a few years ago when the supervisor had gone off her post during the twilight hour and the male tenants had organized a boxing event in the downstairs laundry room. One of the cleaning people had found about fifteen residents gathered around a makeshift boxing ring, cheering and hooting and hollering while two male octogenarians took swings at each other with oven mitt-clad hands. Fortunately, no one had been seriously hurt, but since that time, the supervision duties were observed more diligently.

"What were you thinking?" the supervisor on call had inquired of the fight club members.

"We needed to feel alive," they had responded. Monica knew exactly what they meant. She wished she had the gumption to do something as brave as they had.

As Monica entered the community center, she spotted the once-dashing Mr. Louden, picking up speed with the aid of his walker as he chased Mrs. Johnson around the lounge area and tried to pinch her sagging behind. His primary challenge was that in order to have a free hand to reach her, he had to stop his walker, at which point his prey scuttled further ahead.

Mrs. Johnson looked flushed with girlish anticipation. She glanced coquettishly over her shoulder, somehow giving the illusion of scurrying away from her suitor. Even in her fog of dementia, she always remembered to apply lipstick. Tonight it was a brilliant shade of red. No doubt Mr. Louden was in high hopes that those scarlet lips would soon be pressed against his. That is, once he chased her down and held her in his once-muscular arms, now turned spindly.

On the couch nearby sat a whisper of a woman: Edna, curled up with a ragged baby doll. "Ice cream," she murmured. "We want ice cream." Her eyes brightened as she saw Monica. She patted the seat next to her, beckoning Monica to join her and the doll. Monica was aware of this subterfuge and normally avoided moving toward Edna's lure. For some reason, however, tonight her resolve wasn't firm. She collapsed on the worn divan next to the child woman.

As soon as Monica was within reach, Edna released the baby doll with one hand and latched onto Monica's arm with frail, claw-like digits.

"Ice cream," she pleaded as she looked directly into Monica's eyes, her sharp grip tightening. "We want ice cream."

Monica knew better than to try reasoning with Edna, but she responded. "Edna, you know we don't have ice cream at this time of day."

"Ice cream," came Edna's mournful response, the increasing grip on Monica's arm defying the frail appearance of the small bird-like woman.

Monica's attention had only been turned away from the group for a minute or so. She looked up just in time to see Mr. Louden push his walker out of the way and dive headlong toward Mrs. Johnson's waist. Mrs. Johnson tittered like a middle school girl and lithely sidestepped the advance, causing Mr. Louden to grasp only air and fall headfirst into the table at the end of the couch.

Edna, nonplussed, continued her mantra, "Ice cream. We want ice cream."

At the same moment, Mr. Forbes yelled: "*Fire!*"

Pandemonium broke out from all corners of the room as Monica tried to extract herself from Edna's death grip. Blood poured from Mr. Louden's head, one of those gushing, non-threatening surface wounds. Mrs. Johnson continued to circle around the room, giggling all the way. Mr. Forbes climbed on a nearby chair, shouting about the imaginary fire.

"Mr. Forbes, get down, please! You'll hurt yourself." Monica tried to put an air of authority into her voice. "Edna, let go right now."

The residents weren't listening. The chaos carried on: thumb-sucking, wailing, and all variety of hilarity. One man sat in the corner gently rocking to and fro, calling for his mama. Edna was relentless in her cry for ice cream, and even as the noise in the room intensified, she maintained her steady mantra and her ironclad grip on Monica.

Chairs were knocked over. The man in the corner wet his pants. Blood dripped from Mr. Louden's wound onto the carpet. A woman began to cry hysterically and scream: "Dead! Dead! We're all dead!"

Monica's eyes darted wildly around the room as she finally yanked her arm free, shaking her captor like fresh sheets. Edna, unfazed, quietly reattached to her doll and disappeared into the sofa's corner. Monica reached for the alert button in her pocket just as Mrs. Johnson strolled up to her and peered directly into her eyes.

"Hi, honey. Do you know you're the spitting image of my daughter Ethel?"

With that single sentence, the room went dark and the pandemonium ended for Monica.

DAISY

Daisy's host, the peacock, looked at her with wise eyes and an air of gentle compassion. "Where are you? Well, that, my dear, has a simple answer. You're in the land of Tausi." He swept his elongated neck through the air, inviting her to take in the brilliant landscape that surrounded them. To Daisy's left, pale blue sand stretched for miles along a Caribbean-blue expanse of water. To her right was a forest filled with blue-tinted vegetation, such as ten-foot tall navy-blue mushrooms with white polka dots. Aqua palm trees towered alongside classic evergreens. Blue magnolia blossoms floated above the mossy ground where Daisy pushed herself to stand up.

"Tausi?" Daisy scrunched her forehead into a flattened question mark. "I've never heard of it, but then again I've never heard of talking peacocks."

"There's no reason you would have known about either. Unless, of course, you speak Swahili, or you've ventured beyond the limits of your rational mind in the past." Her host spoke with a regal air that both welcomed and sobered her.

"Well, I don't speak Swahili. And while I *can* say I've felt a little crazy before, it's nothing compared to this, ginormous talking peacocks and blue stuff everywhere. And what's Swahili got to do with anything?"

"Swahili is the birth language of Tausi, which is the word for *peacock* when translated into your English language. In other words, Swahili is the original language of the peacock." The bird nodded with authority.

"Um, right. I get the translation thing, but since when did peacocks even begin to talk? And why would Swahili be their language? I mean, aren't peacocks from India or someplace like that?" Daisy remembered that fact from visiting the zoo with her mother.

"Very well considered, my dear. By the way, what *is* your name? I could keep calling you 'dear' and the like, but it seems as though we might be together for a while and I'd prefer to be polite and use your given name. Which is?"

"Daisy. What do you mean, we're going to be together for a while? I'm not sure I like the sound of that." She took a step away from the bird.

"Now, now, Miss Daisy, don't get all concerned. Tausi is really a lovely place to be stranded, if one *must* be stranded."

"Stranded? What do you mean, *stranded?* I'm still not sure this isn't some crazy dream or a figment of my imagination." Daisy began to pace back and forth in front of the peacock while furtively glancing around.

"Regardless, wouldn't it be more pleasant to simply be curious and enjoy your surroundings rather than battling to get back to somewhere you don't even like?"

"How do you know I don't like where I'm from? As a matter of fact, how do you know so much about me? This is confusing. You seem to know lots of things, but you didn't even know my name. Oh, and speaking of that, please don't call me Miss Daisy. It makes me feel like I'm an old Southern lady who needs a chauffeur." She scrunched her nose in distaste.

"Of course, Mi . . . my apologies. Of course, Daisy. As for what I know and what I don't know, it's all quite basic. People typically arrive here for similar reasons, like not being happy in their original environments, so it's easy to assume you're here for an analogous purpose. Theoretically I'm not psychic, so discerning your name falls out of my normal capacity."

Daisy furrowed her brow again. Just as she was about to dive back into her line of questioning, a movement in the forest's sun-dappled undergrowth caught her attention.

"Something moved over there." She jumped backward a few paces. "Are we safe here?"

"Certainly, we're safe," the peacock responded. "At least, on this side of the island," he whispered under his breath.

"I guess I'll have to trust you on that one." Daisy squinted her eyes.

"Oh you can trust Albert unequivocally," came a voice from the underbrush.

"Who said that? And who's Albert?"

"I said it," replied the voice, "and Sir Albert is your royal host there."

"Sir Albert?" Daisy cocked an eyebrow at the peacock. The white angles on the sides of his face turned a blushing shade of pink under her gaze. The color rose from the base of the white feathers and radiated to the tips of their once ivory expanse. Daisy had never seen feathers change color before. It was quite magical.

"Shhh, Chauncey. You know I don't like to behave all high and mighty with our new guests."

"Whatever," replied the voice, as its source emerged from the underbrush.

At Daisy's eye-level appeared the face of a giraffe, but unless the beast was a giraffe less than five feet tall, something was terribly amiss. What came next was a horse-like neck, fuchsia in hue. As Daisy's confusion grew, a green and white zebra's leg stepped its way into the clearing.

"What the heck?" Daisy gasped. The creature opened its mouth and out swung a tongue long enough to clean out his own ears.

While the length of the tongue was bewildering in itself, a reminder of how she'd started this day surged through her mind. She had never witnessed anything quite like this, although her list of "firsts" was swiftly expanding. The exaggerated tongue attached to this patchwork giraffe-horse-zebra was astonishing on its own, but instead of a normal pinked-up tint, the attachment extending from Chauncey's mouth revealed a bright shade of azure blue.

Blue! What is it with this place and the color blue?

MONICA

Monica winced at the ache in her temples and opened her eyes. The not-quite-white, not-exactly-gray ceiling and recessed fluorescent lighting let her know she wasn't at home, and neither was she at Stratford Estates.

Stratford Estates? Oh my God. What happened? The last thing she remembered was Mr. Forbes yelling fire.

A sharp pain pierced her skull from temple to temple and she closed her eyes again, trying to make the throbbing lessen. No such luck. Gingerly opening her eyes again, she brought her gaze downward from the corner of the ceiling and noticed a large metal clock with a white face and black hands that pointed to 8:52. *Morning or night?* she wondered. *Where am I?*

"Well, look who's awake. Good morning, Ms. Levin. How are we feeling today?" chirped a nurse in Minnie Mouse scrubs who was leaning over her.

"Where am I?"

"You're at Northwest Hospital, honey. Don't you remember?"

"How long have I been here?"

"Hmm. Let me think. You came in Saturday night and it's Monday morning. So, oh, let's see, that'd be about thirty-six hours."

"Thirty-six hours? What happened?" Monica's head throbbed as she struggled to remember the last day and a half.

"From what I heard, there was quite a lot going on at Stratford Estates on Saturday ni—"

"Nurse Simmons, that will be all for now," spoke a dark-haired man as he entered the room.

"Yes, Dr. Oliver. I'm glad you're awake, Ms. Levin," the nurse murmured quietly, before departing the room like a shamed puppy.

"Good morning, Ms. Levin. I'm Dr. Oliver. How are you feeling today?" The man's tone, bright and professional, exuded the understated confidence of someone used to being in charge.

Monica gaped open-mouthed at the handsome doctor who bore a striking resemblance to McDreamy from *Grey's Anatomy*, all wavy hair and dimpled smile. She squirmed under the itchy hospital sheets and reached to smooth her scrambled hair into place.

"I, uh . . . my head hurts."

"On a scale of one to ten, how severe is the pain?"

"A six, maybe?" she answered. She tugged at the open back of her hospital gown, even though it was hidden beneath the sheets.

"Is there something unsatisfactory with your bed, Ms. Levin?"

"Huh? Oh no, I'm just not used to sleeping in strange beds." She immediately felt the color creeping up her neck toward her cheeks. Reaching toward the forming rash on her chest, she scratched distractedly at her clavicle.

"Are you experiencing itching or discomfort? It looks like there's a rash on your chest I hadn't noticed before."

"Oh, that? It's nothing really. It just happens sometimes."

"Could you be more precise about what those times are?"

Seriously? Is he trying to torture me or is he totally oblivious to how gorgeous he is? "Sometimes when I get nervous, it happens. It's kind of like a blush that starts at my chest. It'll go away in a few minutes." *As soon as you leave, no doubt.* Monica wished she could pull the covers over her head without appearing foolish.

Mercifully, Dr. Oliver was the picture of diplomacy. If he knew he was the cause of her increasing color, he never let on. "You don't appear to have a fever. I'll have Nurse Simmons keep an eye on it, just to make sure we're not dealing with anything more severe."

"Thank you. So, Doctor, why *am* I here? The last thing I remember was one of the residents at Stratford Estates yelling 'fire.'" Monica paused for a moment. "There wasn't actually a fire, was there?"

"No. No fire, Ms. Levin. It appears that in the midst of the commotion, you collapsed, and the responding paramedics brought you in."

Dr. Oliver explained how she'd been brought in to the hospital emergency room unconscious. Once she'd been checked in, they'd taken a CAT scan, run the standard tests, and monitored her closely for the past thirty-six hours. Their current prognosis was that she'd had some form of anxiety attack and was suffering from exhaustion.

"What I'd like to recommend, now that you're awake, is a consultation with one of our referral psychologists."

"A psych consult? That won't be necessary. I'm sure I just needed some rest. I'll be fine once I get home, but thank you anyway."

"I'm afraid it isn't that simple, Monica. May I call you Monica?"

"Yes, of course." She felt the blush on her chest deepen. "What do you mean, it's not that simple?"

The doctor diplomatically explained that since she had no other physical symptoms, they were compelled to explore the emotional implications of her anxiety and stress so she could receive the best care and move toward full recovery and avoid any recurrence. Her employer, in fact, had insisted on exploring all possibilities.

It all sounded reasonable when he said it, even though she had no interest in seeing another therapist. Especially since she'd quit seeing her former one nearly ten years ago. It felt like she'd spent eons in that square room with the leather sofa, and she didn't relish the thought of starting over again. But maybe Dr. Oliver was right. She'd definitely been on edge for the last several months since . . . she remembered the other figure lying somewhere in this same hospital.

"Okay," she sighed. "I'll do the consult."

IZABEL

Izabel's cottage lay just east of Deer Harbor, with a sweeping view of West Sound and Orcas Village. The fifteen acres allowed plenty of room for her to maintain her privacy, and her dream of one day adding a horse and a couple of large dogs to her furry family.

Entering through the French doors, she dropped her pack on the multi-colored bench inside the hallway. She'd discovered the bench last summer at the farmer's market and had spent the fall re-styling it in brilliant shades of gold and garnet. One of these days, she'd consider listing it for sale at Beth's Café and Gallery in town. In the meantime, however, she loved having it adorn her entryway with its sunny disposition.

"Lucas? Hey, babe, where are you hiding?" Out of the corner of her eye, she noticed a shadow drift across her bedroom threshold. "Hey, sweet kitty, you in there?"

"Meooooowwww," purred the huge, tortoise-colored cat, as his six-toed paw stretched out to stroke the side of Izabel's leg.

"You hungry, puss? I'm sorry I was gone so long. That sweet little girl just wasn't ready to pop out. You know how those mommies get. They're all certain the baby's ready to be born and then it's hours until their babies finally arrive."

"Puuurrrrr."

"I know, baby, that's no excuse for you missing your dinner, is it? I'm sorry. How about a can of your favorite salmon fricassee?"

Once she satisfied Lucas's hunger, Izabel leisurely shed her clothes as she headed toward the shower. Tiles of multi-hued ocean blue covered the luxurious bathroom. It was the one room in the house that she had insisted on expanding and totally redoing when she had taken possession of the cottage a few years ago. *A woman should be able to luxuriate in her own toilette* was her motto.

Izabel looked around the room she'd made her sanctuary. She remembered lifting the sledgehammer to knock out the hallway closet so she could enlarge the bathroom to add an oversized, princess-style, claw-foot tub. She reached into the stand-alone shower to turn on the water, and then stroked the handcrafted tiles on the smooth walls. Once inside, she always felt as if she was immersed in a tropical sea. This feeling was enhanced when she glanced toward the molded shelving that showcased her collection of handmade candles and gathered seashells.

The mirror over the pedestal sink was adorned with white shells collected from various local beaches and lovingly attached by Izabel herself. Natural light came through skylights in the ceiling, and the inlaid cobblestone floor resembled a London alleyway where her shadow now lay. Everywhere she looked, there was a stamp of her unique touch. There was nothing in the room that didn't hold special meaning for her.

Stripped of her clothes and with her strawberry curls streaming down her back, Izabel resembled Ariel from *The Little Mermaid*. Today, however, she didn't have the energy or inclination to open her mouth to sing. Instead, her attention turned to the area just below her navel as she began to rub her stomach in an oddly familiar way. Stroking her belly tenderly, she felt like a woman who had just taken a pregnancy test and discovered the plus sign in the "you are pregnant" window. She knew this was impossible, since she'd completed her cycle last week.

What is this strange sensation?

Izabel continued to stroke her belly and heard the word "push" as clearly as if someone were in the shower with her. Her mid-section tightened in a spasm. She doubled over and let out a primordial scream that poured from deep within her soul.

The scream lasted for several seconds and left Izabel on the floor, sobbing and sputtering for breath. Lucas slunk into the bathroom and sniffed his way around the crumpled mass lying in a fetal position outside the shower. Then he scampered away like his tail was on fire.

Wrung out from exhaustion and confusion, Izabel crawled toward the bedroom, naked and shivering. She pulled the handmade quilt off the end of the bed and wrapped it around her damp body in a weak attempt to dry off. In slow motion, she reached for the down comforter, pulled back a corner as she rose on her knees, and rolled into the feather bed with the weight of a dead body being tossed off a pier.

DAISY

Time on Tausi drifted by like snowflakes on a cold winter day. You knew it was passing by, but it couldn't be pinned down. There was no way to determine any precise second, minute, hour, or era. For now, Daisy accepted her residence on the island with a *laissez-faire* attitude and sat astride the loveable and odd-looking Chauncey. While they wandered past blue-tinted vegetation and listened to strange twittering noises in the jungle-like forest, he told her he was a descendant of the mysterious and rare okapi species. Sir Albert strolled beside them at what seemed like a snail's pace for him, since a single stride of his lengthy legs could equal four of Chauncey's normal steps.

Wrapped in a faux mink stole, with a felt fedora on her head, Daisy posed like a celebrity in a holiday parade. Everywhere she turned there was something to catch her eye. Brilliant color flooded her senses, and creatures she had never seen before strolled the perimeter of their pathway. In the distance, cerulean waves contrasted against violet-covered sands bordered by a backdrop of luscious lime and jade-colored palm fronds. She had the eerie sensation that she was not the only one doing the watching.

"Hey Albert, did I hear you say something earlier about the other side of the island? It seems as though we've been going in circles forever. Chauncey arrives at a certain point and always turns around or veers in a different direction. What's the deal with that?"

"I don't know to what you refer, Daisy my dear."

"Seriously, Albert? Just because I'm young doesn't mean I'm stupid. I can tell when something's not right."

A whinny escaped Chauncey's snout. He began to paw at the ground with his left hoof.

"See. Even Chauncey knows something's up. Come on Al, it's time to come clean. What's with the other side of the island?"

"It's really no concern of yours, my dear. Trust me. There's nothing you'd be interested in."

"Clearly I *am* interested. And even more so now that you're pretending like nothing's up. Maybe I'll just go explore for myself."

"No!" the peacock blurted. "I mean, that wouldn't be such a good idea, Miss Daisy."

"Not a good idea, huh. Why not, Al?" Daisy raised an eyebrow in response.

Chauncey lifted his head from staring at the ground and said, "You might as well tell her, my lord. I don't think she's one to easily give up."

Albert tilted his head and looked skyward. "Let me consider how this might best be put," he started. "I guess one might say that the other side of the island is less friendly than this one."

"That's an understatement," muttered Chauncey.

"Come on, Albert. Would you please stop sugarcoating and get to the point? What's the deal? Is there some evil witch who casts spells on all the unsuspecting creatures who live over there?"

"How did you know?" piped Chauncey.

"Really?" Daisy stared at the okapi. "I was just kidding. There's *seriously* a witch who casts spells on this island? I guess I shouldn't be surprised, considering that I'm standing here talking to a giant peacock and a patchwork donkey. It can't get much weirder."

"Well, my dear. He's not exactly a witch. One might call him more of a sorcerer, although he refers to himself as The Master."

"So what does this 'Master' do? And why are you so worried about him?"

"It's not me I'm concerned for, Daisy. You see, The Master has a penchant for beautiful young girls and has a way of luring them into his spell if they come too close."

"Okay." Daisy narrowed her eyes at Albert. "Then what happens?"

"Unfortunately, I'm not certain. Once the young ladies cross through the barrier, they never seem to return."

Albert hoped his explanation was enough to quiet the young woman, who continued to stare at him with a puzzled expression. Like Chauncey, Sir Albert understood Daisy was not one to be easily deterred.

MONICA

Monica stared at the sign on the generic office door in front of her: *J. T. Higgins, Ph.D., Psychotherapist*. Her body went rigid for a moment, and then wavered like a balloon slowly losing air. *Am I going to faint again? No. No. No*, she whispered to herself.

For several moments, Monica stood immobile. Finally she reached out her right hand, touched the doorknob, and then jerked it back as though she'd been shocked with an electric current. No matter how hard she tried, she couldn't make herself cross the threshold into the therapist's office. She was like a piece of gum on the wall at Pike Place Market: shiny, sticky, chewed up, spit out, and going nowhere. She couldn't imagine that anyone could really help her, or for that matter, that anyone would want to. Slowly, she turned and walked back down the hallway and out to the parking lot.

Now what? Monica thought. Her supervisors at Stratford Estates had recommended she "take her time" before returning to work. In fact, the supervisors weren't entirely certain they wanted Monica returning to her position. The pandemonium and aftermath of that night was costing Stratford Estates thousands of dollars in damage and incidentals. Not to mention the potential outstanding lawsuit from Mr. Louden's family, who wanted a detailed account of the events that had resulted in their father needing five stitches in his head. And who knew what else was pending?

Fortunately, the director of Stratford Estates had a friend at the local newspaper and had been able to squash the story that had been about to print: "Saturday Night Fever: Residents Hustle Heartily at Local Stratford Estates." It was not a charming story about randy residents, but rather a scathing piece on inadequate care for elders. The pipsqueak reporter had taken the position that Stratford Estates charged thousands of dollars per month for exclusive care (which was true), but then reduced staffing to a skeleton crew who let the dementia-fogged seniors run amok while the staff sat back and watched (which was not true).

Monica's immediate supervisor, John Paul DuPont, was unclear as to what had really happened. Particularly regarding how Edna, a mere whisper of a woman, had supposedly single-handedly prevented Monica from calming the raucous behavior in the common room. Apparently John Paul had never been in close proximity to Edna when she was intent on having ice cream. The end result was that Monica found herself with extra time on her hands, aware that her job status was in a highly precarious position.

For the present, she transferred her gaping at the therapist's doorknob to single-pointed focus on her car's steering wheel. Her beige Toyota Camry idled quietly as she sat in the bland office center parking lot across the street from Northgate Mall. Monica felt as if she was fading into nothingness. Even her clothes were neutral: tan slacks, cream-colored sweater, and beige handbag. Juxtaposed against the neutral hue of the gray Seattle sky and the lackluster office building, the effect was such that an artist or photographer trying to capture the scene would have been hard-pressed to find a strong focal point in the vicinity of Monica or her vehicle.

Putting the car into reverse, Monica glanced over her shoulder and waited for a blue-haired driver to inch past her rear bumper. Then she navigated the Camry out of its parking space.

As she circled the adjacent lot in front of Nordstrom's department store, a slight pinkish tint began to return to Monica's cheeks and her heart picked up its pace. Sweat seeped out of her palms onto the leather steering wheel. She felt a thrill of excitement as she parked the car, unlike any she'd known for several weeks.

Monica entered through the double doors on the south side of the store, stepped into the familiar handbag and accessories department, and inhaled deeply. Leather. Michael Kors. Marc Jacobs. Kate Spade. She knew all the designers. Patent leather. Calf hair. Faux leather. Suede. Like a stealthy cat in the jungle, she moved through the aisles, occasionally reaching out a hand to caress the scrumptious treasures.

"May I help you?" asked a clerk, not more than twenty-two years old. Monica was always disturbed by these young assistants. What could they possibly know about the finer things of life? She keenly balanced her superiority against the jealousy she felt toward these young creatures who got to spend their days surrounded by luxury handbags and accessories.

"No, thank you. Just looking." She tilted her nose into the air and turned away without making eye contact.

Monica strolled past the Clinique and Esteé Lauder counters, inhaling the luscious aroma of cleansers, creams, and specialized perfumes. The shoe department was straight ahead, but she knew it wasn't quite time to move in. She stalked the perimeter like a cougar circling a deer, waiting for just the right moment.

"Have you been helped?" asked a male clerk in an ill-fitting suit and Windsor-knotted tie, breaking her focus.

"Just looking. Thank you." This time Monica flashed him a smile before stepping away and heading toward the escalators. It still wasn't time. She had things to arrange.

Moving past Men's Shoes, she inhaled deeply before putting her fawn-colored pump onto the escalator going up. Savvy. Individualist. Encore. Lingerie. She allowed her eyes to nonchalantly scan each department.

The Nordstrom café was buzzing with activity. It was approaching lunchtime for the early shopping crowd. Monica trained a perfected, casual glance toward her target: the occupied tables of the cozy restaurant. The advantage of dressing like a fair-shaded ghost was that people hardly noticed her, which came in quite handy for today's excursion. After surveying the situation to her satisfaction, she stepped up to the host's podium and pretended to scan a menu.

"Table for one?"

"Yes, please. Do you think I could have something over by that corner? I need to keep an eye on my daughter in Brass Plum." She winked conspiratorially.

"Of course, ma'am. Right this way."

"Perfect. Thank you very much."

"Your server will be right with you."

Monica nodded again.

Next to her table, less than two feet away, sat a pair of neatly coiffed women, deep in conversation. They were probably somewhere in their mid-fifties, a decade or so older than she.

"Did you hear that Christy's getting some work done? She says it's medical, but I'm betting it's purely optional. Although you could hardly say those drooping bags she calls eyelids are 'optional.'"

"I know, right? I don't know how she can even see anymore. Her lids look like they belong on her Shar-Pei."

"Seriously! That's why you should own cute dogs. People always end up looking like their dogs and spouses. Poor Christy."

"Yeah, she's kind of screwed on both counts." Both women chuckled.

And so the conversation continued, the gossiping women trading stories back and forth as they munched their gourmet salads and sipped second glasses of Chardonnay. They didn't notice Monica finishing her tea and picking up her handbag, along with one of their Nordstrom shopping bags filled with a single box of shoes.

Kate Spade. *Excellent,* Monica thought. She smiled to herself as she strolled out of the café and back to the sales area.

"Hello again. I see you're back. How can I help you?" queried the kid in the ill-fitting suit.

"Wow. You have a good memory," Monica replied. She was used to not being noticed at all, much less remembered. She wondered if this was going to be a problem.

"I see you bought a pair of shoes already," he said, nodding toward her shopping bag.

The young man was putting a hitch in her normally smooth routine. *It's all about the thrill, isn't it?* she reminded herself. She'd just have to be creative and improvise today.

"Oh, I picked these up for a friend, but when I called to let her know, she said she'd found them at Bellevue and bought them there this morning."

"Would you like to return them?"

"How about an exchange? I think I could use a treat today." She giggled girlishly.

"Sure. No problem. Do you want to look around?"

"Yes, thank you."

The goody store was open. No beige pumps or plain black slings today. Color. That was what Monica wanted—what she *deserved* for all the trouble she'd put up with over the past several months.

This time, she circled the footwear displays in earnest. She'd sneaked a peek at the receipt and realized that she had an exchange budget in the four-hundred-dollar range. *Not bad.* Monica paused for a moment and wondered if the woman had discovered them missing yet. She doubted it. Sometimes Monica felt a little guilty for her chronic propensity to pick up other people's shopping bags, but not today. The woman in question was so horrible and gossipy, anyway. *That woman actually deserves to be punished for being such a witch, doesn't she?* The thought actually emboldened Monica, prompting her to do something she rarely did: allow the clerk to help her.

"Color, please," she told the young man. "I'm feeling the need for something bright today. It's so gray outside. At least my feet can be happy."

"Awesome," her unknowing partner in crime piped up. "I get super tired of selling sensible black pumps. What can I bring you?"

"How about we start with Kate Spade and Jimmy Choo? They seem to have some great color this season."

"Excellent. What size?"

"Seven and a half."

The clerk disappeared into the storeroom to fetch the shoes, and Monica settled back into the sofa-like seat. Closing her eyes for a few minutes, she sank into the luxury of the moment. From an outsider's perspective, she was just another mid-week shopper buying new shoes. After several minutes, the young man returned with half a dozen boxes. Just as Monica opened her eyes, she caught a glimpse of the two matrons coming down the escalator and held her breath.

As she watched them pass, they were still chatting away. Undoubtedly the two-Chardonnay lunch had loosened their tongues even more and impaired their ability to count the number of shopping bags they carried. It would probably be several hours, or days, before the woman realized she hadn't made it home with her new shoes, but by that time it would be too late for her to do anything about it. *Too bad, so sad*, Monica mused from her vantage point.

The clerk spread out an array of salacious offerings. Glittering Jimmy Choo slingbacks with a peek-a-boo toe. A cute red Valentino with a couture bow.

Flame-colored Ron Whites sporting a five-inch heel. Crystal-embellished Gucci platforms.

"What do you think?" asked her assistant.

"Hmmm. They're all wonderful, of course, but—"

The clerk smiled and opened the final box.

A little gasp escaped Monica's pursed lips. "Perrrrfect."

Kate Spade had done it again. Swoon-worthy satin formed a stylishly tied knot on the radiant peep-toe pump. It was the epitome of sculptural elegance. Three-and-a-half-inch heels, not too high, and best of all, the color: cobalt blue.

"I'll take them," Monica cooed without hesitation.

IZABEL

Izabel cozied up on her sofa in the soft, terry cloth robe her friend from the Rosario Resort had "borrowed" for her. She was painting her toenails and listening to Norah Jones. Lucas purred and nuzzled his face against her leg. Roasted root vegetables and pork tenderloin were baking in the oven, and the delicious caramelized smell filled her house. A deep sigh of contentment escaped her parted lips. It was the most settled she'd felt in days.

She knew Buck was scheduled to arrive in town this afternoon, but she hadn't yet decided whether she would agree to see him or not. She knew he'd be heartbroken if she said no. But a residual and eerie feeling had continued to haunt her since her meltdown in the shower the previous week, on the night the Anderson baby had been born.

Putting down the nail polish and gently pushing Lucas aside, she crawled off her overstuffed sofa and waddled into the kitchen on her heels. The vegetables were coming along nicely. After stirring them with a wooden spoon, she opened the fridge and poured herself a glass of freshly squeezed lemonade from the farmers' market. Buck drifted into her consciousness.

The two things she loved about him were the sex and the fact that he was married. Even though she felt guilty about their dalliance, his marital status had proven to be the glue that made this her longest-lasting relationship ever. At two years, it could hardly be considered a world record, but it felt like one to her.

Ring. Ring. The phone burst to life on the kitchen counter, and Izabel reached across to grab it.

"Hello," she answered with a gruff voice that made her sound like she had a horrible head cold.

"Izzy? Is that you?"

"Hey, Beth. Yeah, it's me."

"What's the matter with your voice? It sounds like car tires on a gravel road."

"Oh, it's nothing. I thought you were Buck."

"I was wondering when you were going to finally dump that guy. It's about time. I've never seen what the attraction is. I mean, he's such a—"

"Whoa, Beth. Slow down. I'm not dumping Buck. I just haven't decided whether I'm going to see him tonight or not."

"So what's the deal? Female problems?"

"Geez, Beth. What wound you up tonight?"

"Sorry. I just hadn't heard from you in a while and thought I'd check in. No one's seen you and Rosie cruising the island this week. Everything okay?"

"Yeah. I've just been busy, that's all."

"Busy? Doing what?"

Clearly it wasn't going to be easy to steer the conversation in another direction. The last thing Izabel wanted to do was tell megaphone-mouth Beth about the weird physical pains she'd been having.

"Look, Beth. I've gotta run, honey. I'll swing by the gallery in a day or two. How's that sound?"

"Sounds good. I've gotta go anyway. Charlie's bringing in a bucket full of oysters, and I need to get shuckin' so later we can get fu—"

"Bye, Beth." Izabel quickly turned off the call, smiled, and shook her head in response to her brash friend.

Ring. Ring. No sooner had Izabel put down the phone than it sprang to life again.

"Grand Central Station," she answered without thinking.

"Hey, babe. It's me." Buck's Southern drawl purred out of the speaker.

Even though he'd lived in the Pacific Northwest for more than twenty years, he'd still kept his Oklahoma accent, never picking up the flattened dialect of those residents raised in the local region. It was a tone and way of speaking that always weakened Izabel's resolve when she heard it. Along with the accent, he still preferred his shabby black Stetson to the ball caps or stocking hats worn by the other men on the island. His soft gray eyes and skin slightly pockmarked from adolescent acne combined to create a portrait of someone both gentle and rugged. That was exactly how he treated Izabel in bed, both tender and firm, and it was the principal reason she heard herself saying: "So are you coming over for dinner, or are you hanging out at Willy's all night?"

"I'll be there in about half an hour, if that's okay with you?"

"All right. I'll see you then," she answered softly. *Damn. Damn. Damn*, she thought as soon as she hung up the phone. *What was I thinking?*

Apparently you weren't, responded her inner critic. But her fate was sealed for the evening. Instead of burying herself in worrisome thoughts, Izabel tried to imagine herself burrowing into the thick mound of man-fur on Buck's chest. The image reminded her of a photo she'd seen in *National Geographic,* where a grizzly bear tenderly stroked a newborn cub. Buck's gentleness was one more reason she stayed with him. Normally, he wouldn't question her need to be quiet, if that's what she required. He would spend the whole night caressing her in his strong fisherman's arms.

Maybe inviting him over wasn't such a bad idea after all.

— — —

When Buck arrived, Izabel was standing by the oven, stirring the vegetables and sipping her lemonade. Her Ariel-like hair fell to her waist, rippling like waves on the ocean. Ballet slippers adorned her feet, and a pink chemise skimmed her hips, landing precisely at the top of her shapely thighs.

Buck gave a gentle tap on the front door's watermarked glass in an attempt to not startle Izabel before coming in.

"You really should keep this latched," he said, closing one eye and cocking his head toward her with a mock frown. "You never know who could wander in."

"Buck, honey!" Izabel squealed with delight as she jumped into his arms and wrapped her legs around his waist. Her moods seemed to swing from one side of the pendulum to the other in rapid speed these days. Right now, she was happy to see this big bear of a man and be held in his caress. She was tired of being alone with her thoughts.

"Whoa, babe! It's great to see you, too." He chuckled and buried his nose in her lavender-scented mane.

Izabel was overcome with emotion at how safe she felt when she saw him. Her eyes began to tear up and a small hiccup escaped her throat. Buck mistook her reaction for passion and hungrily sought out her lips as he began to slide his hand under her shirt.

"Stop it, Buck!" She slapped his hand away, releasing her legs and dropping to the floor. The pendulum had reversed.

Buck stared at Izabel, looking bewildered by the mixed message. This had never happened before. Theirs had always been a love of equal ardor. More times than not, dinner was burned in the oven and their lovemaking ended up happening on the pine plank floor.

Izabel was more prepared for her snappish response than Buck was. Even though she'd been riding her emotions up and down, and back and forth, for the past several days, it still felt confusing to her. "I'm sorry. I just . . . "

"What's wrong, Iz?"

"I'm just tired. That's all." The area below her navel clenched, and a grimace crossed her face. *Oh God,* she thought, *please don't let him notice. I can't bear to talk about this right now.*

"Look, honey. I may be just an old cowboy from Oklahoma, but even I can tell this is more than you just bein' tired. Did something happen while I was away?"

"No. Yes. I don't know." *How can I explain what I don't even understand?*

"Do you want me to stay, or should I go? I have to be back in Anacortes tomorrow night. There's some meeting at the boys' school that Felicia insists I can't miss."

"Would you mind staying?" she said in a childlike voice. "I don't really want to be alone."

Buck looked at her wide, tear-filled eyes and stroked the side of her girlish face. "Of course, I'll stay, honey. You know you're my best girl."

Buck and Izabel sat at the rough-hewn table and quietly ate their vegetables and pork. He nursed a beer, and she sipped her lemonade. Izabel attempted to make conversation, but each time she began, she was reminded of birthing babies and the odd pain in her belly threatened to return.

Buck seemed to sense her discomfort. He chatted away about his fishing trip and the antics of his shipmates, making polite conversation to fill the void hanging in the room. Izabel couldn't bring herself to tell him about the agonizing physical pain she'd been experiencing. She knew he'd be overly concerned and try to figure out how to fix the problem. The last thing she wanted to do was see a doctor or talk to anyone else about the weird pains. She was afraid, however, that if she didn't say something, he'd want to make love once they crawled into bed. They'd never had a night together that hadn't included passion-filled, sweet lovemaking, but there was a first time for everything.

As they climbed into her overstuffed bed and Buck reached across her to turn out the light, she plucked up her courage and said, "Buck, could you just hold me tonight?"

"Sure, Iz. If that's what you need." Confused, but always the gentleman, he wrapped his sinewy arms around her body and prayed for restraint.

Once the lights were out, they lay nestled together. They both pretended to sleep, but neither succeeded.

Breaking free of the claustrophobic spoon, Izabel tossed and turned in the bed beside Buck. Around midnight he gave up on the futile attempt to comfort her and dropped into an exhausted slumber.

Beside him, she stretched and rolled and tossed the covers off until she was shivering. Then she pulled them back on until she felt as though her body was cooking from the inside out, prompting her to swing one leg over the top of the down comforter. As she drifted off to sleep around 2 a.m., an unsettling thought lingered in her mind: *I wonder what else might arise.*

She dreamed of a pint-sized girl with hair the color of freshly harvested wheat and emerald eyes. The girl romped back and forth in a front yard sprinkler, a laughing man in cowboy boots and chaps cheering her on. Something about them both seemed familiar, but Izabel was certain she'd never seen them before. The girl stayed in her dreams all night, growing older and older and taunting Izabel as she grew.

Izabel awoke early and exhausted. The island lay wrapped in its morning shroud before the sun peeked over Mount Woolard. She extracted her lean body from the gentle grasp of Buck's solid arms. Just like the *National Geographic* grizzly, Buck, in his predisposition to care for the weaker being, had instinctively curled back around her during the night. Now he dozed with a raspy snore, and rolled into the space she had vacated.

Izabel stumbled into the bathroom and stared into the mirror. Charcoal-colored half moons marked the area under her eyes, and her face looked like someone had elongated her features with a blunt pencil. The person looking back at her was unsettling. She scarcely resembled the angel of Orcas Island who rode her bike with carefree pleasure through the rolling countryside. Something was shifting. It felt like tectonic plates had moved deep inside Izabel's soul. It all seemed to have begun with the birth of the Anderson baby girl. At least that's where she thought it had begun.

DAISY

Time was an ethereal commodity in Tausi. Daisy was slowly becoming used to accepting things as they were in each moment. When she ventured out from her pink-domed tent, she never knew what would greet her. Indeed, she had no idea whether day and night even existed anymore. It might be clear and brilliant with cerulean blue skies one moment, and dark as ebony the next. In the blink of an eye, rain could start to fall, or a rainbow could magically appear in the palm of her hand.

It was an enchanting land. With so much to experience simply by opening her eyes, it hardly seemed reasonable that Daisy would find herself bored. But she had never been considered reasonable. Even though a change of scenery had occurred, her penchant for exploring and never being completely satisfied hadn't changed one iota.

The primary obstacle standing in the way of her exploration was Sir Albert. He conducted himself more like a mother hen than a royal peacock. Whenever he had duties to attend that Daisy couldn't participate in, he made sure that Chauncey was close by her side. Her only chance for escape (and she felt guilty about even considering it such, because they were so kind to her) would have to come when Chauncey was in charge. Albert was too vigilant, and the okapi was considerably more distractible.

— — —

"Hey, Chauncey, what's that golden round thing all shiny in the distance?" Daisy asked in a childlike voice. "I don't think I've ever seen it before."

Her softened tone made Chauncey act like a wise older sibling. He puffed out his chest. "They call it the dome of Maki."

"What's inside it?"

"Oh, I don't really know. Important stuff, I guess."

"And what about that tree over there. What's it called?"

"Um. Fizzle brush, I think."

Daisy continued her line of questioning until she saw Chauncey's eyelids begin to get heavy and sag.

"Mmmmm. Yoowwwww. Oh, my." Daisy yawned as she stretched her arms. "I think I could take a nap."

"Me, too!" said Chauncey. He seemed grateful to have the game of question and answer over for a while. It was hard work being in charge.

"Would it be okay if we lie down under this fern and took a little snooze?"

"Yes, please! I mean, I think that would be all right, Daisy."

"Thanks, Chaunce. I'm not sure I can keep my eyes open much longer." Daisy crawled under the lavender-tinted fern, and patted the ground beside her.

Chauncey dropped to his multi-colored haunches, gave a quick whinny, and was fast asleep before Daisy even pretended to shut her eyes.

— — —

While Daisy had started her inquiry with the dome of Maki, she was really interested in the hazy cloud that rose above Tausi in the opposite direction, over the far side of the island. She'd have to be quick to make it there before anyone noticed she was gone.

Oh man, I hope Sir Albert doesn't find out I'm gone. He'll be furious with me and with poor Chauncey. I'll just have to hope he's not too hard on Chauncey for losing me. Poor guy, Chauncey's so dang sweet. It's not his fault he's gullible. If Albert's mad, it's his own damn fault.

Creeping like a cat burglar in the night, she moved away from Chauncey's side as the okapi's chest rose and fell in contented sleep.

— — —

Deep in the jungle of Tausi, in the center of what appeared to be a mammoth beehive, sat a creature unfathomable to human eyes. From the waist down, he resembled a massive Humpty Dumpty. Porcelain white skin with an eggshell-like appearance protruded from beneath a wide leather belt. Veins and cracks wove their way throughout the creature's lower half. Some of the cracks oozed purplish goo, and small winged insects resembling goldfish dove in and out of the sludge, unheeded by the beast.

Stripes of gold and black extended upward from the garish waistband, approximating a bumblebee's lines that had gone through a drawing stencil vertically instead of horizontally. Atop the considerable beelike torso was the distinct head of a man, full and round with the texture and color of a robin's egg, accentuated by a bulbous nose, one sapphire-blue eye, and one onyx-dark eye. Cloven feet protruded from the lower body, and apish hands erupted from the striped torso. He rested, with a look of bemusement upon his face, watching the smoke rise from his fire and out the top of the hive.

Here sat The Master, and this was his domain.

The creature twitched inside his grotesque Humpty Dumpty body and leaned his bulk toward a collection of jars haphazardly arranged on a split and rotting oak. He squinted through his blue eye and scanned the contents of each jar one by one. A severed finger with a blue polished nail. An ashen lock of hair. The heart of a bird.

"Ah, yes," he murmured through rotted teeth when his eye landed on an antique jar filled with golden honey. Inside the gilded vessel, a picture was forming. A single figure twisted and morphed until it sharpened to reveal the mid-sized girl. Or was she a woman?

Fascinated, he watched the girl-woman make her way through the jungle. His nose twitched when she came to a dead end. Each time she paused, he ran his yellowed fingernail along the jar to manipulate a pathway for her.

Silly thing, he thought. *She has no idea who's in charge here. She's like a pawn on my personal chessboard.*

Watching her with greedy eyes while absentmindedly flicking at the goldfish creatures diving in and out of his purplish goo, he opened and closed each trail with his finger so that she was directed precisely where he wanted her to go: the center of his lair.

Such a charming young thing, he thought. *I can't wait to meet her.*

MONICA

Ah, Friedrich. You're the man. Monica mused as she turned Nietzsche's words over in her mind. She hadn't thought of the nineteenth-century cultural critic since her first semester philosophy class at Briar Cliff, but today she found comfort and solace in the philosopher's timeworn words.

In truth, who could say I actually stole those brilliant Kate Spade shoes? Or if I'm actually a thief? Didn't I simply pick up an extra shopping bag when I gathered my own purse? The tag-along parcel was merely a purchase acquired from a woman who had more bags than she could manage. One might consider that I simply lightened that woman's load, freed her a tad bit from gluttony, and saved her from the potential agony of back strain.

That self-righteous woman doesn't deserve to have such gorgeous shoes at all. It'd serve her well to be more generous with womankind. I just gave her an opportunity to be charitable, to make a gift to the community of Monica.

There are donation boxes all over town asking for gently worn shoes to support the homeless. So the woman's charity toward me was an excellent stepping-stone toward helping the underprivileged. While I'm not exactly homeless and the shoes hadn't been worn yet, I could definitely be considered less fortunate than that polished matron with the overactive credit card.

Monica's reverie accompanied her the few miles toward home, until she pulled into the driveway. She glanced around to make certain her neighbor, Jenny, was nowhere in sight. Seeing the curtains flutter on the duplex window next door, she ducked into her passenger seat so Jenny would think she'd already gone into the house. Monica didn't want the busybody asking questions or putting a damper on the buoyant mood she was experiencing after such a long time. Once the coast was clear, she gathered the spoils from her afternoon at the mall and quietly exited the car.

Inside the house, she flipped on the living room light, revealing clean and sparse surroundings. Natural light and lots of white furnishings and accessories made the miniature abode feel airy and unified. It was considerably more compact than the house she'd grown up in on Sunset Hill, but the price was affordable and it was close to work. Despite the limitations of living in half of a duplex, Monica had done her best to make it feel like home with the resources she had.

Instead of crowding the compact kitchen with overhead cabinets, Monica had asked the contractor to mount a deep shelf across the windows. Since she lived and cooked frugally, she only needed minimal storage space for kitchen goods. Glancing toward the end of the faux-marble counter, she noticed the blue message light on her land-line phone flashing. *Probably a solicitor.* She picked up the receiver and dialed her own number to check the message.

"Hello, Ms. Levin. This is Dr. Higgins's office calling about the appointment you missed this morning. We'd like to reschedule at your earliest convenience, so if you can call us back, that would be wonderful. Thank you so much. And we look forward to hearing from you soon."

Monica shuddered at the thought of returning to the therapist's office. *How can some stranger "help," when there isn't anything wrong with me?* After pushing *delete* on the answering machine, she busied herself preparing a Cobb salad, washing each knife and measuring cup as she finished using them.

Lost in reverie, she jumped when the phone rang. *Oh geez. What now?* Plunking the damp dishtowel onto the cabinet, she automatically reached for the phone to pick it up on the second ring.

"Hello."

"Good evening, Ms. Levin. This is J.T. Higgins. I'm calling because you seem to have missed the appointment we had scheduled this morning."

"Yes, I'm so sorry. It must have slipped my mind. I just picked up your office's message."

"No problem. These things happen. How are you feeling this evening?"

Oh, here it comes. All of the "how are you feeling" B.S., Monica thought to herself. "I'm quite well, thank you. I honestly don't think there's any need to reschedule my appointment. I'm sure Dr. Oliver was just being thorough when he suggested a follow-up with you."

"Possibly. It sounds like you've had quite the case of exhaustion and that you also collapsed at work. While I appreciate your wish to not waste time, I'm wondering what might have led to the collapse and if there's anything you'd like to talk about or check out."

No, I don't want to check anything out. And you're making me feel exhausted right now. "Well, who can argue with two doctors?" Monica replied in a cheery voice that belied her irritation.

"Great. How's next Wednesday around the same time? Say ten-thirty?"

"That sounds perfect. I'll see you then. Now if you'll please excuse me, someone's at my front door."

"Certainly. I look forward to meeting you."

Monica's hand shook as she replaced the phone in its cradle. Standing in the middle of the kitchen, she furrowed her brow and turned away from the salad on the counter. She didn't like the idea of someone peering into her psyche. Wrapping her arms around her body, she twitched with a shiver and shook her head to try and clear her thoughts.

Leaving her dinner untouched, she walked to the front entryway, picked up her shopping bag, and made certain the latch on the door was securely in place. She peeked inside the box. Her eyes caressed the blue satin lines as she inhaled the scent of expensive leather. Her shaking slowed to a tremor and her breathing began to calm as she passed through the orderly living room toward her bedroom.

"Come on, babies. You're going to love your new home," she cooed, as she hugged the box to her chest.

The living space of Monica's duplex was just large enough for two small bedrooms, given the compact size of her kitchen and living room. On the rare occasions when guests visited, they were often confused because there appeared to be a large area of unaccounted-for space in the home. Monica's bedroom was the only sleeping room and there was no spare room or office space.

Stepping into the modestly sized bedroom, she closed the door and tugged on the white brocade curtains until they covered the window. Like a spy on a mission, she glanced around the room to make certain everything was in order. Cornflower blue pillows lay meticulously fluffed atop the antique-white poster bed she'd slept in as a child.

Her eyes glanced across the matching nightstand, taking an inventory of its contents: a digital clock (7:32 p.m.), Terry Tempest Williams's *When Women Were Birds,* and a floral box of tissues. Satisfied everything was as she'd left it, she reached beneath the nightstand and pressed a concealed button.

Like something out of a James Bond movie, the wall that housed her matching white armoire slowly rolled away, revealing an entrance into another room.

Monica stood at the threshold of the hidden space. She twittered with delight and clapped her hands before throwing them wide open. "Welcome home, girls. It's time to meet your new friends."

What appeared before her was a feast for her eyes and a balm for her aching soul. Dozens of elegantly aligned shelves were spaced around the area. This secret closet had replaced the second bedroom of the duplex. But Monica did not think of it as a mere closet. It was more like a posh boutique transported directly from Rodeo Drive in Beverly Hills.

From floor to ceiling, there rested over three hundred pairs of shoes, color-coordinated and arranged according to style and type. Pumps. Boots. Spiked heels. Active wear. Gucci. Louboutin. Alexander McQueen. Prada. And, of course, Monica's favorite, Kate Spade. Feathers. Sparkles. Bows. Patent leather. Suede. Platforms. Designer canvas. Nothing was missing.

Monica flipped a switch on the wall, and a crystal chandelier glided downward from the ceiling. Her hazel eyes filled with tears at the sight and sparkled in the glowing light. With the push of a small lever, the existing shelves began to rotate to reveal even more storage space. *Ah. So beautiful.*

In the center of the room lay a stack of silk and embroidered pillows that resembled a small altar space. Monica cradled her new cobalt blue shoes in her arms, lowered herself onto the mound, and nestled into the pillows.

She settled her eyes in a soft gaze as if preparing for meditation, slid off her pumps, and began to hum Lucinda Williams's "Sweet Old World" until she drifted into slumber. Softened by sleep, she looked like a fairy princess amidst her court of watchmen named Lou, Alex, and Kate.

IZABEL

Just before sunrise, Izabel moved into the kitchen on feet quieter than Lucas's. Hands shaking, she hastily scrawled a note for Buck: *Gone for fresh air. Back soon.* Her movements were slow and deliberate, like those of an ill person recently back on her feet. She winced and clutched her chest as she pressed the green button to start brewing coffee for Buck. It felt like the cottage walls were closing in on her, and fresh air was all she could think of as she slipped out the door into the morning glow.

Pulling Rosie out of the small storage shed, she swung her leg over the seat and steered toward the road leading to the beach. Izabel loved the healing properties of Orcas Island. Each day, she had the opportunity to experience mountains, forests, and the ocean, all in one compact area. Today, the sea was calling to her.

Once she was outside, her energy rose like lifting mist. Her legs turned like pistons and worked hard to pump oxygen into her aching chest as she climbed to the top of one of the rolling island peaks. Once she was there, her heart beat like an excited child pounding on a new tin drum until she dropped to the other side and coasted down the hill, feet lifted off the pedals, curly mane flowing behind her. She repeated this process several times until she finally arrived at her favorite peak overlooking the ocean.

Once there, Izabel carefully laid Rosie on her side. She removed her shoes, dug her toes into the mossy loam, and opened her arms wide. There she stood like a five-pointed star, breathing deeply as the moist ocean air flowed over her exertion-dampened skin.

The Indian summer of extended warm weather and cloudless skies was threatening to come to a close. For several weeks, the daytime temperatures had hovered in the low seventies, perfect for long bike rides, midday paddleboarding, and kayaking. For the past few days, however, the highs had dropped, and Izabel could feel the chill in the early morning air.

She thrived in the San Juan Island environment. It was astonishingly more inviting than the mainland Pacific Northwest to the south. Visitors were always surprised to learn that the sun shone here almost two hundred and fifty days of the year, thanks to the rain shadow effect of the Olympic Mountains to the south.

This morning, however, wasn't one of the shiny days. Izabel pondered whether the climate gods had sensed her mood and concocted this day to match exactly how she had felt: gray and foggy.

The girl in last night's dream had seemed so familiar, yet not. Izabel wrapped her arms around her body to ward off the chill that pressed to crawl in. Staring into the misty distance, she allowed the dream to come back into focus, which she recalled in precise detail.

A red-haired teen stared at the ceiling of a room where she lay on a four-poster bed. Another girl, dark-haired, sat cross-legged in a window seat, nonchalantly removing black polish from her nails.

"God, I'm sick of ruffles and pink shit. I hate being trapped in Barbie's nightmare. Thank God my parents are dead!"

The girls gasped in unison, then tossed their heads back and cackled like witches gathered around a cauldron.

"Wow. I can't believe I said that out loud. Oh, Mommy, I'm so sorry." The red-haired girl turned her emerald eyes skyward.

"Are you really sorry?" The other girl looked puzzled. "I thought you hated your mother."

"Yeah, but—"

"I mean, sorry. I know you're probably not glad they're dead, but, like, I wouldn't blame you if you were." The dark-haired girl nonchalantly continued filing her nails.

"No, you're right. I did hate them. Well, not both of them. Daddy was a saint, but Mother? Oh my God. She was a royal b-i-t-c-h!"

"Damn straight," the other chimed in. "She kinda, like, scared me."

The girls sat in silence for a few moments, the dark-haired one focused on her nails.

"This is so fucked up! What am I supposed to do?" The red-haired girl burst into tears. Slamming her fists into the pillows, she stood on her knees and grabbed a fistful of fabric in each hand, like a caveman brandishing his weapon. With force incongruent to her petite stature, she banged the pillow against the mattress and the headboard until feathers flew everywhere. She ripped the bedding at the seams. Ticking tore into shreds and pink taffeta floated amidst feathers.

"Whoa." The dark-haired one stared slack-jawed at her friend. She seemed unsure whether to stop her or egg her on.

"Fuck, fuck, fuck!" Miss Red-hair bellowed. "I wanted them to die and now they're dead. I killed them. I killed them. I killed them." She screamed at the top of her lungs, and then collapsed in a sobbing mess on her tattered bed. Makeup streamed down her face as her chest heaved up and down. Her friend sat with the nail file in mid-air, mouth still agape.

The red-haired girl reached over and flicked on the radio. Heavy metal blasted into the room. The girl lifted her head and started pounding it against the headboard.

"That's enough!" Miss Dark-hair lurched across the bed and grabbed Miss Red-hair's head between her palms, but Red-hair shook her loose and looked around the room like a feral cat.

"Where the fuck are my cigarettes? Is there any of that joint left from last week? Oh, God, what am I gonna do?" She spoke as if no one else was in the room.

The girl pulled herself off the bed like a zombie out of the grave and lurched down the hallway to a master bedroom. She made her way past a king-sized bed and into the en suite bathroom. She opened the medicine cabinet and reached for a bottle marked Alprazolam that was tucked behind an assortment of vitamins and fish oil.

"Oh, God, I hate my life," the girl moaned. In clearer light, she looked about eleven instead of the seventeen that Izabel instinctively knew she was. Hair covered her eyes, and her pink nightgown hung off her waif-like shoulders. She was pencil-thin.

"Damn! Damn! Damn! Damn!" The girl started throwing things and thrashing about like a junkie desperate for a fix. This time she pulled every item out of the medicine cabinet: toothpaste, night creams, cotton balls, Excedrin, tweezers. Every imaginable thing flew onto the bathroom floor or landed in the sink. A jar of foot cream splashed into the toilet. The medicine chest was nearly empty, and still the girl raged on. Her gaze landed in the upper left corner, and a glimmer of turquoise blown glass caught her eye: a tiny pipe.

"Well, lookie here. Mommy dearest wasn't just into narcotics. Looks like she was a pothead, too." The discovery of the pipe seemed to slow the girl down momentarily and take her focus off of the prescription pills she'd tucked into the flimsy pocket of her nightgown. She glanced around the tiny bathroom of the old house, looking for something to put in the pipe.

She noticed that a few bent candles lined the tile around the claw foot tub. Shampoo and conditioner sat next to bath beads and lavender bubble bath. The girl moved toward the door as if to leave, and then her eyes landed on a black canister of deep conditioner. Like a fish snapping at bait, the girl reached for the slick black jar and turned the lid. Inside was at least an ounce, maybe two, of marijuana.

Izabel shook her head and tried to focus on a small motorboat in the distance. Her chest tightened when she thought about the dream. She felt shaky all over. Bending her knees, she sat on the mossy ground and hugged her sweatshirt tighter around her torso. "What was that all about?" she whispered into the breeze.

Sometimes, like today, something happened to remind her that she had no memories of the first part of her life. It was like she'd woken up one day as a young woman. Almost two decades ago, the Franciscan nuns of Shaw Island had taken her in when she'd arrived on their landing with only a backpack, bewildered and too thin. They'd brought her into their fold and cared for her lovingly.

Izabel's fondest memories from that time revolved around working alongside the sisters at the ferry dock and greeting wayward travelers and curiosity seekers as they visited the island. She'd been a regular fixture at Little Portion, the store that was Shaw's only commercial establishment. It was named after the Italian church Portiuncula, meaning "a little portion of the earth," the place where St. Francis of Assisi had lived and died.

Shaw had been Izabel's "little portion" for nearly five years, until she'd moved across Harney Channel to Orcas Island. She'd been heartbroken when the nuns had ultimately left the island. It had been the end of an era for the local residents, and created yet another rupture in Izabel's personal history. She regretted that she hadn't been one of the eighty islanders who'd gathered to see the remaining four sisters depart from Shaw Island.

Sister Gabrielle would know exactly how to comfort me, Izabel mused. Sister Gabrielle had become a surrogate mother to her, and had been the one who'd encouraged her to get a paying job so she could afford to pursue doula training. That had been the main reason Izabel had left Shaw in the first place. She hadn't felt right, continuing to rely solely on the small sisterhood to support her.

It all seems so long ago, she thought, staring at the gray sea that blended into the steel-colored sky. Sister Gabrielle would know what she should do, just like she'd known when Izabel was a lost young woman.

After Izabel had been on Shaw for a few months, Sister Gabrielle had suggested she help out at the pre-school with the youngest children on the island. It had felt foreign to her at first. As far as she'd known, she'd never had any interaction with little ones.

"I don't think kids like me," she'd said to the nun.

"Nonsense. Children love anyone who loves them back. All you have to do is be with them and let them know you care."

"I'm not sure I know how."

"Nonsense." *Nonsense* had been Sister Gabrielle's code word for *You've just lost this argument; now get on with it.*

Izabel pushed herself back up to her feet and let the harsh morning wind blow over her. Dressed only in capris and a thin cotton hoodie, she shivered like a dying leaf, attached to its branch by the narrowest of stems. It was the kind of chill that went deep into the marrow of her bones, reaching into the darkened long-ago where her memories lay buried.

I wonder what'd happen if I jumped from here. Izabel startled awake. The idea of jumping from the ridge had never before entered her mind. *Crazy! Shake it off! Go find Buck and climb back into bed. You just got up too early, that's all. Shake it off and everything will be all right.*

The unnerving spirit enveloped Izabel as she mounted her bike and turned toward home in the lifting morning mist. Since most of the return trip was downhill, she coasted with her feet lifted four inches off the pedals and imagined her spirits lifting too. Everything felt so hard. She thought she could use a little "lift" in her life.

Once back at the cottage, she leaned Rosie's tires against the front steps and tiptoed inside, hoping not to awaken Buck. She could hear him snoring in her cozy bed. She knew it might take the apocalypse to rouse him today. It was always like that when he returned from a fishing trip. He would be filled with energy and exhilaration to see her, but once the excitement wore off—usually after a night of gentle lovemaking—he would conk out and sleep like an Egyptian mummy long into the following day.

Izabel wasn't certain what to expect today, since their night had settled into restless cuddling rather than soul-soothing sex. Peeking through the bedroom door, she saw Lucas curled close to Buck's head, six furry toes resting proprietarily on the sleeping man's shoulder. While Lucas adored Buck, he was without a doubt Izabel's cat. Or, more aptly put, she was his person.

"Come on, kitty." She motioned with her palm and whispered softly. "Come on."

The cat stretched lazily, gave a parting glance at Buck and the cozy nest they shared, then leapt panther-like from Buck's pillow to the floor at the foot of the bed in one fluid motion. Izabel gingerly closed the white paneled door, grateful she'd oiled the creaking hinge a couple of weeks ago.

Padding into the kitchen on bare feet, she filled the teakettle with water from the tap and turned on the ancient gas stove, being mindful to catch the pot before it screamed its boiling signal. She peeled a banana and ate it as she stared out the window and waited for the water to boil. Reaching into the cabinet, she pulled out a pottery mug and turned it over to read the inscription on the bottom: *The Universe Knows.* A groan escaped her throat.

With tea in hand and Lucas at her heels, Izabel entered the living room and snuggled onto the overstuffed sofa. She didn't have the energy to make a fire, so she lit the candles on the rustic wood coffee table. Then she pulled the worn patchwork quilt she'd discovered at the local farmers' market over her legs. Lucas burrowed into his usual spot in her lap.

What's going on with me? she mused. *My life feels out of control. My emotions are out of whack and my body . . . well . . . I don't even know what to think about that.* Lucas reached out a paw as if to touch her arm in affirmation.

The boundaries are so blurry. Lucas's breath feels like mine. Who was the girl in the dream? The cat's spine twitched as if sensing his mistress's mood. They were both restless and calm at the same time.

Lucas nipped gently at Izabel's hand. An internal voice whispered to her. *Be still.* Izabel shook her head. *I don't know who I am anymore. What is happening to me?*

"Hey, babe. What's going on?" Buck's voice preceded him into the room. He paused in the doorway, leaning on the doorjamb with one lanky arm. "You're up early."

"So are you. I thought you'd sleep until at least noon."

"You know I can't sleep when you're not with me. Why don't we go crawl back in that feather bed of yours? I promise I'll make it worth your while." A rakish grin crossed his face.

Even though Izabel knew he would be gentle and she could get lost in the folds of his competent caresses, she hesitated.

"What's wrong, Iz? Did I do something?"

She winced. It broke her heart to think he might be blaming himself for her sallow mood. Buck had never been anything but kind to her. If anything, *she* was the one in the wrong for allowing a married man to share her bed.

From somewhere in the depths of her memory, a Joyce Carol Oates quote arose. "There was a man she loved with a violent love, and she spent much of her time thinking about his wife." Felicia. Buck's wife. Why was she present in Izabel's mind this morning? Who was the other woman? Izabel? Felicia? Or was there someone else?

When she thought about *the other woman*, it was neither Buck's wife nor her own image that haunted her, but another woman from long ago. This time the pain was not in her gut, but in her heart's center: a sharp, stabbing penetration. She knew, just as fall followed summer, that she and the other woman could never be separated.

"Iz? Did you hear me? Did I do something wrong?" Buck had crossed the room and was standing before her, looking bewildered.

"Oh, sweet man," she whispered to Buck. "No. You haven't done anything wrong." Izabel reached up and stroked his whiskered cheek. "I'm so sorry. It's me that's wretched. Absolutely wretched." When the final word was out of her mouth, Izabel's hand dropped to her side like a dead weight. Her shoulders heaved with wracking sobs.

"You're scaring me, Iz. I don't know what I'm supposed to do. Can you tell me what you need? And who says you're wretched?"

"Oh, Buck. Will you just hold me?" That was the only thing she could think to say.

No sooner had the words escaped her lips than his strong arms encircled her. He scooped her up and headed toward the not-yet-cold feather bed.

Lucas sat on the sofa, leisurely licking his Hemingway paws. Then he slunk onto the floor and followed them into the bedroom.

DAISY

The Master perched precariously atop the busy hive. Absentmindedly stroking his golden stripes with one hand, he watched Daisy slog through the overgrown pathway of ferns and other luscious vegetation. He was becoming bored with the game that the girl didn't even know they were playing. Her focus was single-minded as she put one foot in front of the other, not even noticing the brilliant colors dulling and becoming increasingly monochromatic as she forged ahead. Her intense concentration was pointed toward the other side of the island. She'd lost sight of her reference point, the hazy cloud, and was having trouble getting her bearings.

Daisy had always been tenacious in her pursuits. Her mother had said she was the epitome of a feral dog with a bone, never letting go once she'd sunk her teeth into something. The Master chuckled with renewed anticipation as he read her thoughts.

Around the next corner, a bulldog appeared in the center of the path, startling Daisy out of her trance. The dog was the most normal-looking creature she'd seen since arriving in Tausi. She wasn't sure how to respond. His squat body was a standard size, unlike Sir Albert's giant stature, and his fawn-colored torso stood in sharp contrast to the blue-green surroundings.

Moving cautiously, she took a step toward the familiar-looking pup. "Hey buddy. Where'd you come from?"

With alacrity and a wagging tail, the dog trotted toward her. As he neared, she noticed something protruding from his mouth. Daisy stumbled backward as her gangly feet wrapped around each other. Eyes wide, she held her breath and covered her mouth to avoid vomiting up the scarce contents in her stomach. His face was indeed that of the breed she'd pictured in her mind, but instead of the doe-eyed pup she'd expected to see, there stood a brutal carnivore. Extending from his jaw was the leg of a freshly killed deer-like animal. Daisy thought the appendage might still be kicking, although any movement was most likely an illusion caused by the pup's jaws chomping up and down on the fuchsia and black striped leg. *Chauncey?* Her heart sank. *No. Chauncey's leg is green and black, but gosh, I bet it's at least a distant cousin.*

"Oh, that's gross," she sputtered aloud. "Get outta here!"

From his lofty perch in the beehive, The Master snapped his fingers. Just as quickly as the vision had appeared, the bulldog and his gruesome chew toy were gone.

Daisy stood still and shook her head, touching a palm to her temple. *What the heck? My mind's playing tricks on me. I must be dizzy from hunger.*

No sooner had the thought of food formed in her mind than a banquet appeared on a platter alongside the pathway: Peanut butter and jam sandwiches on white bread, cut in star and heart shapes. Fresh baby carrots with ranch dip. Frosted pink animal crackers with sprinkles. Apple juice in a tiny box with a straw.

Daisy squealed with delight like she had the first time she'd opened her lunchbox in kindergarten to find the exact same lunch. Wait. This was, literally, the *exact* same lunch. *What is happening here?* she thought.

The Master cooed into a microphone that fed directly to where Daisy stood.

"Oh, sweetie, you know you get all fidgety when you wait too long to eat." It was her mother's voice, but where was it coming from? "Go ahead and eat up, Daisy, the bread gets soggy if it sits too long."

"Mom? Mom, is that you?"

"Yes, pumpkin. It's me." A woman appeared on the pathway where seconds before there'd only been ferns.

"Holy shit!" Daisy staggered backwards.

The woman wore short cutoff overalls with a tight, white t-shirt beneath. A wildly colored cross adorned the center of the bib. Her streaked hair flowed like waterfalls down her back, and her flawless skin was unadorned except for a hint of pink gloss on her heart-shaped lips.

While the woman seemed familiar, she definitely wasn't Daisy's mom. Her mother wasn't nearly this exotic, and she wouldn't have been caught dead in shorts, much less cutoff overalls.

"Who are you?" Daisy asked. No sooner had the words escaped her mouth than the woman vanished.

"Little fool," muttered The Master.

"Daaaaaaisy? Where are you, Daisy?"

With a flash of guilt, she recognized Chauncey's worried voice. She considered fleeing in the other direction, but the relief of hearing a familiar voice won her internal tug-of-war.

"Chauncey, I'm here! I'm right here!"

Chauncey emerged from the jungle beside her. Daisy virtually threw herself onto the okapi's neck and squeezed him tightly.

Sir Albert appeared in the space behind them. He cocked his peacock's brow and the plume atop his head quivered with an I-told-you-so air.

"Miss Daisy." The majestic bird nodded.

"Hey, Al." Daisy looked down and scuffed the ground with her left toe.

"Did you have a nice nap? Chauncey here, has been trying to convince me you were sleepwalking. Is that indeed the case?" Sir Albert paused for a moment, waiting for Daisy to respond. "Certainly you weren't attempting to visit the other side of the island, now, were you?"

"Damn it!" The Master cursed. "One flick of the goo and she's gone! Blasted child! And curses to that blue-feathered Thanksgiving turkey! His power is clearly stronger than I've given him credit for."

In his hive, the beast began to gyrate wildly until it seemed he would literally come apart at his goo-soaked seams. As parts of his posterior began to break open, the earth parted in the jungle floor near where the reunited trio stood.

Sir Albert squawked in alarm as the damp ground cracked and shook around them. "Daisy, quick, grab my neck. Chauncey, sprout your back-up wings. We've got to fly before the whole place opens up!"

"What's happening?" implored Daisy.

"Apparently you've made someone quite angry, my dear, and frankly I'd prefer not to tarry lest we find out what else he's willing to destroy. Jump on, now!"

MONICA

As Monica tossed and turned on the floor of her inner sanctum, she dreamed about a faceless man with the voice of J.T. Higgins. He strolled into her bedroom and cavalierly pressed the hidden control for the closet. As he moved toward the opening, she lunged at him and yelled: *No!*

She flung her arm outwards and slammed it against the corner of a shelf. *Ouch!* Opening her eyes, she surveyed her wrinkled clothes and stiffened body as the odd sensation that this man could see inside her hidden secrets stirred wildly within her belly.

Oh, thank God I was just dreaming. What if he really found out?

Her passion for shoes had started out so innocently, with that first tiny pair of black patent leather tap shoes. As she glanced toward their place of honor near the center of the room, her mind dipped into the era of sweet memories before things had become difficult the second time around. Actually, she'd lost count of the "difficult times," but she knew a measure of relief had begun with that pair of heel-tapping soles.

Monica shifted her body on the loosely scattered pillows and reached for the child-size shoes. As her hand touched the smooth leather, her memories returned to her as a tiny tot merrily dancing heel-toe-heel-toe across the kitchen floor. The lyrical sounds and enthusiasm had worn out long before the shoes. In a desperate attempt to hold onto the sweet memories, Monica remembered how she'd created her first shoe shrine when she placed the tiny shoes atop her old jewelry box and placed a candle in front of them.

In the closet, next to the shiny tappers, resided the sparkly slippers that were a perfect replica of Dorothy's from *The Wizard of Oz*. A brief smile crossed

Monica's face. Her eyes scanned the other few child-size pairs that resided in her let's-not-panic room, and her breathing calmed.

Ahhh. This is more like it. But the tug of war inside her brain persisted— Happy. Sad. Calm. Anxious. Peace. Despair. Finally she lifted herself off the cushions and moved to the kitchen. She shook her head as if shooing away a fly, and focused on the day's task at hand: finding something to keep herself occupied.

I've got to get out of this house or I'm going to lose my mind!

Monica prepared a cup of tea to settle her mood. Then she sat down at the kitchen table to sort through yesterday's mail. As she placed bills in one pile and junk mail in another, she paused at the adult education brochure from the local community center. *Hmm. I could always take a class*, she thought. Monica's eyes scanned the class catalogue as she lifted her teacup for another sip. Beginner's French. Introduction to Photography. Creative Writing. *Creative Writing. Hmmm. It's been years since I've written anything besides a boring status report.* Her eyebrows lifted and her chest heaved with a deep sigh.

Might as well. What've I got to lose?

—   —   —

Two days later, Monica pulled into the parking lot of the North Seattle Community Center. The creative writing class she'd convinced herself to sign up for started in fifteen minutes. She fidgeted in the driver's seat for a few minutes, adjusting her hair, reapplying lipstick and checking between her teeth for stray spinach. For the fifth time, she checked her satchel to make sure she had everything the class outline had recommended: loose-leaf paper, three-ring binder, pens and pencils, eraser, dictionary, and a bottle of water.

Her stomach was performing Olympic-scale gymnastics as she entered room 203. She adjusted her black-framed glasses and tugged at the navy pencil skirt that annoyingly rode up in the back when she walked. *Reminder to self: lose five pounds or give this skirt to Goodwill*, she thought.

With her white button-down shirt and one-inch navy pumps, she looked like a secretary from the early eighties. The rest of the class seemed to be wearing various combinations of loose flowy things and stonewashed denim. She felt overdressed as usual, but her mother had always said, "Better to be overdressed than underdressed." Monica had never been underdressed in her entire life. Even in bed she wore full-length pajamas and nightgowns.

She glanced around the tables that were arranged in a U-shape. She couldn't decide where to sit. Everyone looked at ease and prepared, like they did this kind of thing all the time.

"First time?" came a male voice over her right shoulder.

"Um, yes. How can you tell?"

"It's either your first community class, or you aced Girl Scouts for always being prepared," he said, as he peeked into her open satchel that rested near his chair.

"I thought that was the Boy Scouts?" She heard a flirtatious tone in her voice that she hadn't used since, well, a long time ago. *Get a grip, Monica. You're here for class, not romance.* The thought was both exhilarating and sobering.

"My mistake." The man reached over and pulled out a chair for her.

It was a challenge to keep her gaze forward *and* glance sideways to survey the oddly appealing man. He appeared to be in his mid-forties. His salt and pepper hair curled wildly in all directions. A slight paunch rested at his mid-section. *Probably sits at a desk all day. Hmmm. I wonder what he does?* He appeared to be about five-foot-ten. Standard khaki slacks. Blue button-down shirt. Oxford tassel loafers. Together, he and Monica looked like poster people for business casual attire.

"Jack," he said, reaching out his hand for hers.

"Monica," she answered, as they clasped hands in a welcoming grip.

Another voice spoke up suddenly. "Good evening, my children. And welcome to Creative Writing. I believe this is the beginner's class, although I dare say you look long past the beginner stage. But then everyone deserves a chance to be creative, I suppose."

The words came from a grand madame who stood no more than five feet tall. Regardless of her petite size, the woman carried herself with the posture of a prima ballerina. She looked as if she might lift *en pointe* at any moment. Her distinct perfume declared that she wasn't a proponent of the "no fragrance" policies that had sprung up all over Seattle these days. Monica was positive that a hint of Shalimar had entered the room several seconds before its wearer arrived. The septuagenarian's voice purred like a regal beast as she addressed the class of spellbound students. "I am Ms. Tisha, and I shall be your guide for the next eight weeks."

She was wrapped in layers of fabric and volumes of pattern and color. It was like her clothes had been constructed in a jellybean factory and she hadn't been able to decide on the flavor of the day, so she'd chosen them all. Fiery reds competed with rich purple, fluorescent green, and an array of psychedelic paisleys and exotic batiks. A white and bubblegum-pink turban with an onyx jewel in the center wrapped her head. Monica was so taken with this strange creature that she failed to realize Ms. Tisha was calling on her.

"*Hellooooo.* You there, Miss Prude and Proper. Why are you here?" The teacher pointed at Monica's nose with her crimson fingernail.

"Ex-excuse me?" Monica stuttered.

"Oh, I'm sorry. Did I offend you? I thought *I* was the teacher and *you* were the one who was supposed to be paying attention. I can see we've got our work cut out with you, my dear, beginning with the notion of creativity. Did you know its classic meaning is to transcend *traditional* ideas?" Tisha's heavily mascaraed eyes narrowed and scanned Monica from head to toe. Monica felt her limbs go numb as she felt the red rash begin to creep up her chest.

Ms. Tisha continued, "You could always start with your clothes. Lighten up a bit. Have some fun. Toss in a little flair. We can't be creative in our writing if we're all battened down behind buttons and tight skirts, now, can we?"

Her face ashen, Monica tugged at her skirt, adjusted her glasses and stared at the purveyor of words with her mouth ajar. The bluntness caught her off guard, even though she knew Ms. Tisha's words held a grain of truth. *Say something, you idiot!* she thought.

"Well, fortunately this is not a speech class. Hopefully you're more verbose on paper than you are with speech. I guess we'll see." Ms. Tisha tossed her head and turned away from Monica with a flip of her scarf. "You there. In the pink. Why are you here?"

Monica was reminded of an incident in her neighborhood during nesting season. One moment, she'd been strolling along, minding her own business, and the next an angry mother crow had flown directly at Monica's head from behind and whacked her on the shoulder. Then the bird had circled around and done it again. Ms. Tisha was like that bird. Monica couldn't grasp what she'd done in either instance to deserve an attack without provocation.

"You okay?" Jack whispered, as Ms. Tisha directed her attention toward the other side of the room. "That was pretty brutal."

"I'm okay," Monica whispered back. *Oh dear God,* she thought, *if he's nice to me I'm going to lose it, and she'll have a field day.*

"Oh! I see you two are friends. How did I miss your twin Oxford shirts? My mistake." Ms. Tisha whipped back around to focus on their corner. "Did the pair of you think a little creative writing class might put some spice back into your marriage?"

"But we're not—" Monica began in defense.

Jack stood, grabbed her hand, and hissed, "Get your things. We're outta here!" Then he spoke aloud, "Thank you, Ms. Tisha, but we're going to take our non-creative selves elsewhere. Good evening, Madame Bitcherfly. We'll be leaving now."

Monica followed him out, feeling a little stunned. Once they were out in the fresh air of the evening, she released the breath she'd been holding and looked up into Jack's mischievous eyes. They both burst into loud guffaws, like naughty school children that had left a rotten apple in the teacher's drawer.

Monica clutched her side as she recovered from the fit of laughter and spit out, "*Madame Bitcherfly?* I could never."

"Well, she deserved it. I can't believe she was so rude. I knew she had a big personality, but geez, that was over the line."

"Do you really think so? I mean, maybe she was just being honest? I don't know why I even signed up for the class. I'm no creative writer. Actually, I'm no creative *anything*. Ms. Tisha was right."

"Are you kidding me? That woman wouldn't recognize fine writing if it was stenciled on the inside of her eyelids. Did you read her autobiography?"

"Actually, I did. She sounds like quite the vamp, doesn't she? Do you think she really had an affair with Ronald Reagan?"

"Who knows, but can you imagine her going up against Nancy back in the day? The pure fashion clash would've been enough to bring the reporters out of the woodwork and send poor Ronnie running for cover! I bet she was making it all up. She couldn't have been more than a kid when, I mean if, it happened, and then she waited more than half a century until all the witnesses were dead to tell the story. My hunch is that autobiography is her version of a 'creative' story!"

"You're funny! I think creative writing is perfect for you!"

"Thanks, Monica, but I'm sure not going to study it with Madame Tisha. An abbreviated evening with her is enough to last me a lifetime! So whaddya think? Where should we go now?"

Is he asking me out? "Um, well, I was planning to go home, I guess." Monica turned the tip of her pump against the ground and twisted her body sideways.

"Home? Are you kidding? We should at least go have a celebratory coffee or something. My treat."

Oh wow, he's persistent. Monica stared at her companion under the parking lot streetlamp, and the gymnastic routine returned to her stomach. It had been years since she'd been alone with a man, other than the aged residents at Stratford Estates. Even stepping foot inside the creative writing class had tested her adventurous limits, and being attacked by the escapee from the jellybean factory had left her feeling drained and exhausted. Even though Jack had been a gallant knight, the tug to return to her inner sanctum was strong.

"That's very generous of you, but—" she began.

"But you have to get home to what? Wash your hair? Walk the dog? I'd say meet your husband, but I don't see a ring."

"I'm sorry. Maybe another time?"

"All right. I know when I'm getting the brush off." Jack hung his head. "Another time it is."

Before she could change her resolve, Monica tightened the grip on her satchel with one hand. She realized she was still holding Jack's firm hand in her other. "Good night," she whispered, eyes downcast. "Thank you for everything."

"Good night." Jack let her slender hand ease out of his grasp. "Can I call you?"

"Yes," she whispered. With heart pounding inside her chest, she disappeared into the Camry with the agility of a ninja and turned her car toward the protection of home, realizing a few miles down the road that she'd failed to give him her number.

— — —

Once inside her house, Monica kicked off her sensible pumps, uncharacteristically left them by the kitchen doorway, and poured herself a glass of wine. "Hello, Chuck," she said to the cheap white elixir. "Nice to see you tonight. Wanna take a walk with me?"

Monica had developed her eccentric behavior of talking to nonhuman things—wine, furniture, the birds outside her window, and, of course, her shoes—after she'd started living alone. The difference with the shoes, however, was that she was certain they reciprocated the conversation. When she was in her inner sanctum, it was as if the chatter inside her head made sense like it did at no other time. She knew others might deem her crazy, but she could hear the silk pumps telling her she was beautiful. The heavy boots convinced her of her strength. Flip flops encouraged her to go outside and play, and the Louboutin heels spoke of exotic places she longed to visit.

Wine glass in hand, she padded to her bedroom. Flipping on the light and then pushing the secret button, she watched the closet roll open. Tears came into her eyes at the sight of the glowing chandelier, and her nostrils filled with the intoxicating aroma of fine leather and plush carpet. "Heaven," she whispered.

As she examined the glass in her hand, she remembered the feeling of Jack's palm in hers. How long had it been since she'd held a man's hand? *Wait. I know exactly how long it's been.* Taking another sip of wine, Monica remembered the night her college roommate, Jessica, had placed that inaugural beer in her hand. It had been the night of her first college party, and the night that had changed her life.

Monica sat in the middle of her closet and marveled at how vivid the memories of that night remained in her consciousness. In fact, when she closed her eyes for a moment, she could feel the world spinning like it had that night at The Commons, and she remembered it all.

— — —

Monica looked in the dorm room mirror and patted her frizzy, permed hair. "Um. I think I'll stay home," she groaned to her roommate. "I'm not feeling so good."

"Ah, don't worry. It's just jitters. We can take care of that in a jif." Jessica shook her fluffy curls, reached into her bag, and produced a can of Pabst Blue Ribbon and popped the top. "Here ya go."

"Uh, thanks," Monica glanced sideways at her friend.

"Go ahead, sister. Chug-a-lug." Jessica had been drinking since she was fifteen, and assumed everyone else did the same.

Monica brought the lukewarm can up to her pink-tinted mouth and caught a whiff of the nasty-smelling brew. Her impulse was to hold her nose like she did with cough syrup, but she thought twice since Jessica was watching. Instead, she closed her eyes, tilted her head back, and steadily poured the liquid down her throat. A slight cough escaped her lips when she finished.

"Whoa. Look at you go. You're a natural. The Lambda Chis are gonna love you!" Jessica handed her another beer.

Monica's mouth lifted upward into a Cheshire-cat grin. Maybe I'll fit in after all, she thought.

The Lambda Chi house was on the far side of campus away from the dormitories. It was located on the infamous Fraternity Row that could be found on every college campus. At a reasonable pace, it took about twenty minutes to walk there, but the cans of beer the girls gulped on the way slowed their progress.

"This is fun," Monica giggled. "Oh, look at the cute duckies," she cooed, as they walked past one of the campus ponds. "My parents got engaged at Theta Pond at OSU. I wonder if it looked like this?"

"Probably." Jessica shrugged.

"How many duckies do you see, Jeshca?"

"What? Ducks? Two. Why?"

"Nushing. I thought there smore." Monica tipped sideways and followed the pond and the ducks onto her side. "One of 'em looks shtuck to me."

"Mo? What the heck? You okay?"

"I push need to take a lil ress here with the duckies. Ah, thish feels nice." Monica lay still and watched the pond and ducks start to spin slowly.

"Come on, Monica. We're almost there." Jessica bent down to lift up her friend. Monica's body wobbled like a hundred-pound jellyfish.

"Push napping. Mm okay." Monica waved Jess's hand away with a flick of her wrist.

"Well, if you're sure. Party's right down the block. Come on over when you're ready." Jessica tottered upright.

"S'kay," mumbled Monica, but her friend was already disappearing in a blur, heading merrily toward the party.

Ugh, make the spinning stop! Monica curled onto her side and felt the bile *rise in her throat. Her back jerked like a bronco in a rodeo as she began spewing beer and ramen noodles all over the pathway.*

In the moist night air, she heard the chatter of people coming toward her. Wild-eyed and mortified, she hoisted herself to her knees and crawled like a spooked animal into the foliage alongside the path.

"What was that?" squealed a jumpy girl.

"Nothin', babe," a boy's voice answered.

"I know there's something there. What if it's the ghost of The Commons?"

"Ooooooooooo. Come out, Mr. Ghost. Come out, come out wherever you are," the boy teased in a spooky, high-pitched voice.

"Jimmy, stop it! I'm scared."

"Ah, come on, babe. It's probably just a raccoon. Let's get to the party. You've got me to protect you from any old ghost."

The voices faded away while Monica hugged her knees to her body underneath an azalea bush. The bitter aftertaste of vomit and beer lingered in her mouth. The distinct sound of her mother's voice spoke up in her head: That's what you get for trying to fit in, Monica Gayle.

God, her mother was like a bad spell that couldn't be broken. Whenever Monica tried to break free, the voice of her mother showed up to prove Monica could never make it on her own.

I mean, look at you. Your first night out on campus and you're throwing up beneath a bramble bush. I thought I raised you better than that. Might as well turn tail and come back to Washington, honey. These Ivy League guys won't look twice at you.

"I'm not here looking for a guy, Mother. I'm not you!"

Oh, I can clearly see that, Monica Gayle. I'd never be caught dead puking under a bush. I was raised to be a lady, and so were you.

"A lady? Are you kidding me? The only thing you raised me to be was a slave and your punching bag! Well, I'm going to prove you wrong! I'm going to be a great writer and you're going to wish you'd been nicer to me."

A writer? Oh, there you go again. Who do you think you are? Emily Dickinson? You know she died an old maid, right? And Virginia Wolfe stuffed rocks into her pockets and walked into a pond. On second thought, you might make a good writer after all. Hm. Old maid. Suicide. Looks like you're on the path already, Missy.

"Go away!" Monica screamed. "Leave me alone!"

"Hey! Who's there? Everything okay?" came a voice from the pathway.

Oh dear God. Did I say that out loud?

"Anybody there?" It was a boy's voice. Monica heard feet rustling alongside the bushes. After a few moments, she heard a "Humph," and footsteps moving away. Monica breathed an inaudible sigh of relief just as a tiny mouse scurried across her hand.

"Aaaaaagh!" Her voice reverberated across The Commons as she frantically scrambled out of the bushes. The wide-eyed boy simultaneously dove toward the scream, causing their heads to bump together in the murky dark.

"Ouch! Get away from me!" she yelled, as he grabbed her arms to steady her. "I'll scream."

"Wait. I promise I won't hurt you." The boy dropped her arms and held his hands up in mock surrender. "Are you okay?"

"What? Yes. I don't know. Go away, please." Monica covered her face with her hands. Unclear on what to do next, she peeked over the top of her fingers and found herself looking into the kindest eyes she'd ever seen.

"Is someone else in there?" The boy nodded toward the bushes.

"What? No. Just me."

"Oh. I thought I heard you telling someone to leave you alone."

"Um. Uh. Nope. You must've been hearing things." The embarrassment was starting to make Monica's head clear. She hoped this boy hadn't stepped in her puke in the dark.

"Are you sure you're okay? What were you doing in there anyway?"

Having a nervous breakdown. Puking my guts out. Embarrassing myself for eternity. The usual. *Monica shrugged.*

The boy looked at her like she was a fawn that had just lost its mother. "You're shivering," he said. Monica saw that he was trembling, too. She stared back at him through heavy glasses askew on her makeup-smeared face.

He gingerly removed his denim jacket, and wrapped it around her shoulders. "There you go. That should help."

"Thank you," she whispered.

"I'm Jeremy."

"Monica." She glanced sideways, noticing his denim shirt and cowboy boots

that were in sharp contrast to the preppy frat boys in their Oxford shirts and penny loafers.

"Hey, Monica."

"Hey." *Her shivering had finally stopped, thanks to the jacket.*

"Where you headed?"

"Oh, I was kind of, like, going to a party with my girlfriends."

"Oh." *Jeremy looked around.* "Where are they? Do you need to go meet them? Can I walk you?" *Once the words started flowing, he kept them coming. The stream of awkward conversation tethered them together as they stood in the moonlight.*

"Um, no. I'm not going to the party."

"Oh. Okay. Could I walk you somewhere?"

Monica had never had such a cute boy ask her that. During high school, she'd kept her nose in the books studying so she could get out of Seattle. She'd hated the rain and the grunge music scene. She'd hoped that when she got to Briar Cliff, things would be different.

"Sure. I guess." *She swallowed hard. Her mouth still tasted of vomit and beer.*

"Okay. Great!" *Jeremy's face broke into a smile, followed by a wide-eyed slow-down-boy grimace.* "Um. Cool. Where do you want to go?" *He looked down and kicked the ground with the toe of his left shoe.*

"There's a coffee house on Briar Lane where I like to study. We could go there if you want." *Where I like to study? Geez, Monica. Could you say anything nerdier?*

"I know that place," *said Jeremy.* "Marty's, right? It's one of my favorites, too."

"Really?" *Monica couldn't believe her luck. She wondered why she hadn't seen him there before.*

"Well, let's go and get something to warm you up."

Monica turned her eyes downward, a mix of slight fear and anticipation coursing through her body. She started to tremble again from the cold night air and her wave of emotions, then hugged Jeremy's jacket to her chest. "Oh my gosh. I still have your jacket. You've got to be freezing. Here, take it. Please."

"No, ma'am. Besides, this is hardly what you'd call cold back where I come from."

"Which is?"

"Billings, Montana."

"Are you kidding me? I thought everyone here was from Connecticut or New Hampshire!"

"Me, too. Where are you from? You don't sound Yankee to me. No offense."

"None taken. I'm from Seattle."

"We're practically neighbors."

"Yes, sir."

Monica and Jeremy walked through The Commons, chatting as though they'd known each other since childhood. As they neared Fraternity Row, they could hear the raucous yells of drunken partiers amidst music blaring from gigantic speakers perched precariously in second-floor windows and along porch railings.

"Which party?" *Jeremy nodded toward the houses.*

"Huh?"

"Which party were you going to with your friends?"

"Oh, the Lambda Chis, I think."

Just then a girl came stumbling down the sidewalk toward them. "Mo Mo. Zer you are."

"Hey, Jessica. You okay?" *Monica stared at her disheveled roommate. She could smell beer and smoke coming off her.*

"You betcha! Renny and I are juss headin' down to the pond for a dip. Wanna come? Hey, who's the hottie?" *Jessica nodded toward Jeremy.* "Way t' go, Mo. I didn't know you had it in ya! Sure ya don't wanna come for a dip?"

"No thanks. We're going for coffee at Marty's."

"Coffee, schmoffee. I'm goin' swimmin'."

"Okay. Be careful. I'll see you later."

"Later, alligator. Oh, Mo Mo, you've got leaves in your hair. I like it! Maybe I'll get some at the pond."

Monica reached her hand toward her head and felt twigs and dried leaves in with her hair. "Oh my God. Why didn't you tell me?" *She glared at Jeremy.*

"Well, since we just met, I thought maybe it was your personal style. Your friend seemed quite taken with it. Who am I to judge?" *He winked.*

"Oh dang. I need a mirror. Where's my purse?"

"I didn't see one. Maybe you left it under your bush?"

Monica rewound the events of the evening in her mind, going back to just before she left her dorm. Her memories were fuzzy from the beer. "Nope. I left it *at home, so I wouldn't lose it at the party. I can only imagine what my makeup looks like if I have twigs in my hair."*

Jeremy looked at her like she was precious treasure, instead of the mess she imagined.

"You've got to get the twigs out of my hair or I'm going home right now."

"Stand still." Jeremy drew close and started delicately picking leaves out of Monica's hair. The ebbing effect of the alcohol made her sway on her feet a little.

"There you go," Jeremy said as he removed the last leaf from her crown. "Now that I've acted as your personal valet, I guess I should ask if you prefer to have mascara running down your cheek or not?"

"What? Oh, no. You must think I'm a total loser!"

"Absolutely not." Jeremy began to wipe the smeared mascara from Monica's cheeks with the end of his shirtsleeve, until her face was clean of telltale trails. With each movement, he held her gaze. "All done."

"Thank you," she whispered. "Am I presentable now?"

"Perfect." Jeremy held out his open hand. "Shall we?"

"We shall." Monica grinned and put her hand in his steadfast grip as they strolled toward Marty's.

— — —

In her closet, Monica turned her hands palm side up and examined each one. On the left was the hand Jeremy placed in hers that night so long ago. For a moment, she felt his tenderness, and then her palm began to burn as she fast-forwarded and felt the heat of betrayal. He'd said it was a mistake, that he loved her and wanted her to be his wife. A stream of tears rolled down her face. Squeezing her eyes shut, she curled her palm into a fist like a scribe rolling and sealing a hidden message.

Inhaling and exhaling several times like a yogi preparing for meditation, she opened her eyes and looked at the hand Jack had held tonight. Perhaps it was a new beginning. A deep sigh moved through her body as she reached for her wine glass. Even though she'd ceased crying, her hands shook. Chardonnay sloshed onto the creamy carpet. The past wouldn't let go. There would be no new beginnings for her. Her shoulders rose and fell, and a tragic wail filled the room.

She curled into a ball, her mind racing with all the wild thoughts of what had been. She'd thought she could forgive the betrayal, but time had never allowed her to forget. Two decades later, she lay on the floor of her inner sanctum with a stinging palm and watery eyes, surrounded by the only things that brought her any comfort.

IZABEL

As Izabel stood on the deserted beach, her only company was a stranded log and the heavy, burning feeling inside her belly. She shifted from foot to foot with agitation, before planting her sandaled feet into the rocky sand to steady herself. She couldn't stand that she'd hurt Buck with her standoffish behavior the last time they were together, and she couldn't shake the deep feeling of shame about being someone's mistress. She imagined that even if Felicia didn't love him anymore, as he said, she would still be hurt by the betrayal.

Narrowing her eyes at the stalwart log, she thought it looked as if it might raise an ashen-gray branch and point at her accusingly. She could see the massive trunk had tumbled for years, if not decades, in the Strait of Juan de Fuca. Depending on the prevailing currents, the mighty conifer had made its passage either from the coastline of northern Canada or the Pacific Northwest's Olympic Rain Forest.

No roots. Izabel stared at the orphaned log. *I know that feeling.* A burning sensation rose like bile in her throat. She held her paddleboard underneath her right arm and wiped a tear from her cheek with her left. The longing to drop the board and rest on the weathered log was strong, but the call for revenge against herself and punishment for her deeds was more virulent.

The waves in the Strait were white-capped, spitting their own salty tears her way. Only a fool would enter the sea today, or a woman with nothing to lose. Izabel believed she was both.

Kicking off her sandals, she dug her toes into the pebbled beach. Her blue rash-guard covered her torso, acting like the thinnest shield against the raging wind. Her long legs sprouted goose bumps that stretched like tiny pin dots up a flesh-colored map. One foot in front of the other, she inched her way toward the rocking sea. She thought about Virginia Woolf filling her pockets with stones and strolling into a river to meet her watery death.

Izabel didn't want to die, at least not yet. A tiny niggle inside whispered she had something greater to live for, even though a louder voice cursed and railed and told her she must be punished for all her wrongs.

Behind her, the dried-out log reached a lone branch her way like a beggar pleading for alms. The frigid water nipped at her ankles as she inched into the sea, and a shiver rattled up her spine. Before long her whole body would be numb. She kept moving.

She waded waist-deep into the water and dropped the board, hanging onto the separate paddle. Normally, she would attach the board to her ankle with a strap, but today she felt reckless and left it undone. If the board washed out to sea, so be it. She no longer cared.

Using her upper body strength, she pulled herself into a seated position atop the board, rocking in the churning water. Raising the paddle perpendicular to the water, she began to push away from shore. Even this close in, the waves pushed her to and fro. For a split second, Izabel rethought her decision to paddleboard today.

Once she was about ten feet from the beach, she gained her footing and stood on the board. Her balance was good, and she rolled instinctively with the waves that crashed and threatened to tip her over. *Years of yoga were good for something,* she thought. Dipping the paddle into the sea, she dug deep like a determined gravedigger. *One two. One two. One two.* She found her rhythm in the pounding waves and headed outward at a ninety-degree angle from the shore.

Izabel paddled nonstop. Despite the cold morning air, her body warmed, and she broke into a sweat beneath her rash guard. She guessed she was about a mile from shore when a crackle of lighting flashed to the south, followed by a deafening boom. Izabel dug her paddle deeper into the navy sea, not letting up even when the skies opened and needles of rain pricked at her bare skin.

Yes. Yes. That's more like it. Bring it on! She looked up at the sky. *Hit me with what you've got!* It felt like she was in a wild contest with the sea. She would paddle a few feet, slow the board slightly, and look up into the sky, rain blinding her with driving force. Then the sky would flash and crackle in response.

Izabel lifted her paddle with both hands over her head and shook it at the sky. "What do you have to say to me?" she bellowed into the wind.

The sky lit up. Thunder boomed. And a four-foot wave caught Izabel from behind, knocking her feet out from under her and hurling her into the churning sea.

Down she went, spinning and turning, panicking when she realized she couldn't tell which way was up. Everything was a muted shade of slate blue, sky and water, a soup of confusion.

This is it. I'm going to die. So be it.

At the moment Izabel let go of the fight, she remembered to watch her bubbles and see which way they floated. When she gained her focus, she relaxed and began to float upward until she pierced the surface, gasping for breath. Her board was nowhere to be seen, but the paddle floated about ten feet away. It wasn't much, but she'd take it.

Izabel reached the paddle easily and slipped it beneath her arms like a toddler's pool noodle. She rested for a moment and caught her breath, before scanning the horizon again. The waves had calmed, and the whitecaps were peaking at about one foot instead of three. The rain stopped as abruptly as it had begun, and a window opened up in the cloud cover to reveal a hint of sunshine.

Izabel flipped onto her back, hugging the paddle across her chest. With her ears below the waterline, the world took on a muted hum and she felt herself relax. Drifting in the open sea without agenda, she thought about the previous weeks: the Anderson baby's delivery, her disturbing dreams, the inexplicable stomach pains, and the gnawing feeling that she was cheating on more than Buck's wife. It was too much. She considered just letting go of the paddle and sinking to the bottom of the sea.

If she'd been on her stomach, her position would have been a dead man's float. Instead, she rocked with her face turned toward the sky while the waves tossed her body to and fro. She clung to the paddle and wondered if today might be the day she died.

Who would miss me? Buck? Miriam? Beth? I don't have any family, none that I can remember, anyway . . .

A large wave splashed across her chest, filling her open mouth with salt water. She gasped, inhaling the briny sea, and struggled to gain her breath. Her feet shot downward into the frigid water, and she almost lost her grip on the paddle.

Once she stopped coughing and gained some semblance of composure, Izabel realized how cold she was. She could feel her core temperature dropping, and she wondered how much longer she could last out here. *Twenty minutes?* She recalled something about that being the length of time people could survive with a lowered temperature, at least before they lost consciousness.

Don't let go, came a muffled voice from somewhere outside her. Had the hallucinations started? She'd heard that was what happened when you started to lose consciousness. You heard things.

Hang on, Izabel. There it was again. The voice. She closed her eyes tight and tried to ignore the hallucinatory voices.

"Izabel? Is that you? You okay, honey?"

The voice was getting louder and she could feel her panic rising. *Stay calm.* Then she felt something bump against her elbow. Kicking her feet down and raising her torso, she saw a life jacket floating next to her, and Hank the handyman coming alongside her in his small fishing boat.

"Whatchoo doin' out here in this mess, girl?" He reached out his grizzled hand.

Izabel tipped the paddle toward him. He took hold of it and pulled her closer to the boat before reaching under her arms and lifting her in.

"I picked up this here board 'bout a hunnert feet out. Is it yours?" Hank pointed at her paddleboard balanced across the stern of his boat. She nodded.

Hank took off his jacket and wrapped it around her. "Geez, Iz. You're shiverin' like a leaf in a windstorm. You okay?"

"I'm f-fine. Th-thanks, Hank." Her teeth were chattering so wildly, it was difficult to get the words out.

"I'm worried about you, girl. First you try to get yourself killed on your bike, and now I find you out here in the middle of a storm. What's going on?"

"I'm okay, really. Just bad timing," she said, trying to soothe his worried expression. "I owe you two now, Hank. You're my hero."

"Aw, thanks, honey. I'm just glad I could help. Whaddya say we get to shore and get you home?"

"Sounds good." Izabel clutched Hank's jacket around her shivering body. *Why did I do something so stupid?* she thought dully, as the boat turned for the shore.

DAISY

Daisy squinted her eyes and looked at the object perched at the fringe of the beach, where pink-tinted sand turned into blue jungle. About twenty feet long and half as wide, it looked like a giant loaf of bread on wheels.

Psychedelic paint was splattered across the sides, punctuated by spirals twirling outward into paisley pinwheels. There were oodles of fluorescent pink flowers entwined with lime-green frogs whose lithe tongues juggled aqua, lemon yellow, and raspberry tinted eggs. All of this was plastered along the sides and over the top of the classic-yet-not school bus. Even the tires, which a person might expect to be black, were mottled shades of purple and magenta.

The effect was dizzying. The riot of color threw Daisy off kilter, and she blinked her eyes to try and steady her gaze.

Daisy stood motionless in the sand, weighing whether or not to approach the multi-colored bus. It seemed to be abandoned, but the words printed on the side kept her rooted to the ground, swaying ever so slightly: *We're Coming to Take You Away.*

Who, me? she wondered.

"Yes, you, my dear!" a voice bellowed as the door swung open and a bawdy character appeared on the top step. Daisy gasped and took a slight step backward, as her hand flew to her O-shaped mouth.

The creature's appearance was confusing. At first glance, he appeared to be dressed like the hat merchant from one of her favorite children's books, *Caps for Sale*. Unlike the mild-mannered salesman in the book, however, this man seemed anything but.

Black plaid pants rolled over his pear-shaped hips, giving the illusion of a moving checkerboard as he stepped out of the bus. His topcoat glimmered like a midnight sky, but when he turned to the side, a riot of colors—red, tangerine, fuchsia, and lime green—flashed down the sides of the streaming tails. He looked like an electronic billboard, changing appearance every few seconds.

Daisy held her breath and kept her cat-green eyes fixed on where he stood. A small hairy hand reached through the doorway behind him. It was followed by another, and another, until the passageway was filled with a mishmash of hairy human-like creatures.

Monkeys, at least a dozen, rolled onto the sand as if they'd been poured from a giant barrel. A bold one wearing hot-pink lipstick and a feather boa charged toward Daisy, stopping abruptly at the girl's feet. Then it reached for the loose braid hanging down her back and hoisted itself up onto Daisy's shoulders.

"Get off me!" Daisy flailed her arms, trying to take a swing at the clinging primate.

"Tsz, tsz, tsz!" The monkey laughed through gritted teeth, tightening its grip on Daisy's neck.

"Go away!" she shouted again, twirling in circles and swatting at the beast.

"Tsz, tsz, tsz!" The monkey beckoned, motioning its chattering friends to join in.

Daisy shook and squirmed and swatted as she tried to untangle the hairy hands from around her neck without success. Four more monkeys joined the party, each one wrapping around one of her arms and legs.

Daisy shrieked and spun like a whirling dervish. The monkeys laughed and hooted as if they were on a wild carnival ride. The girl stumbled and crashed into the sand. The monkeys clung on, unwavering. Images of being eaten alive flashed through Daisy's mind as her captors bared their menacing teeth.

Her shoulders heaved up and down as wracking sobs escaped her body. The monkeys cackled and gave each other high fives over her prone form.

"Albert? Chauncey? Help!" Daisy wailed before planting her face into the pink sand, grit filling her mouth.

As she went down, the boa-clad leader waved its arm like a cowboy riding a bucking bronco and beckoned the rest of the pack toward Daisy. A dozen monkeys romped across the beach and gleefully joined the pile atop the small heap of a girl.

Daisy could feel herself disappearing, like the life was seeping out of her body. Sand filled her mouth and her lungs pressed into her ribs with the weight of her captors. She wiggled a finger from beneath the furry pile and crooked it up toward whatever she might reach.

She touched something that felt like a brass button, perhaps from one of the monkeys' coats. The word *Push* flashed through her brain. *Push.* There it was again. Her eyes were blocked by sand and monkey fur, so she wiggled her finger toward where she'd felt the button. Reaching with her last ounce of strength, she found the smooth surface and pushed.

Daisy's body rose without effort from beneath the huddle of monkeys, reversing her spinning actions from moments before. The mischief-makers spun with her, holding on as if she were a lone tree rooted in a hurricane. Their bodies flew parallel to the ground, straining to maintain their grip. One by one, sideways gravity pulled them free and flung them off, each monkey vanishing in a tiny cloud-like puff until only the boa-clad one remained.

The two locked eyes, Daisy's gaze burning and the monkey matching her intensity. Round and round they spun, Daisy feeling stronger with each rotation.

Steps away, the man in his checkerboard pants made a move toward them. Daisy had forgotten about him, but as soon as he appeared in her peripheral vision, she screamed.

"*Albert! Chauncey!*" Her roar filled the jungle.

The startled monkey released its grip and flew outward into the man, knocking him over. The two rolled together like a tumbleweed, across the sand and up into the open door of the magic bus.

The bus shuddered upon impact, then dissolved into nothing, like a sandcastle doused with a crashing wave. Daisy fell down onto the sand and lay still, panting.

"Hello, my dear. You called?"

She looked up. Sir Albert was standing by her side, looking completely unruffled.

"Wha-what just happened?"

"Lovely boa you have there." The peacock dipped his beak under the monkey's boa, now around Daisy's slender neck. She stared at the white feathers, dumbfounded.

"Shall we take a walk and go find Chauncey?" Sir Albert knelt in invitation.

Daisy shook her head again, then swung her leg over the peacock's body and wrapped her arms around his long neck. "Yes, let's," she whispered.

MONICA

The time away from work dragged by. Monica attempted to busy herself with getting fall chrysanthemums for the outdoor planters. Sweeny's Garden was always a great place to stroll and get lost for a while. With acres of plants and trees, it typically took the salespeople and gardeners a while before they noticed she'd been wandering aimlessly without adding anything to the red wagon she pulled from section to section.

Monica spent hours wandering through Sweeny's Garden, like a cat examining a mouse hole. Next to shoes, plants were her biggest delight, and the good ones cost a small fortune. That was something she needed to consider more seriously, now that her job appeared to be on shaky ground. She hadn't quite figured out how to shoplift garden plants without being noticed. The big ones were bulky and difficult to manage, and pilfering one small cyclamen hardly seemed worth the effort. She found it amusing that it was easier to carry home a four-hundred-dollar pair of shoes than pocket an eight-dollar zinnia.

"Is there something in particular I can help you find?" asked a young man in the nursery's signature green polo shirt and dirt-dusted khakis.

Monica glanced up and saw that his nametag read *Jeremy*. She inhaled a half breath and coughed like she'd just swallowed a bug, then replied, "No, thank you. Just looking." She turned back to the zinnias, feigning interest in their bright spiky blooms as the salesman walked away.

Thinking of Jeremy, *her* Jeremy, put her on edge. She walked in circles, picking up plant after plant, and putting them back down.

Somewhere in the nursery, a cell phone rang, a tinny familiar ringtone, that took Monica back to her Briar Cliff dorm room and the first time Jeremy had called her.

— — —

"Hey, Monica."

Her knees weakened when she heard Jeremy's voice, and she could feel the color rise up her chest. She hated that about herself. Fortunately, he couldn't see the blush through the telephone lines, but she thought he could probably hear it in her voice.

"Whatcha up to?"

Her dreamy-eyed self murmured internally: Laying here thinking about you. "Nothing. Just studying."

"That's my girl. Hitting the books on Saturday afternoon."

His girl? Monica liked the sound of that. "You know me. I can't get enough of women's history."

"So, what are you doing tonight?"

Monica's heart fluttered. Saturdays at Briar Cliff were reserved for official dates. Unless their initial meeting at the pond counted, Jeremy and Monica hadn't yet had a weekend rendezvous.

"Oh, not much. Studying maybe." She didn't want to reveal she was supposed to hang out with her roommate and some of the girls, in case he wanted to ask her out.

"Wish I could join you. I promised the guys I'd hang out with them tonight."

Great. Now I sound like a loser with nothing to do. "Sounds like fun. I may go with Jess and the girls down to The Cliff. I don't know."

"Well, I just wanted to call and say hi. Maybe I'll catch ya later?"

"Yeah, later." She couldn't hide the disappointment in her voice.

"Hey Monica, I really meant what I said. I wish I could be with you instead."

"Really?" Warmth rose up inside her, and she smiled.

"Really. I would never lie to you. Ever."

— — —

Tears formed in Monica's eyes, blurring the flowers in front of her. Jeremy's promise had seemed so solid back then. Her chest tightened and she knew it was time to leave Sweeny's Garden. She lowered her head to avoid making eye contact with anyone and scurried back to her car. Turning the key in the ignition, she glanced into the rearview mirror, wiped the smeared mascara from beneath her eyes, and smoothed her auburn hair.

She stared stonily through the windshield as she drove home. Even though she'd sworn a personal oath that the cobalt Kate Spades would be her last acquisition for the season, the memories of Jeremy were taking their toll. As if that wasn't enough, her nights continued to be filled with vivid dreams of faceless men and tap dancing girls. Meeting Jack at the writing class had been exhilarating, but they hadn't exchanged phone numbers, so he had no way to reach her. *Just as well. I'm better off on my own.* Without her job to fill time, the hours seemed to drag by like old women climbing Machu Picchu.

Once home, Monica sat at the computer and opened her favorite website, Zapatos. Shoes in every size, color, and style popped onto the screen. She immediately felt her chest relax and the pounding in her head lessened. Closing her eyes, she imagined inhaling the new leather aroma. Her nostrils flared and a contented sigh escaped her lips. Monica knew this was like setting up an open bar in front of an alcoholic, but she forged ahead. It felt so good. *I'm just looking. There's nothing too expensive here anyway. What's the harm?*

Scrolling through page after page, she spotted a sparkly blue pair of Ugg boots. Giggles rose as she glanced down at her bare toes and imagined curling them inside the cozy lamb's wool interior.

Without hesitation, she reached for her near-the-limit credit card and entered the sixteen digits. Complimentary next-day delivery. *I love Zapatos! I always feel so bad when I tell them the package never arrived or pretend to ship it back with a UPS receipt from work.*

Okay, she would allow the charge to stay on her credit card this time. She wasn't at work, and there was always the concern someone might catch on, since she'd done the same thing just two months ago with the Ferragamo pumps. *Just a little something to take the edge off.* She wrinkled her brow. *Surely I can afford them.*

Just as the order confirmation popped up on the screen, her phone rang. She groaned, then answered, forcing fake cheeriness into her voice. "Hello?"

"Monica. This is John Paul."

Monica rolled her eyes. John Paul was the son of the owner of Stratford

Estates, and the very fact that he had a directorial position was a prime example of who-you-know and not what-you-know getting people ahead.

"Hey, John Paul. How are you?"

"Well, *I'm* just fine, but I'm calling to see how *you* are. I checked with Dr. Higgins's office, and they said you hadn't made it in yet."

Checking up on me? Isn't there some kind of doctor–patient privilege thing that applies? "Well, um—"

"You know, Monica, it's extremely important that you comply with the plan we made for you to return to work. I can't keep picking up the slack forever, you know?"

"Yes, John Paul, I understand." Monica rolled her eyes again and drummed her fingers on the desktop. "I have an appointment with Dr. Higgins first thing tomorrow morning."

"I'm not sure you *do* understand, Monica, since you failed to keep your appointment last time." *Blah blah blah,* she thought, tuning him out. His voice droned on like the grown-ups in the *Peanuts* cartoons. "And furthermore, I'm not sure you recognize the severity of the charges that may be brought against Stratford Estates due to your negligence."

Monica made a face. *My negligence? Are you kidding me? I passed out from doing your job and mine!* Biting her tongue, she responded like the good girl she'd been raised to be. "I'm sure you're right, John Paul. I don't understand all you've been through in my absence, but I promise to see the doctor tomorrow and get it all fixed up so I can get back to work." *And start doing your job again,* she added.

"Well, that sounds more like it. Take good care, Monica. Ciao."

"Good-bye, John Paul," she said through gritted teeth.

—   —   —

The next morning, the sun rose in one of those ethereal dawns that spread pink light across the lightly frosted rooftops. The final vestiges of golden leaves stubbornly clung to a few trees, and the world resembled an impressionist painting for a few glowing moments.

Strains of Pink Martini's "Sympathique" floated *à la française* from Monica's iPod shuffle as she stared out the kitchen window. She envisioned herself strolling along the Seine in Paris with a Hermés scarf wrapped around her slender neck and a West Highland terrier by her side. In her dreamlike state, she held her breath to extend the magic. When her lungs began to beg for mercy, she reluctantly released her breath, exhaling like a deflating balloon. In real life, her only visit to the City of Light had been in her imagination, and her only knowledge of the language was a mere vestige from high school French classes.

The golden light shifted to pale yellow and the diamond-like frost turned splotchy and dull. *J.T. Higgins. Ugh.* She couldn't put the meeting off any longer if she wanted to get her job back.

Do I want it back? Not really, but what other choice do I have? Monica's shoulders rose and fell with a deep sigh. She was sick of the mundane tasks. The smell of impending death and unwashed bodies. John Paul. *I was born for more than this, but I lost my choices for achieving anything great when I left Briar Cliff . . . even though it wasn't much of a choice. Whatever. I need to pay the bills.* It was a conversation she'd had with herself a zillion times. The voice of reason always seemed to win: *be responsible; pay the bills; do what everyone expects.*

Just once, she'd like to tell the voice of reason to shove it. In fact, that's what she'd done last week when she walked away from the therapist's office at Northgate, but Reason had tracked her down and thrown her failures back in her face. If she wanted to hold onto her mediocre job at Stratford Estates, she'd have to at least make an appearance at J.T. Higgins's office.

The teakettle whistled in unison with the ding of her egg timer, followed by the toaster's *pop* as her whole wheat bread sprang up. She had her breakfast regime down to a fine art. *I'm not so worthless after all*, she thought.

Unwrapping the packet of English Breakfast tea, she methodically placed it in the Wedgewood cup cradled in its matching saucer. "How are you this morning, my lovelies?" she inquired of the heirlooms she'd inherited from her grandmother. Some mornings Monica wished she were Belle in *Beauty and the Beast* and that her dishware could talk back. "Maybe meeting with the therapist won't be so bad. At least he's someone to talk to. No offense, my lovelies, but you're not the most loquacious companions a girl could ask for."

With breakfast finished and the kitchen tidied up, it was time to get dressed for her command performance with J.T. Higgins. She was ready to turn the incident at Stratford Estates into a distant memory.

Monica dressed with great care, as she always did. Making the perfect impression and managing what others thought of her was always her top priority. *Today,* she thought, *I must appear impeccable, competent, and calm.* She needed to come across as rested and ready to go back to work and create the illusion that she was in no way the same woman who'd passed out in the middle of the elderly riot at Stratford Estates.

She considered whether it would be beneficial to play up her feminine side, in case she needed to resort to flirtation in order to win her case. While she wasn't exactly desperate to resume work, she *was* eager to ensure she had a regular paycheck coming in.

Maybe I should fail the test? Let them prove I'm incompetent rather than exhausted. Get myself fired. I could collect unemployment if I were laid off. I wonder how long that would last. Oh, you silly fool. No one else would hire you, and then what would you do?

Monica returned to the task at hand: finding the perfect outfit. *Skirt or slacks? Button down or pullover? Color?* Today she needed something with a little pop.

The pale-blush Ann Taylor blouse peeked out from behind a row of starched whites. With a hint of silk instead of the usual cotton blend, it added the feminine touch she desired while not seeming overly soft. She paired it with a black tweed pencil skirt and sheer gray-black nylons.

She eyed the ebony Jimmy Choos with the six-inch heels and imagined donning them, a slick of matte fuchsia lipstick, and slinking into J.T. Higgins's office. *If only I had the nerve.* Instead, she reached for the classic Salvatore Ferragamo pumps in black patent leather and dusted her lips with petal-pink gloss.

With that finishing touch, she patted her hair, adjusted her glasses, picked up her purse, and walked out the door. She had exactly twenty minutes to arrive at her destination. Perfect timing, as always.

IZABEL

Beth's Gallery and Café was as eclectic as Beth herself. Nestled in the center of Eastsound, the exterior boasted a Cape Cod-style porch with oversized floral baskets hanging year-round. Wicker chairs waited patiently for weary citizens to stop and sit a spell, and an old pickle barrel, long empty, completed the picture. Faded red paint and black hardware decorated the saloon-style door that evoked a warm feeling of welcome.

Izabel and Beth had been friends ever since Izabel had moved to the island. They were a striking pair, as Izabel measured five-foot-eight, and Beth was no taller than five feet in heels. Izabel adored her friend, but she'd never been able to figure out how Beth got away with her no-nonsense, sometimes vulgar talk, and still amassed a store full of loyal customers and friends every day of the week.

Her café was legendary with both locals and tourists who mingled together in the interior, a wild mix of country and modern. Just as Beth was brash, so was the modern art that begged for attention from the rustic brick walls. The crowded and curved aisles mimicked her figure. Mismatched tables with red-checked cloths were tucked into one corner, where Izabel and her friends sat sipping coffee.

Separating the gallery space from the café and country store was an aisle of old-fashioned candy jars filled with everything from lemon drops and tootsie rolls to Harry Potter jellybeans. Beth hustled down the aisle by the ladies' table, feather duster in hand, and tilted her head to hear the conversation.

"You have to let your mind rest," Miriam said, looking into Izabel's tired eyes. "And your body, too. I heard you got stuck out in the storm this week."

"It was nothing," mumbled Izabel, focusing on her teacup to avoid eye contact with her mentor.

Miriam Petroni was the island's resident crone. With ivory-steel flowing hair and eyes to match, she was the epitome of wisdom and grace. No one knew how old she was, nor did it really matter. Izabel knew that Miriam was an old soul and had probably been ministering to others since she was a mere tot.

Many islanders called her Gaia, after the Earth Mother incarnate. No one knew exactly where she lived, but rumor was she resided deep in the enchanted forest on Mt. Picket amongst the spotted deer and barred owls. Whenever she arrived in town, she brought a feast of foraged mushrooms and other heavenly forest delights, some of which she'd dropped off today for Beth.

Miriam trained her piercing gaze on Izabel until the young woman released a sigh and looked toward the corner of the room. "I know, I know. But Sister Gabrielle always said, 'If you're not moving, then you're not doing.'"

"I agree with Sister Gabrielle," Beth said as she scooped up the women's empty mugs. She wiped the table and headed toward the sink tucked behind the main counter.

"Are you kidding me?" Marly piped up, twisting a strand of her ebony hair. "That sounds like my days in Silicon Valley. Work. Work. Work. With no time for ideas and dreams."

Marly and her husband, a pair of former dot-comers from California, ran Eugene's Thrift Store, a few doors down from Beth's. A stunning African-American woman, today she was wrapped in scarves of burnished red and sea-foam green. Intricate braids ran like dried river beds along her scalp and connected at the base of her neck with a gold satin ribbon. She raised an elegant eyebrow at Izabel. "Seriously, you have to make time for dreams."

"I dream while I'm sleeping," chuckled Beth, as she whooshed back by the table. "What about you, Izzy?"

"Ugh. I can't even sleep these days."

Miriam reached an age-spotted hand across the table and laid it atop Izabel's. "You have to let your mind rest." She tilted her head to capture the younger woman's gaze.

"I hate it when I close my eyes these days," Izabel continued. "I keep having these crazy, erratic dreams with birds everywhere."

"Oh, spooky. You mean like Alfred Hitchcock birds?" asked Beth, as she straightened a painting on the wall.

"No. More like peacocks and parakeets. It's really weird. Last night I dreamed about a giant peacock telling me to clean up my mess. When I saw where his beak was pointing, there was a dead crow lying next to Rosie. It looked like I'd run over it." Izabel shook her head, and a little shiver ran up her spine.

"Gross!" said Beth. "Birds are nasty. There's this cockatiel at my mother-in-law's nursing home in Seattle. It's pretty and all, but it's always getting out of its cage and causing the patients to freak out. It's kinda funny though, 'cuz there's this super prim and proper administrator who always ends up having to get it back in its cage. It's quite a sight watching Miss Prissy Monica Levin scoop that bird up with her nice white cardigan."

Izabel's head jerked up as she looked to where Beth was rearranging a display of hand-crafted lamps. "What?"

"Huh?" Beth wrinkled her forehead.

"The lady. What's her name?" Izabel pressed.

"Who? Oh, Miss Priss? Her name's Monica Levin. A real piece of work. She's constantly telling me and Charlie to quit bringing stuff into Mom's room. Says it puts pressure on the staff to keep things in order. She's always fussing over something."

"I bet she is." Izabel stared at a knothole on the floor between her feet. She felt her chest constrict and her emotions go numb.

"Are you okay?" Miriam rose from her seat, came up behind Izabel, put an arm around her shoulders, and pressed her cheek against her friend's pallid face.

Miriam's touch reminded Izabel of their first meeting almost ten years earlier, when she'd been supporting a particularly difficult birth near Otter's Pond. The family had opted to have only Izabel assist, without a midwife or the local doctor on call. It was one of Izabel's first births and she'd been in deep trouble, kind of like now.

"Miriam, do you remember the night we met?"

"Yes, I remember." Miriam smiled at the memory.

With the change of topic, the color returned to Izabel's face. "I was so arrogant back then. I'd never considered what could possibly go wrong in childbirth. I still believed mothers went into labor, wailed or stoically gritted their teeth, then bore down and pushed out a healthy baby boy or girl. Boy, that night I found out *exactly* what could go wrong."

"What happened?" asked Marly.

"Well," continued Izabel, "the mother had been laboring for more than twenty-four hours and was exhausted. 'Can't push. Too tired,' she said, and then passed out.

"'What's wrong with her?' screeched her husband, as he grabbed me by the shoulders. I assured him she just needed rest and then tried to stay calm. The house sounded weirdly quiet without the mother's screams. Her raspy breath was the only sound in the room.

"I'd never considered myself a praying woman, but I closed my eyes and began to whisper, 'Dear God, forgive me. I need help. This woman's gonna die if you don't send someone right now.' Not more than a minute later, I heard this blood-curdling barn owl scream, and then a solid knock on the door.

"I yelled at the husband to answer it. When he did, there stood Miriam, wrapped in flowing robes, a Mary Poppins bag over her arm and a twinkle in her eye."

"How'd you know?" Beth asked Miriam.

"Oh, I was passing by and thought I heard screaming. I decided I'd better check to see if everything was okay. Izabel basically pushed the poor man out of the way, pulled me into the room, and asked if I knew how to deliver a baby."

Izabel giggled. "Do you remember the look on his face when he realized I didn't know what to do?"

"I remember he started shouting at you. Then we both hissed at him to be quiet, and I thought he might pass out. Poor papa, he was so stressed out." Miriam's eyes twinkled as she joined Izabel in laughter.

"What happened next?" asked Marly.

"Well, the mother revived almost instantly upon Miriam's touch. The baby arrived within minutes, perfectly pink and healthy. I used to wonder why you were passing by that remote home on a dark night with your birthing talismans." Izabel eyed her old friend. "But then I just acknowledged you were a gift from God."

"If not the Goddess herself," Beth chuckled, as she set a plate of warm scones in front of her friends. "How'd we get on the topic of babies, anyway? I thought we were talking about weird bird things."

Izabel's mood sank again and she felt like she might pass out.

"You okay, honey?" Miriam asked gently, brushing a loose strand of hair from Izabel's face.

"I'm fine. Beth, could you please get me a drink of water?"

"Sure thing," Beth wove her body between the narrow aisles, dusting and straightening along the way. "Seriously, you should see this Levin woman with a bird wrapped up in her sweater. She looks kinda like you do right now."

"Enough." Marly made a cut signal with her hand across her throat. "How ya doing, honey? You look like you just saw a ghost."

Izabel glanced down at her feet, then looked back up to find Miriam's knowing eyes trained on her own tear-filled ones. Turning slightly to escape her friend's gaze, she pasted a half-smile on her face. "I'm fine, Marly. I think I may be coming down with a bug or something."

Miriam reached across the table and squeezed Izabel's hand. "Come on, honey. Let's get some fresh air."

DAISY

Daisy stretched her arms above her head and tried to turn over in the cot, only to discover it had turned into a wobbling hammock while she slept. Shaking her head, she rolled her eyes and remembered that linear time had no meaning in Tausi. She could no longer think in terms of day and night, or sleeping and waking. She remembered the stories she'd read about out-of-body and near-death experiences: floating figures, wordless encounters. Tausi was like that.

She opened her eyes to the familiar blue haze and intertwined her fingers with the loosely woven ropes fashioned from the island's blue-tinted bamboo. She turned her gaze toward the shore, or at least where she thought the shore should be.

Instead, she saw a vertical sheet of water, a lake turned on its side. Unlike a waterfall, there was no downward flow. As Daisy squinted, she noticed that the water was moving upward, as far as she could see.

She sat upright in the hammock to make sure she wasn't the one tilted. Nope. A wall of steel-blue water rose skyward from the ground.

"Fascinating, isn't it?" It was a woman's satiny voice, coming from somewhere over Daisy's left shoulder. Daisy knew the line between waking and slumbering here was elusive, so she pinched the inside of her left forearm to check her current status. In slow motion, she lowered one foot and then the other onto the ground, until she stood on loose sand.

"You're awake," said the voice, but this time it came from within the wall of water in front of Daisy.

A shimmery, diamond-like shadow began to form inside the liquid barrier. Daisy stared, brow furrowed.

Like a sailboat steering toward land, the shape floated closer to Daisy, and two bare feet came into focus. They had feminine, yet gritty toes, rough and worn like those of someone who lived for barefoot beach walks. Each toe sported a silver ring with distinct patterns: a waffle weave, the head of a lion, and on the pinky toe, a tiny beaded daisy.

The girl shook her head. How could the being's toes be in razor-sharp focus when the rest of the being was still blurry?

A laugh like reindeer bells at Christmas erupted from the watery vision. Daisy thought this person, if it *was* a person, was enjoying Daisy's confusion. The hair on the back of her neck stood up, and she ground her teeth in frustration. Then she squinted to see what else might manifest.

The toes now rested atop a sleek paddleboard with vibrant yellow and red stripes. The water continued its vertical lift, and the board emerged horizontally, like a heron's beak piercing the watery perimeter that reached toward the shore where Daisy stood. She jerked backward at the unreal composition and the appearance of the new colors. She'd grown accustomed to the singular blue palette in everything around Tausi. *Hmm. Something feels different here.*

Again, the voice like tinkling bells sang out: "Yes, things are different now."

Daisy paced back and forth along the pastel beach without taking her eyes off the floating figure. She knew by now that in Tausi, the blink of an eye could change the whole scene, and she was intent on bringing this one into focus.

The ethereal form continued to draw nearer, and random parts became more clear. It definitely looked like a woman. She appeared to be wearing a flowing evening gown. Daisy couldn't tell if it was black or a deep shade of midnight blue. Her hair was twisted into a classic up-do, and tiny clips, the shape of teardrops, twinkled in her glowing, strawberry-blonde hair like fireflies dancing at sunset. The face remained unclear.

"Why don't you take a picture? It'll last longer," a childlike voice cackled from behind Daisy. She swung around to see who'd spoken.

Her gaze landed, not on a child, but on a camera with a long lens nestled in the palm tree above the hammock. Daisy somehow knew that if she could grab it, she'd be able to sharpen her view of the woman's heart-shaped face.

Rising to her full five-foot-three, Daisy flexed her toes and lunged toward the lens. Her fingers brushed against the cool metal casing, then tangled in the palm frond. The force pitched her forward onto her knees, where she came face to face with her mirror image instead of the sand she'd expected. It was as if the wall of water had slid beneath her. Instead of falling in, however, she levitated about six inches above it in a crouched position.

Daisy closed her eyes, head swirling with vertigo. She took a deep breath, and reopened them to find a face that wasn't her own peering back at her from the steel-blue pond.

"Mother?" she whispered to the still water.

No response.

"Mother?" she asked again.

This time, the water buckled as if someone had thrown a stone into the center of the reflection. Only ripples radiating out from the center remained. Daisy watched them spread outward until the surface smoothed over like glass. A single tear dropped from Daisy's face into the pond.

There was a soft *pop,* and the water turned back to sand. Daisy dropped in a heap onto the gritty beach.

Daisy's mind scurried back and forth. *Who was that woman?* She wasn't concerned about vertical, up-flowing water or disappearing ponds. Instead, it was the undistinguishable face of the woman that captured her attention. Daisy instinctively put her hand over her heart and wondered about the odd sense of connection she'd felt. While it was bewildering, it was also comforting, almost as if she'd seen a photo of someone she knew and had forgotten. Someone she loved.

"But I don't recognize her," she murmured, shaking her head.

"Don't recognize who?" Chauncey's shadow appeared on the sand next to Daisy.

"No one." Daisy shook her head like a dog emerging from a pond.

MONICA

Monica felt a familiar dampness in her palms as she reached for the doorknob of J.T. Higgins, Psychotherapist. The standard-issue chrome knob felt cold to her warm hands. Like skin drawn to dry ice, her hand clung to the fixture. *Just turn the knob, Monica, and we can have this behind us in an hour.*

She got the inevitable paperwork from the receptionist and sat down in one of the waiting room chairs to fill it out. She more or less knew what to expect, but she still hated the intrusive questionnaire:

- *Briefly describe the issues or concerns that have brought you here.*
- *Please check any current or past issues that affect you.*
- *Current medical problems.*
- *Have you previously seen a therapist?*
- *Have you ever been hospitalized for physical or mental issues?*
- *Suicide attempts?*
- *Is there a history of mental illness in your family?*

Oh geez, do I really have to do all of this again? Short. Simple. Sweet. In and out, Monica, and we're done.

"Here you go." Monica returned the forms to the receptionist, along with her insurance information.

This Higgins must make a pretty good living, Monica mused as she looked around at her surroundings. She knew what kind of overhead it required to hire even one not-very-well-paid assistant, and the woman in front of her looked like she was doing better than just okay. Her nails were professionally manicured, and her highlighted hair was definitely not Miss Clairol. She was dressed with a style that spoke of professionalism, but exuded creativity and a strong feminine flair. *I wonder if Ms. Tisha, or Mother, would approve? I wish I had the nerve to pair boots with a riding skirt and wear antique earrings. Maybe someday.*

"Thank you," the receptionist piped. "It'll be just a few minutes. Please make yourself comfortable."

Monica settled into the microsuede armchair and flipped through the latest *Time* magazine. Her palms weren't quite as clammy as when she'd entered the therapist's office. Nonetheless, she was anything but comfortable. She was grateful that no one else was in the waiting room.

She heard the assistant murmur into a phone and then announce more audibly, "You can go in, Ms. Levin. Right through this door." She motioned down the short hallway to her right.

Monica gathered her handbag, stood up straight, patted her hair, smoothed her skirt, and headed down the designated corridor. The door to a nondescript office stood ajar as she approached.

At the cluttered desk, with his back toward the door, sat a man with curly, somewhat familiar hair. He appeared to be watching something outside the window. The floor creaked as Monica stepped into the room and he spun his chair toward her while speaking.

"A blue jay was sitting on the bran . . . ch. Um. Monica, is that you?"

The color rose in Monica's cheeks. *Jack!*

"What are *you* doing here? I mean, nice to see you. I, um, meant to call, but I didn't have your number. Gosh, I thought you were my ten-thirty appointment. Wish I could talk now. Gee, it's great to see you. I already said that, didn't I?"

Monica's knees wobbled. *Breathe, Monica. Breathe. What the hell?* "Are you Dr. Higgins?"

"Yes, that's right."

"J.T. Higgins?"

"Yes. What's wrong?"

"I thought your name was Jack."

"Well, it is. Short for James. James Travis Higgins. J.T.'s my professional title. Why?"

"I'm Monica Levin."

"Yes? Monica Levin. I like the sound of that . . . *oh.*" He halted as his brow furrowed. "Monica Levin. My ten-thirty appointment."

"Yep. *C'est moi.*" She delivered the words with a shrug and upturned palms.

"Oh. Wow. Isn't this something? Who would've thought we'd meet again so soon, and like this?"

"I guess you could call it 'something,' but I'd call it downright embarrassing." Monica shifted from foot to foot.

"Please, have a seat." Jack motioned toward the cocoa-colored sofa. "There's nothing to be embarrassed about."

"Okay. If you say so." Monica started to sit, then changed her mind. "I really don't think this is such a great idea." She eyed the door like a cornered rabbit looking for a hole in the fence. *If I run really fast, he probably wouldn't catch me.*

"Please stay." His voice was gentle, as though he had read her mind. "Can we just talk a bit?"

"Talk?"

"You know. Talk. I'll say something, and then you answer. And then you ask me a question, and I'll answer. Conversation. Back and forth. You and me. People do it all the time."

"But what about the appointment? I mean, you're supposed to be my therapist. Aren't there rules about that kind of thing?" Monica clutched her purse to her midriff.

"How about if you start by sitting down?" Jack gestured toward the couch. "I promise I won't bite or ask you any therapy questions about how you're feeling." He winked.

I'm not feeling so good was what Monica wanted to say. Instead, she turned her body sideways and perched on the edge of the couch.

"Awesome. Feel better now?"

"Not really. I'm not sure what we should do. You know, about the appointment and everything."

"First, we're going to consider your appointment canceled. Sound good?" Jack closed a folder on his desk.

"Yes." Monica sighed. "Now what? I don't want to take up any more of your time."

"Oh, you can't pull the I've-got-to-be-somewhere-else routine this time. I know for a fact you have nowhere else to be for the next forty-five minutes, and neither do I. I'd call this a happy coincidence." She saw a twinkle in his deep brown eyes.

"I'm not so sure about that. I don't feel so happy about landing here as another one of your crazy clients who needs to talk about her deep dark secrets."

"Crazy clients? My guess is you have a low opinion of therapists, or at least of the people who come to see them." Jack lifted an eyebrow and tilted his head in her direction.

"I'm sorry. It's nothing personal. It's just that my company said I needed to come in if I want to go back to work. Really, there's nothing wrong with me. I was just tired and forgot to eat lunch and hadn't had time for dinner and got a little woozy in the community room. Everyone totally overreacted. Seriously, there's no real reason why I should be here, except some silly paperwork." Monica heard the words flowing out of her mouth like someone had turned on a faucet full blast.

"I see."

"Oh, please don't start with the therapist routine." Monica rolled her eyes.

"Sorry. I haven't heard you speak that many words at one time since we met. I was just taking it in."

"No, I'm sorry. It just feels awkward here in your office. I still can't believe *you're* the shrink they referred me to."

"Shrink, eh?" Jack's eyebrows lifted again, and a smile curled the corners of his mouth. "To set the record straight, I'm a psychotherapist not a psychiatrist. No medical school. Thus, no shrinking."

"Sorry again."

Jack opened his mouth, and then closed it again. Monica wondered if he might ask her to stop saying "sorry." Instead, he pressed the call button on his intercom. "Patty? What time's my next appointment?"

"One o'clock."

"Thanks." He released the call button and turned back to face Monica. "Let's get out of here. Coffee? My treat?"

"Um. Well. I guess that would be okay." *Oh geez, why didn't I wear my Hermés scarf?*

"Shall we?" Jack said, as he held the door open for her.

— — —

"Morning, Carl."

"Morning, Jack. What'll it be today?"

Jack leaned toward Monica, close enough that she could feel his warm breath on her ear. "Ms. Levin, what's your pleasure?"

"Oh, hmmm. Lemme see. I guess I'll have a non-fat latte. Tall?" Monica wasn't used to ordering coffee. She was more of a tea drinker, but since she was standing in a place called Crazy Carl's Coffee, she could hardly bring herself to ask for English breakfast tea.

"You heard the lady, Carl, and I'll have my usual triple grande caramel macchiato, extra whip."

No wonder he has that paunch around the middle, Monica thought.

"I should probably cut back on the extra whip," Jack said, as he patted his belly. "But it's so tasty, I can't help myself."

As Jack chatted away with the barista, Monica looked around the independent coffee shop. She noticed it lacked the sleek, consistent appearance of the one-on-every-corner Starbucks. Half a dozen faux cherry tables rested on the commercial-grade carpet, with matching seats that looked like elementary school chairs on steroids. The entryway had a synthetic floor designed to look like maple, and two large rugs with an avatar of Crazy Carl himself provided ample space for patrons to wipe their rain-soaked feet. The tables were flanked on the north side by a bar with five more seats, and on the south by a cozy sitting area. It was interesting how people in Seattle lined up on one side or the other of the great coffee debate, Monica thought. Independent versus conglomerate. Local guy versus corporation. The amusing thing was that Starbucks had actually originated as an independent, right here in the Emerald City.

The clientele were a side of Seattle she wasn't used to seeing. Normally, at eleven a.m., she was slaving away at Stratford Estates. *Who are these people who can hang out in the middle of the morning?* Monica wondered. *Don't they have jobs to go to? Maybe they're all independently wealthy.* There seemed to be a lot of that around here: people who worked from home, or who had made their money in the eighties when Microsoft was king. Monica doubted that Microsoft millionaires were hanging out at Crazy Carl's Coffee. But who knew?

She saw these independent types all the time at Stratford Estates: once-young executives, now turned middle-aged, who were finding themselves smack in the middle of the sandwich generation. Their parents were aging, and they had kids beginning high school or starting college. They showed up at Stratford Estates to privately stow away an aging mother or father they'd chosen not to accommodate in their six-thousand-square-foot McMansions on the east side of Lake Washington.

And, of course, there were the pompous narcissistic types who considered themselves to be modern-day Adonises. These were the guys who traded in their first wives to reinvent themselves at fifty-plus, watching peewee soccer with their Gap-clad kids and perky young trophy wives. Monica knew the wealth of these particular types was probably not as great as they wanted everyone to think. If they had an elderly family member to deal with, they chose the more modest Stratford Estates over one of the elaborate complexes on the east side of the lake or a posh high-rise in the center of downtown.

"Penny for your thoughts," Jack said, as he turned toward her with two steaming cups.

"Oh, I was just wondering who comes for coffee in the middle of the morning. I'm typically stuck at my desk this time of day."

"Well, today, *we* do. Let's sit, shall we?"

Jack put the coffees down on a table and wandered over to the self-service bar for napkins. Just as Monica settled herself into the chair, a sweet-faced child with coal-black hair and wide, cinnamon-colored eyes walked up to her with outstretched arms.

"I got ice cream," the girl proudly announced.

"Yes. I see that." Monica leaned down to meet the child's eyes, thinking of Edna and her passion for the creamy substance.

Before they could continue the conversation, the child toddled off in her puffy pink coat to join her mom on the cozy sofa in the corner. A faux fireplace offered its illusion of warmth. Monica thought the picture of mother, child, ice cream, and fireplace would have made a lovely portrait. *They grow up so fast.*

"Cute kid. Do you have any of your own?" Jack sat down across from her.

"She *is* cute, isn't she? She wanted to show me her ice cream. Do all coffee shops carry ice cream now?"

Jack didn't miss Monica's diversion tactic, but he didn't pursue the topic. Glancing toward the door, they saw a father enter with two little boys. One was strapped to the dad's broad torso. The other little guy strolled in proudly, wearing rubber firefighter boots. All three wore stocking caps, an indicator that the weather was definitely changing.

"I'm so fascinated by how busy this place is at this time of day. What do you think all these people do?" She really wanted to ask Jack whether or not he had children, or a wife. But that was a slippery slope, since she wasn't prepared to reciprocate the conversation.

"Well, let's see. How about them? Whaddya think their story is?" Jack nodded toward a pair of women seated kitty corner to them, engrossed in conversation. One had flaming red hair cut in a stylish curly bob. The color belied her age, which was clearly on the other side of seventy. The second woman wore a stocking cap with braids hanging from either side. Heavy orange glasses perched on her beaklike nose.

"How would I know that?" Monica sputtered.

"It's a game I like to play sometimes. You know, making up stories for people I see. I usually do it alone, but this seems even more fun. Let's give it a try."

"Oh, I couldn't possibly."

"Let's pretend it's an exercise for our creative writing class."

"Ugh. I'd rather forget." Monica closed her eyes and shook her head.

"Come on. It'll be fun. Otherwise, I might have to start asking questions about you."

"I guess if you put it that way . . . How about you start?" Even though this game was extremely uncomfortable, it was better than discussing her personal life.

"Here goes. So, the flaming redhead is a former striptease diva. She started dying her hair in the fifties to match her favorite poodle skirt after an unfortunate incident in Clinton, Oklahoma where she was head cheerleader, class of '56. Red was highly aware that the panties she wore under her uniform were way too tight, so she quit wearing them during the day and only put 'em on for football games.

"One night she was in a hurry and forgot to wear them to the big game. When it came time for the first cheer, she leaped high into the air, right in front of the principal, who was a staunch Southern Baptist. Shocked out of his gourd, the principal, a former lineman, jumped to his feet and tackled Red before she knew what hit her. Her watching parents rushed down to the field, wrapped their daughter in her father's coat, drove to the bus station, and bought Red a one-way ticket for Reno. Upon her arrival, she dyed her hair the color you see today and never looked back. Your turn."

"Are you kidding me? How am I supposed to follow that?"

"Your choice. You can either continue with her story or start with the braided lady."

Monica closed her eyes for a moment, took a deep breath, and prayed something creative would come out. "The braided woman is a feminist from the seventies who recently heard about Red living here in Seattle. She's a reporter for a women's magazine and wants to write about the outrage of Red being banished from her town in the fifties. At first she was intrigued about Red being tackled by a Baptist, but then she decided it wasn't a strong enough angle for her article. Instead, she's switching gears and going with the environmentalist angle. She's really more of a tree hugger than a bonafide feminist. She's curious about the potential carcinogenic impact of using red dye for more than fifty years. She's a passionate researcher and is intrigued by the potential connection with the 'Orange Number 1' debacle of the fifties." Monica paused to see Jack leaning toward her, elbows planted on the table, chin resting in the palms of his hands, with a bemused grin on his face. "Do you see how she's leaning into Red's personal space? This woman is like a cat in a garden filled with catnip. She's rolling all over the place in near hysteria. Red is about to tell her to get lost, I think." Monica pressed her lips tightly together, drew an exclamation point with her head, and let the hint of a smile cross her face.

"Wow! 'Orange Number 1' debacle? Are you sure you've never played this before?" Jack clapped his hands together.

"That was fun. I think I might like this game." Monica blushed under Jack's approving gaze. "And for your information, Orange Number 1 was actually banned in 1956. The same year our Red was head cheerleader." Monica finished with a proud nod.

"Bravo! We'll have to do this again sometime. You're really very creative. What does Ms. Tisha know anyway, other than the color of Ronald Reagan's briefs? But for now, I was wondering if you'd be willing to tell me a little about yourself?" His voice sounded like a kid asking for a later curfew.

Monica shifted in her seat and reached for a packet of sweetener. She ripped the blue packet open and stirred her latte with vigor, avoiding eye contact with Jack.

"Feel free to share anything. Anything at all." Jack opened both palms in a peaceful gesture. "Where were you born? How about you start there?"

Monica glanced at her wristwatch and then looked back across the table. "Look at the time. I've really got to be going." She jumped up like Cinderella realizing the clock was about to strike midnight. "And you've got to get to your one o'clock appointment."

Jack checked the time on his cell phone, and then looked back at Monica, who was already five feet away. "I guess you're right. We'll have to continue this next time."

"Yes, next time." She smiled through the jarring of her pounding heart.

IZABEL

Sitting on a cliff high above the sea, Izabel looked at the passage she'd copied in her journal the night before: words from Sue Monk Kidd's *The Dance of the Dissident Daughter.*

"The truth is, in order to heal, we need to tell our stories and have them witnessed . . . Sometimes another woman's story becomes a mirror that shows me a self I haven't seen before."

Izabel stared out across the open water and wondered what wound it was that she needed to heal. While she had seemed to return to a reasonably normal routine after the period surrounding the Anderson baby's arrival and her restless, dream-filled nights, she couldn't shake off the feeling that there was another story inside her begging to be freed and witnessed. She wondered if it had to do with the "other woman" she'd sensed before.

Miriam. I need to call Miriam. Last week at Beth's coffee shop, Miriam had led her out the door for fresh air and helped her steady herself when Izabel paled during the ladies' coffee gathering. Before they'd parted ways, Izabel had hinted to Miriam that things were more troubling than she wanted to admit, and she'd vaguely mentioned how her own body had mimicked Shannon Andersons's delivery pains. She hadn't been able to bring herself to say any more at the time, even though she trusted Miriam more than any other person. Miriam was always available to listen, but Miriam never pressed Izabel until she asked for help.

Izabel stared toward the horizon, where the shadow of a setting moon floated like a beach ball, and wrapped her arms around her petite frame. She whispered: "Miriam, I need you," and trusted her friend would soon answer her prayer.

— — —

Izabel pedaled home in the growing light. As she leaned Rosie against the front porch, she heard her phone ring and retrieved it from her bag.

"Hello," she said, still a bit out of breath.

"Hello, my lovely Izabel. A little birdie told me you were in need of some livening up. Is that true?" Izabel could sense Miriam's affection and merriment radiating through the phone's tiny speaker.

Izabel chuckled and wondered who the "little birdie" was who'd relayed the message to Miriam. Perhaps it was the flicker that sat on Izabel's windowsill and watched her cry, or maybe the seagull that had swooped by as she stood overlooking the sea. When it came to Miriam, there was no use in asking questions. Things just magically *happened* in her presence. It was inevitable, so why waste time or effort trying to figure it out? Still, it was fun to imagine the birds carrying their messages like secret spies.

"Oh, Miriam. How did you know?"

"Now, Izabel, you know better than to ask such questions. Do you or don't you require a bit of livening up? That is the primary purpose of this conversation."

"Aren't you one to be calling the kettle black? You know the answer to that question already. Otherwise, you wouldn't be phoning. Am I right, my dear Miriam?"

"I'll take that as a yes then. I have two words for you. Soul. Dance."

Izabel giggled. "Oh, Miriam, you always have the perfect remedy for everything! When? How? Where?"

"Tonight, of course. And leave the rest to me, dear one. Just show up at sunset at Jacob's Landing. I'll take care of the rest. Oh, and wear something dazzling! *La bella luna* is going to be at her most magnificent, and so should we! *À bientôt, mon amie.*"

"*À bientôt,* my Miriam!"

Miriam had an uncanny way of assembling interesting and unlikely characters for any gathering, and Izabel trusted her completely with this special event. She couldn't wait to see who would arrive for the soul dance. It would be an intimate event, no doubt, and she hoped Beth and Marly would be included, but there was no time to worry about the guest list. She needed to find something stunning to wear.

Izabel inspected the contents of her closet, unimpressed. *Nothing. I have nothing dazzling to wear.* She could almost hear Miriam's voice, professing her opinion like Endora from *Bewitched. Well, that simply will not do.*

"She's right, Lucas. This simply will *not* do!" Izabel scratched the cat's ears, then set about gathering what she needed to head into town. She flung her patchwork bag over her shoulder, absentmindedly ran her fingers through her hair, and grabbed her denim jacket. "Okay, kitty. I'm off to Eugene's. Hopefully they'll have something dazzling in stock today."

— — —

Izabel didn't like to spend much time in the hub of the island, but today she was desperate. Ever since Miriam had said, "wear something dazzling," Izabel had envisioned herself drenched in moonlight. Eugene's was her best shot, unless she wanted to hit some of the more upscale shops geared toward wealthy lookie-loos who thought it exotic to buy something on the island. Those shops were overpriced and in no way represented what the locals wore, unless you counted the rhinestone-studded t-shirts featuring black and white whales. The respectable islanders only wore those to clean fish or gather eggs from their chicken coops.

Izabel was grateful that Marly and her husband had made enough money in Silicon Valley to open up their secondhand store and take early retirement on the island. Izabel couldn't imagine they made much of a living selling recycled goods, but they seemed perfectly content to serve the underfunded locals who exhibited a touch of high style and finesse.

While most patrons thought Eugene was Marly's husband, their assumption was wrong. The namesake for the store was actually a two-year-old English bulldog. A framed photo of the wee pup hung over the counter. In it, his squat body sat plopped in a pile of autumn leaves, one pink ear standing on end and illuminated by sunlight; the other dark ear hung limply on the opposite side of his pug face. His entire body was the color of snow, except for the black patch around his left eye that bled into the drooping ebony ear.

Compact in size, the little black and white dog had an active streak, but was perfectly content to while away the days napping in his wicker basket behind the counter or greeting customers with a wag of his short, slightly twisted tail. The attached corkscrew had a way of wiggling his entire body once he put it into motion. At the sight of Izabel, Eugene's bat ears perked up with anticipation of a belly rub.

"Hey, sweet boy," Izabel cooed, as Eugene flipped over and turned belly-up with a whimper. He had no problem allowing Izabel to be the alpha dog in this situation.

"He knows an easy mark when he sees one," came Marly's sultry voice, as she appeared from behind a beaded doorway. "Long time no see. How are you, Izzy?"

"Marly! It's great to see you." The two women gave each other a friendly hug.

"You here for something to wear to the soul dance?"

"Wow, news travels fast, doesn't it?"

"Miriam does have her ways." The two women shook their heads and looked toward the ceiling. Miriam's uncanny ability to intuit things seemed to come from a place far beyond mortal understanding.

"Are you coming tonight?" Izabel asked.

"Wouldn't miss it for the world! It's been way too long since we've danced under the moonlight. I know Veronica and I will be there."

"Great! I didn't know Veronica was in town."

"Yeah, she's back for the weekend."

Veronica was Marly's young sister-in-law who lived on the mainland while she attended the University of Washington. Izabel hoped the group tonight wouldn't be too large. She would have to trust Miriam and her powers of knowing exactly what needed to happen.

"So, what are you looking for today?"

"Well, whenever I close my eyes, I imagine dripping in moonlight. I know that may sound silly, but Miriam said to wear something dazzling, and that's the image that keeps popping up."

"No such thing as silly when it comes to clothes, girlfriend! Sassy or chic? What are you seeing?"

"Both!"

"Then I believe I may have the perfect thing for tonight's soiree." Marly winked. "I'll be right back." She disappeared behind the beaded doorway that led to the back room, and Izabel resumed her love fest with Eugene.

Marly reappeared momentarily, holding a tissue-wrapped parcel in her hands.

"I believe these may have been custom-made for you. They arrived in the mail earlier today. Gift of an anonymous donor. I couldn't figure out the deal until I saw you walk through the door. Heaven Express is what I'm thinking, but I'll let you decide for yourself." With a flourish, Marly bowed and offered the delicate bundle to Izabel.

"Ohh. They're gorgeous," Izabel purred. In her hands she held a pair of 1920s-style salmon-colored satin pajamas. With a broad collar and plunging neckline, you could tell they would hang loosely while also showing off Izabel's feminine physique.

"They're absolutely perfect." Izabel couldn't take her eyes off them, nor could she resist stroking the fabric just like she'd petted Eugene moments before. "Heaven Express, absolutely."

Marly grinned. "Now how about something for your hair? Not that it needs anything."

"What do you have in mind?"

Like a magician pulling a scarf through her sleeve, Marly ceremoniously handed Izabel an ornate arrangement of felt and satin lilies with sparkling sequin embellishments. It was a hairclip that perfectly matched Izabel and the retro pajamas.

"Oh, Marly. This is over the top!"

"You like?"

"Are you kidding me? This is too much! I mean it. I haven't felt this happy in . . . I can't remember how long. Thank you!" Izabel wrapped her arms around Marly's neck, as tears came to her eyes.

"My pleasure. Now you better head home and get ready for your soul dance!"

"But I need to pay."

"No worries. I have no intent of charging you for today's purchases."

"Really?" Izabel stared at Marly.

"Really. After all, how can I in good conscience charge for something I never ordered? Magic is definitely in the air." Marly smiled.

— — —

Back home, Izabel stood gazing at the glamorous creature staring back at her from the bedroom mirror. She had lined her green eyes with kohl and highlights of gold, making her appear like an Egyptian goddess. Her hair fell down her back in a loose French braid, swept up at the temples and held on the right side with the funky-yet-elegant hair ornament that Marly had gifted her. The salmon-colored pajamas draped from her shoulders to a deep V in the center of her porcelain chest. The loose-fitting pants slouched slightly on the tops of her bare feet, and her toes twinkled with golden-pink polish. She felt like a black and white film star bursting into live Technicolor.

"Yoo-hoo, Izabel? You ready to go?" a familiar voice came from outside.

"Beth? Is that you?"

"Yep, it's me. In the flesh."

That was an understatement. When she opened the door, Izabel thought maybe Daisy Duke's long-lost sister had arrived on the scene. Buxom Beth, as the men of Deer Harbor called her, wore a gold lamé, knotted midriff top and low-rise, cutoff jean shorts. Her exposed skin was painted with iridescent glitter, and her hair sat high on either side of her head in little-girl pigtails. High-top orange Converse sneakers and striped mid-calf socks completed her outfit. Izabel wasn't sure how Beth pulled it off, but beneath all the glitter and skin, she managed to convey an air of innocence that was absolutely endearing.

"Oh, Iz. You're a knockout!"

"Thanks. You're looking pretty hot yourself! What're you doing here anyway?"

"Miriam was afraid you'd decide to ride Rosie down to the beach in the dark, so she suggested I swing by and pick you up."

"She does think of everything, doesn't she? Although Rosie and I would be just fine on the road."

"I know. But you wouldn't want to risk messing up those gorgeous jammies, now, would you? Where in the world did you find those? They are H-O-T."

"Marly had them in her shop. I couldn't believe it. They're just so perfect for the soul dance!"

"You bet they are! Speaking of which, we better get scootin' if we're going to make it by sunset!"

—   —   —

The fire-lit sky dripped with shades of pink, apricot, flame, and gold, like a painter had filled a brush with rich colors and cast them across the dying embers of the sun before it dropped behind the horizon and faded into night. The spectacular show appeared as Izabel and Beth rounded the curve at the top of the peak, before dropping down onto the narrow road that led to Jacob's Landing. For a moment Izabel imagined herself sinking into the colorful landscape, too, her salmon-tinted pajamas the perfect camouflage.

"I'm a burning flame," she whispered so low that Beth didn't notice.

"Geez, I'm ready for the moon to rise. Enough of this sunshine stuff. Let's get the party rolling," Beth chirped. "Looks like Miriam beat us here."

As they pulled up to Jacob's Landing, they could see the makings of a bonfire: a deep pit surrounded by stones and filled with driftwood. Larger logs surrounded the pit and formed a circle. Miriam's vintage Volkswagen van was parked off to one side, with the sliding door wide open and the trunk lifted high. In another era, there had likely been surfboards strapped to the top and Grateful Dead blaring from the speakers. Tonight, however, there were no boards on top, and the precious cargo consisted of an assortment of percussion instruments and drums. The only music came from Miriam's deep melodic humming as she joyfully unloaded the instruments.

"Ladies." She looked up and smiled, while hoisting a giant conga drum as if it were a five-pound sack of flour. "Welcome to Jacob's Landing."

As Beth and Izabel edged closer to the venue, Izabel noticed indentations in the sand around the outer perimeter of the logs. Candles. Dozens of candles nestled along the beach. Not just any candles. Freshly made. Miriam must have been here for hours. Each candle had been created by digging a small hole and pouring fresh wax into the "mold." A wick had been carefully placed into the wax and tied off with a small twig. Izabel knew the effect would be stunning when the sun fully set and darkness descended upon the beach.

"What can we do to help?" Izabel asked.

"I've just about got it, but if you'd like to finish unloading the drums and setting them over there, that would be wonderful."

Miriam looked like she had risen straight out of the ocean. She was wearing a toga. It was made of fabric that at first seemed like dark-blue matte, but as she walked gracefully across the sand it shimmered with highlights of sea-foam green. Around her waist, she had tied a scarf stenciled with silver stars and crescent-moon shapes. Goddess incarnate. A band of tiny shells was tied around her head, with a glistening piece of abalone shell in the center, just above her third eye. More abalone shells hung from her ears and settled into the flowing strands of her silver-blue hair.

Everything about her appeared effortless. Her eyes twinkled with deep knowing, and Izabel felt herself relax as she gazed into their depths.

"You are absolutely radiant this evening, my dear." Miriam's words rolled into the air like a sweet caress.

"I was just going to say the same of you, Miriam." Izabel gave a little shiver and lightly touched the hair ornament at her temple. "The beach looks absolutely stunning! How long have you been here?"

"Oh, Izzy. You know time is an illusion." The old woman winked.

"Yoo-hoo. Y'all down there?" a voice called from the road.

"That must be Emma Jean," Miriam said. "Come on down, Emma Jean."

Emma Jean Pendergast was the vision of a woman you might see at an airport on her return trip from Honolulu. In actual fact, Emma Jean hated to fly, so she was rarely at any airport, and she'd never been to Hawaii or anywhere tropical. Nonetheless, she adored wild, brightly colored prints, and tonight was no exception. Age-wise, her odometer had stopped at fifty-nine for as long as anyone could recall, and she always had "just a few more pounds" to lose. Izabel wondered what special diet Emma Jean was trying out this week.

"I brought some coconut milk and rum," she offered, as if on cue. "I recently read that coconut milk is great for boosting your immune system. Or maybe it was coconut water? Who knows, but I bet it'll be yummy mixed together. Kinda like a healthy piña colada, don't ya think?"

Beth leaned in toward Izabel and whispered, "What is that thing on her head?"

Izabel giggled as she looked back at Emma Jean. Perched on top of her tightly woven, beauty-parlor pin curls was a contraption that looked like an Advent wreath. Instead of holly leaves, evergreen branches were woven together into a circle to form an oddly shaped crown. Tiny dime store trinkets were attached along the circumference, and dead center above her forehead was a plastic pineapple about six inches tall. If she had been leaning against a wall, she might have been mistaken for a circus performer waiting to have the pineapple split down the middle by a dashing knife thrower.

Miriam must have sensed that Beth was about to point out the atrociousness of the headdress. She stepped between the two ladies. "Emma Jean, what a unique hat you're wearing this evening. Wherever did you find it?"

"Do you guys like it? I just had so much fun putting it together. I saw something similar at a Hawaiian luau on the Discovery Channel and decided to make one myself. Unfortunately, there aren't any flowers blooming now, so I had to use evergreen branches instead of orchids, but I think they work just fine. Don't you?"

All the ladies nodded.

"What about the pineapple?" Beth couldn't contain herself.

"Oh, that's the best part. I had it from that time Jim and I went to that Hawaiian theme party in Friday Harbor. They used them in the centerpieces and I brought one home. I'd been waiting for just the perfect occasion."

"And here it is." Beth snickered. "Lucky us."

Izabel elbowed Beth and tried to stifle her own mirth as she assessed the rest of Emma Jean's outfit: a matching shirt and capris with a boldly splashed Hawaiian print of hot pink and marigold with lime-green foliage, finished off with her signature runners and white bobby socks. Emma Jean liked to pretend she was on her way to or from a jog at all times of day, even though everyone knew that walking from her couch to the mailbox was enough to raise her heart rate. Tossed over her arm was a puffy purple coat, just in case the temperature dropped.

As the sun completed its descent below the horizon, the remaining guests arrived. Marly appeared like a vision in white flowing linen, sporting vintage cowboy boots, with a headband holding back her raven braids from her glistening face. Beside her was Veronica, the youngest of the odd assemblage. She was petite, all legs and arms, and wore an aqua crushed-velvet romper that barely covered her buttocks. A gold cord was wrapped around her tiny waist, and her hair flowed freely. She looked like an advertisement for the hip clothing store where she worked.

In the rising moonlight, Izabel glanced around at her friends and wondered if she'd ever seen a lovelier sight than this array of women that Miriam had assembled.

Izabel thought about past soul dances that she'd been a part of and wondered what Miriam had planned for tonight. Miriam, in her wisdom, knew Izabel's need was greater than simply spending an evening with women friends. If Izabel was going to release the pain in her body and move toward physical and emotional healing, a shift needed to happen. Drumming and dance were the perfect way to give gesture to those trapped feelings. Miriam knew from personal experience that if there was no feeling moving through the body, then the body would become stagnant and the center of the soul would crumble. Miriam believed the crumbling had begun in Izabel, and she was determined to reverse the progress as best she could.

Soul dance was an ancient ritual that called upon the power of Spirit, the ancestors, and elements of earth, wind, fire, and water alongside the conviction that all things are connected throughout space and time. Not everyone viewed soul dance with the respect it deserved. Most people viewed it as a time of play beneath the moonlight, but this simplified view did not diminish its power. Whenever a group gathered together for each other's best interests, transformation was inevitable. Miriam's role tonight was to set the tone and assign the role-play energies to each participant, with Izabel as the focus of the ritual.

Looking toward the assemblage of modern-day goddesses waiting on the moonlit beach, Miriam nodded her head in affirmation and began to move through the gathering like a lean jungle cat.

Beth stood beside the mini-van, munching on tortilla chips and salsa. Miriam sidled up to her, leaned in, and murmured, "Mother." Beth nodded in acknowledgment.

Emma Jean stood a few feet away, fiddling with her garish headdress in the van's side mirror.

"Father," Miriam said as she drifted past.

"Mm-hm," Emma Jean replied through closed lips.

Marly and Veronica sat on driftwood logs, huddled shoulder to shoulder. "What exactly is a soul dance?" Veronica leaned close to her sister-in-law with wide eyes as she surveyed the surroundings.

"You'll see soon enough." Marly turned her face upward toward the warm October sky.

"Ah, I'm glad to find the two of you together," Miriam said, appearing beside them like a genie emerging from a bottle. "You each have very special roles in tonight's dance."

Veronica's eyes widened as Miriam explained that Marly would represent the sisters or friends of Izabel's life, and Veronica, as the youngest of the group, would be the children in Izabel's life.

"But I don't know what that even means. I didn't think Izzy even, like, *had* children," Veronica's face contorted in confusion.

"No worries, my child," replied Miriam. "Just be yourself. The magic of the night will do the rest."

"Okay." The young woman looked back toward Marly with eyes round as the rising moon.

"Really, it's okay," said Marly. "I was nervous the first time I did this, too, but seriously, there's nothing to be afraid of."

"What if I do it wrong?"

"Impossible!" Marly and Miriam smiled in unison.

Miriam moved to the other side of the circle where Izabel stood staring out at the ocean, the light gleaming off her salmon-colored pajamas. The older woman looped her arm through Izabel's and spoke to the entire gathering. "Ladies, shall we?" She motioned toward the fire pit.

"Yeehawwwww!" Beth shouted, as she kicked off her Converses and moved into the circle. Emma Jean pulled off her runners and socks. Everyone else followed suit.

As if it had been choreographed, Miriam looked to the night sky, then moved to her place in the circle. Each woman followed suit, looking skyward, then walking with reverence before settling behind an instrument.

Miriam picked up the wooden flute with lithe fingers. Izabel stood behind the giant conga drum with her feet buried in the sand and body erect, yet relaxed. Veronica chose a tambourine, giving it a little shake. Beth reached for the cowbell. Marly settled at the djembe, and Emma Jean laughed as she shook the maracas.

The giggling quieted in unison, and the sounds of the night—lapping waves, distant owls, whispering breeze—softly enveloped the band of soul sisters. Each woman looked around the circle into the eyes of the others. A sense of awe passed through them like rustling autumn leaves.

"Inhale. Exhale. Breathe in. Breathe out," Miriam requested.

With everyone's eyes closed, the sentient rhythm of the encircled spirits became one, like a single organism moving in fluid motion.

"Inhale. Exhale. Keep following the rhythm of your breath and feel the earth beneath your feet," Miriam continued, pausing between instructions. "Breathe in. Breathe out."

Her voice was like butter melting in the night air. "Ladies, we are here to drum and dance for Izabel. Each of you has been given a role to embody. Izabel, I will represent you and you will be an observer. This isn't about acting or trying to get the role right. It's about allowing the energy of Izabel's family members to be represented here in this circle." Miriam paused and looked around the group. Everyone except Veronica stood with their eyes closed, chests rising and falling with the rhythm of the waves.

Miriam gave Veronica a nod of assurance and took a deep breath, followed by an exhale. Soon the young woman was breathing in unison with Miriam. She closed her eyes as she relaxed.

"I'm going to invite each of you to simply continue breathing and listen. Follow your heart and allow the rest to come."

When the time was right and not a second before, Izabel lifted her slender hand and placed it on the drum. From out of the silence, the lone beat resonated upward from the ground. Another instrument joined in—the flute.

An image of herself as a teenager flickered through Izabel's awareness.

One by one, the remaining instruments merged with the conga's heartbeat.

As the musicians found their song, the music rose and fell across the Sound. The cowbell rankled the harmony.

The image of a harsh-faced woman flashed through Izabel's mind.

As quickly as the bell had clanked and the face appeared, both softened into accord. The djembe and conga played back and forth.

In Izabel's mind, her six-year-old self danced and a dark-haired, slightly older girl joined in.

Maracas shook *and in Izabel's mind, a man's gentle face etched itself onto the glossy wood.* Izabel's heart quivered with feelings of comfort and tender care. Still, she was lost in the rhythm of the drum as she kept pounding her way through the emotions. Across the sphere the tambourine twittered with delight, and Izabel saw a crown of daisies encircle Veronica's head.

"Daisy," she whispered into the night sky.

Izabel's body wavered like a balloon losing air, and she missed a beat on the conga. She felt as if her world was being consumed with a purifying fire, and if she was to survive, she had to become a flaming phoenix rising out of the ashes. With a deep breath, she steadied herself and prepared to sprout wings.

Instead of a bird, however, it was the moon that had risen. It was as if the women had drummed *La bella luna* into the night sky. She was magnificent. Miriam nodded toward Veronica, who, like an elfin sprite, carried her tambourine and wove in and out among the buried candles, lighting each one as she passed. The sand turned to sky, and diamonds twinkled above and below.

One by one, the percussionists ceased playing, until only the lone flute whispered in the night air. Slowly the women rose from their seats, fluid, like cobras stretching from their coils.

Izabel was the last to stand. As the flame from the fire reflected off her shimmering satin clothing, she could almost swear she *was* a phoenix rising out of the ashes. Strong. Molten. Brilliant. A lifetime's past troubles burning away as she rose with the flames and the lilt of the flute that was her.

One after another, the dancers circled the glowing embers. The moon smiled in response as coyotes howled and night owls screeched their approval. Sorrows fell away. Time dissolved. The night sky shimmered.

PART
TWO

For to cling to the past is to lose one's continuity with the past,
since this means clinging to what is no longer there.

Thomas Merton
Catholic mystic (1915-1968)

DAISY

The twelve-foot Buddha bowed his head prayer-like over the upright Steinway piano, looming like a gentle guardian.

Daisy cocked her head to one side. "I thought God was supposed to watch over me, not Buddha."

From her hidden vantage point, she placed one bare foot onto the jungle path, holding her breath as if that might lighten her footstep. One step closer, she could see the Buddha was molded out of bluish concrete, not the flesh and blood she'd initially imagined.

She let out her breath, but her relief was premature. With the release of breath, she found herself standing on the edge of a steep precipice. Her eyes widened and her vision zoomed back like a panoramic camera until the whole scene lay before her, herself included.

"Weird. I'm, like, in the scene *and* above it."

There she was, in a blue flowing dress, hands on her shoulders, and arms akimbo from her neck. Her hair blew behind her as if she was standing in an easterly wind; but as she looked more closely, she could see the breeze was blowing in all directions. It didn't seem blustery or chaotic at all, which fascinated her.

The precipice Daisy stood on was a dark circle about twenty feet in diameter. It looked like someone had drawn it with a black magic marker. The circle wasn't complete, however, and Daisy stood just above the small opening. Next to her head, the outline of a pentagon floated alongside a crown shape. The random markings looked like someone had drawn them on an upright piece of gray construction paper, except they were moving, not inanimate.

Two tiny hearts appeared, and a circle materialized between them. Daisy reached her finger out and drew an X in the air. The X grew before her eyes, and the shadow of a man soon towered over her from behind.

She jerked her head over her shoulder to see who or what was casting the shadow. Her heart pounded, and the hair on her arms tingled. Nothing there. She looked around the scene for something to erase herself with, but the marker was permanent. The shadow continued to rise into the sky until she was a mere dot in its presence.

Frantic to escape, she peered at the gap in the circle in front of her, and then turned to look behind her. The circle curved like the back of a large whale. Cautiously, she moved her legs out from under her and slid down the backside of the hump. On the way down, her eyes widened as she saw the stone Buddha spring to life and begin to play "The Blue Danube" on the Steinway.

"Yo, Daisy. What's up?" Chauncey greeted her at the bottom of the slide as if he'd been there the whole time.

"Do you hear that music?" she asked.

"Music? You mean like birds singing?" The okapi lifted his multi-colored snout into the air.

Daisy looked back toward where she'd seen the Buddha and the Steinway, but in their place rested two simple sheaves of eggplant-colored wheat.

The Master's skin rolled and cracked as he chuckled from his hive. "Silly girl. She's just like her mother," he said, as he laid the black marker next to his honey jar.

MONICA

"So you went to school on the East Coast, huh?" Jack watched Monica, dark eyes glistening over the top of his caramel macchiato. "How'd you get from Briar Cliff to Seattle?"

Monica twisted the napkin in her lap and weighed whether Briar Cliff was a safe topic for their second coffee date. They'd already dispensed with the pleasantries of weather and drink orders, but Briar Cliff meant Jeremy and her parents—and Lily. It was a huge can of worms, one she'd kept inside for almost twenty years. She wasn't sure she was ready to let it out, but Jack had called every other day for two weeks until Monica had agreed to see him again. Now she sat in Crazy Carl's with a shredded napkin in her lap and an interesting man showing her rapt attention.

"You sound like my dad," she said, glancing toward the ceiling fan of the coffee shop. "That's almost the first thing he said." She looked upward and appeared to drift away into another space and time.

"Briar Cliff? Isn't that on the East Coast somewhere?"

"Yes, Daddy. It's in Massachusetts."

"Humph. What happened to the University of Washington?" countered a disgruntled voice.

"Mom, that was always your plan, not mine."

"You don't have to get all huffy about it, Monica Gayle."

Jack grinned and raised his eyebrows. "Monica Gayle?"

She lowered her eyes from the ceiling and sighed. "Yes. My mother liked to use my whole name to get my attention. I was always getting in trouble for rolling my eyes at her, but that day I resisted because I was so excited about getting accepted to the school I'd always wanted: a women's liberal arts college, three thousand miles away from my family."

Jack pursed his lips in an unspoken question. Monica closed her eyes and squinted back at him, praying he wouldn't ask her about her desire to get so far away from her family. When he didn't say anything, she carried on with her story like it was yesterday.

"Oh, Pumpkin. I know you've always had big dreams, but you know we can't afford a fancy East Coast school. We've got both you and Lily to think about," said her dad.

"And Lily has her dance classes and art lessons to consider. Those are her dreams and we can't break her heart. She's just a little girl and wouldn't understand if her big sister moved to Maryland."

"Massachusetts," Monica interjected, but her mother never missed a beat.

"Whatever," she said. *"Lily has her heart set on going to Paris or New York, and I know she's got a great shot at it. Are you going to be the one to tell her she has to quit training so you can go to some snooty school just to learn how to be a writer? Can't you learn to write anywhere?"*

Jack groaned at Monica's imitation of her mother's caustic tone. "Lily is your younger sister, I take it?"

"Yes, and this was pretty much the same conversation I heard my whole life. Lily was Venus and I was Pluto. If I ever hinted at being in the spotlight or taking something away from Lily, my mom labeled me selfish and inconsiderate."

"So, how did you make it to Briar Cliff?"

I told my parents, "I got a full scholarship." My dad was thrilled, but Mom harassed me about airfare and room and board, reminding me they weren't free.

"I told Mom it was all taken care of. I'd saved my money from babysitting, and I had enough to get me there. Room and board was paid for, and once I got there I'd get a job. What I didn't say was that when I left, I wasn't planning on coming back."

"Yet, here you are." Jack smiled.

"Yes, here I am." Monica sighed, and Jack looked slightly offended. "Sorry, nothing personal. Long story."

Jack leaned forward on his elbows. "I have all the time in the world."

Monica reached for another napkin and began to twist it in her lap. Jack sipped his coffee. "What about your parents? How did they meet?"

Monica smiled. This felt like okay territory, and she kind of liked thinking about her parents as young and in love. "Well, Mother and Daddy met in the late sixties when they both went to Oklahoma State University."

"Oklahoma? Ah, do I hear shades of Red and the story you spun last time we were here?" Jack leaned in.

"Maybe." Monica chuckled. "My dad was a farmer from Washington's Skagit Valley, and Mother grew up in this small town called Ada, Oklahoma. He'd never met anyone like her, so, as the story goes, when she dropped her first 'Hi y'all' with honey-dripping sweetness, he was a goner.

"Her sorority picture shows a girl with mile-long legs and long, ash-colored hair. She was wearing an ivory-colored shift. Most of the other girls had bobs or pony tails and wore cardigans over skirts. June, or Ju Ju Bean as her friends called her, looked like a princess surrounded by her court. She set a pretty high standard for her daughters to live up to." Monica let out a deep sigh. Jack reached across the table and covered her hand with his.

"What about your dad? How did he get to Oklahoma?" he asked gently.

"Well, the big joke around our house was that women's liberation hadn't made it to the Sooner State and Daddy needed a wife to help him run the tulip farm, so he headed south. Plus the fact that OSU had one of the top Ag Engineering programs in the country. So when Mother walked into the fraternity mixer, young Darrell thought his prayers had been answered." Monica scoffed. "Little did he know he'd just laid eyes on one of the most complicated women alive.

"Mother had done her homework. She knew Daddy was a senior, president of the house, and rumored to be on the lookout for a wife to take back to Washington. He was also pretty cute. Dark hair, six feet tall, slender, and according to Mother, he had geeky horn-rimmed glasses that she would take care of later. She made it her personal mission to become his wife, so she could leave Oklahoma as fast as possible. For a while she called him her knight in shining armor. It would've been kind of sweet if it hadn't seemed so calculated, but then again, that was Mother, always trying to get ahead."

"Your mother sounds like a formidable woman." Jack rubbed his thumb along the side of Monica's shaking hand. "What about your dad? What's his side of the story?"

Jack's effect on Monica was calming. It reminded her of the way her dad used to talk about his and June's first few months together. "Daddy used to get all dreamy-eyed when he talked about their time at Oklahoma State: playing pinball and eating chili dogs down on the Strip; stealing kisses by Theta Pond and sneaking into his presidential suite in the Sig Alph house. They were the golden couple on campus. They used to stroll hand in hand through the hedgerows and cheer together at football games. He said he was the luckiest man alive when they got married."

"What do you think changed?"

"Well, Mother managed to hold her façade in place until they arrived at the family farm following their honeymoon. Almost immediately, her disappointment reared its ugly head when she saw that the nice city house she'd imagined looked more like a crummy Oklahoma farm.

"For the next two decades, Daddy spent every waking hour trying to make it up to the woman he'd promised to love, honor, and cherish until death do they part. Mother vacillated between being the sweet girl who'd drawn him in with 'Hi y'all' and Ursula the sea witch, making bargains and deals to get what she wanted most in any given moment: a new house, fancier clothes, another baby.

"I know he was tired and worn out, but he was also a man who honored his commitments. So he stayed." Monica sighed, and a faraway look crossed her face. "Most of the time, he simply tried to keep out of her way, but when I decided to go to Briar Cliff, he stood up for me and said, 'Monica, honey. I couldn't be a prouder father if you'd been elected the first woman president of the United States, and I know your mother feels the same way.' Then he narrowed his eyes at Mother and dared her to say anything negative about me."

"Good for him, but what did your mother do?"

"Oh, she played along and said something like, 'Well, isn't that wonderful, Darrell? Our little girl is growing up. I'm just so proud I could holler for joy. Yay you!' Then she clapped her hands in mock delight and raised them in a V over her head, like an aging cheerleader. Ugh. It makes me sick to think about."

Jack squeezed her hand. "I'm definitely proud of you. That must have been really hard."

Monica sniffled, wiped a tear away with her free hand, and breathed a sigh of relief.

Jack continued. "Where are they now?"

Monica felt her chest constrict, and the weight of a stone settled into the pit of her stomach. She couldn't think of her parents' death without remembering falling in love with Jeremy. The events were too interwoven. Gazing into the distance, she murmured, "They died."

Jack squeezed her hand again. "Do you want to talk about it?"

Monica shook her head, stared into space for a moment, and then began to talk.

"My friend and I had just finished our economics seminar when we ran into one of the girls from my sorority house." She didn't have the courage to tell him "the friend" had been Jeremy, the love of her life.

"Sorority?" Jack said, with a raised eyebrow.

A slight smile rose at the corner of Monica's mouth. "Oh, believe me, I resisted the Greek system my whole freshman year, but then gave into the wooing at the start of the next year. Living with my wild roommate, Jessica, and the other girls was never a great fit for me. Their all-night partying and revolving door of sexual partners wasn't helpful in keeping up my grades.

"Delta Mu learned I was on full scholarship and had won the West of the Mississippi contest, so they invited me to pledge their house. They seemed like a nice bunch of girls, but their primary interest in me was my grade point average." Monica shrugged. "Sisterhood meant lots of study hall hours and weekly dinners with our housemother. I made some casual friends, but mainly focused on school." Monica omitted the part about her growing relationship with Jeremy. Since boys weren't allowed in the sorority house, it had also helped solve the dilemma of saying good night to Jeremy every night.

"Did your parents die while you were at school?"

"Oh. Sorry. Where was I?"

"You were on your way back from economics," Jack prompted.

"Right. When I walked into the house that night, a girl said 'Hey, Mo. There's a note on the bulletin board that says Mom Hays wants to see you after dinner.'

"All through dinner, I had a nagging sense something wasn't right. After I cleared my dishes and left them in the kitchen for the houseboys to wash, I stopped by the restroom, washed my face, and applied a thin layer of lip-gloss. Even though the Delta Mus weren't a flashy sorority, our housemother appreciated a 'well-put-together young lady,' as she often liked to remind us." Monica thought briefly that her stalling that night long ago mirrored her getting to the point with Jack today.

"Go on," Jack urged gently.

"On my way down the hall, my closest friend in the house, Louise, asked if I was going to see Mom Hays. I said yes and asked if she had any idea what was up. Louise winced slightly, and then she said, 'I just know she asked me to come with you.' I thought that was kind of weird, especially when Louise took hold of my hand, then knocked on our housemother's door."

"'Hello Monica. Louise,' Mom Hays said. 'Won't you please have a seat?' She wore her silver hair in a chignon and pearls always draped her crepe-papery neck. She looked more like a high-society grand dame presiding over a dinner party, instead of a chaperone assigned to instill order over sixty spirited girls.

"I can hear her as if it were yesterday. 'Monica, dear, I'm afraid I have some bad news.' I started to panic and barely heard what came next. 'There's been a horrible accident. I don't know how to tell you this, but your parents were killed.'"

"Louise gasped and dug her fingernails into my palm, kind of like you're doing right now." Monica looked at Jack, eyes blurring with tears. It had been years since she'd thought of this story. "I went totally blank and sat staring at Mom Hays as though she'd stripped off her clothes and begun doing a pole dance.

"Louise prodded me to say something, until I finally asked about Lily. Mom Hays said Lily was fine and wasn't with my parents when it happened. Louise burst into tears and threw her arms around my neck, sobbing about how sorry she was. Then she screamed at me when I said it wasn't anything to worry about. Mom Hays reached over and patted both our hands as if we were small children, then had Louise take me upstairs to my room. I heard her whisper to Louise that I was probably in shock and needed some rest."

"Oh, Monica, I'm so sorry. That must have been horrible." Jack scooted his chair a little closer. "You were so young."

Monica stared at the ceiling of the coffee shop, remembering how her housemates had tiptoed around her and whispered amongst themselves, not knowing what to do. None of them had ever lost one parent, certainly not two at once. Jeremy had called daily, but she'd refused to see or talk to him.

"I thought it was all my fault. I'd wished them dead so many times, and it finally happened. After the initial shock wore off, I gathered the courage to speak to Mom Hays again and find out what happened. Apparently they'd been traveling across the Olympic Peninsula toward Neah Bay. Daddy had always wanted to visit the furthest northwest point on the continental United States, and for some inexplicable reason, my mother had agreed to go with him. Lily was away for the weekend participating in one of her thousand extracurricular activities, so it was just the two of them on the road.

"*The Seattle Times* called it 'one of the most bizarre accidents in state history.' My parents had been traveling west on Highway 112 toward Clallam Bay, on the winding roads used by logging trucks. On one of the hairpin curves, a fully loaded log truck approached toward the east. Just before the two vehicles moved into parallel position, a weakened chain on the logging truck snapped. The weight of the single break dominoed until every other chain broke, and the entire truckload released on top of my parents' vehicle. The coroner said they died instantly. It was like crushing a fly with a wrecking ball. The truck driver was hospitalized for minor injuries and severe shock. If there had been any witnesses, they would have declared it a freak occurrence."

"Oh, sweetie," Jack said.

"Just like they met, so they died, fast and furious. June and Darrell Levin were no more."

"I'm so sorry. What happened then?"

"Well, I had to decide what I was going to do about everything. They didn't leave any funeral directives, and I was left in charge. The funeral director recommended cremation, since there wasn't anything left of the bodies. Rumor had it the coroner was still trying to decide which parts belonged to whom. In a snap decision, I agreed, even though I had little doubt that Mother was already burning in a flaming pit of hell." She looked up slightly, trying to gauge

Jack's reaction. He never wavered. "I'm sorry. I wanted to feel sadness about my mother's death, but I just couldn't muster the emotion. Poor Daddy. All he wanted to do was see the place where the big fishing boats came in. I prayed he would rest in peace. I loved him so much."

"And Lily?" Jack asked.

Monica let out a deep sigh.

IZABEL

One of the things Izabel liked about her relationship with Buck was that it wasn't exactly a relationship. He was a married man with a wife and two teenage boys and, even though she struggled with being the other woman, she preferred being on her own. They hadn't seen each other since the night he'd returned home from his fishing trip in Alaska and she'd been daunted with disturbing dreams. While he'd called her several times wanting to come visit, Izabel had managed to keep him from returning to Orcas Island, until today.

Buck knocked at her door unannounced, waking Izabel. He was holding a bouquet of chrysanthemums and smiling with the lopsided grin that never failed to melt her heart. Izabel knew he wanted more from her than she was able to give today, or maybe ever.

"Hey, gorgeous," he said, holding the flowers out to her. "Long time no see."

"Hi." She felt bashful as she reached out to take the bouquet, and slipped beneath his arms when he tried to hug her. Seeing the disappointment on his face, she stood on tiptoes and gave him a peck on the lips, then took his hand and led him into the house.

"This is a surprise," Izabel said, walking through the living room toward the kitchen.

"Yeah, I got tired of waiting for you to invite me."

Izabel busied herself looking for a vase. "Things have been a little crazy," she said over her shoulder, as she reached into a cabinet.

"Crazy how?" Buck said, as he settled onto one of the bar stools.

"Oh, you know, busy. Painting. Doing chores. Stuff."

"I see," Buck twisted his mouth, and Izabel could tell he wasn't satisfied with her answer. "Could we have some coffee and talk?"

Izabel felt panic rise in her chest. Since the soul dance, she'd felt even more out of sorts than she had before it, not quite herself in a way she couldn't quite explain. Her belly continued to clinch at the oddest times, but she hadn't seen a doctor, or told anyone except Miriam that anything was amiss. She was afraid of what might spill out if she started talking. Her other option today was to distract Buck with sex, but that idea made her stomach churn even more.

"Sounds great. How about we head into town and get coffee at Beth's?"

"I was kind of hoping—"

"I'm totally out of coffee beans, and she's got some killer new art in the store. We could get breakfast, too."

Buck's face fell, but Izabel knew she'd won when he said, "Okay. Beth's it is."

—   —   —

The villagers of Deer Harbor didn't credit the success of Beth's Gallery and Café to the proprietress's no-nonsense attitude, or her exquisite ability to combine obscure knick-knacks with world-renowned art. It wasn't about the eclectic décor or the collection of quirky locals who gathered on the large front stoop year round. No. The success of Beth's Gallery and Café could be attributed to one thing: the smell.

Today the featured smell was nutmeg. As Buck held open the saloon-style doors and Izabel stepped across the wooden threshold, she caught the faintest whiff of the spice. She stopped in her tracks as a memory surged up in her mind.

She was thirteen or fourteen, standing at the top of a flight of stairs and peering over the bannister down into someone's living room. The pungent nutmeg aroma came from sprinkles atop the Christmas eggnog two bleary-looking adults were consuming in large mugs. The smell drifted into her nostrils like the angry voices rising up the stairs.

"Here's to that uptight priss leaving the house!" The woman lifted her mug in a mock toast, and Izabel listened across time. "Who the hell does she think she is, going off to that snotty East Coast school?"

"That's no way to talk about your daughter," the man protested.

"Oh, shut up, you old fool. You're no better than she is."

Izabel covered her ears and squeezed her eyes tightly closed. *What the hell?* She wanted to plug her nose to stop the memories.

Buck reached over and took her hand. "What's wrong, Iz? You okay?"

"I just need coffee," she said, looking up into his gray eyes. His kindness managed to quell her bewilderment for the moment. "Let's go sit down."

— — —

After breakfast, Izabel and Buck wove their way through the creatively cluttered aisles of Beth's gallery. Sated from lattes and freshly baked scones, they strolled with Buck trailing slightly behind Izabel, their pinky fingers touching. Each time Buck reached to take her hand, Izabel moved away or picked up a trinket from a shelf. She felt guilty for keeping him at a distance, and the pinky-touch was her best attempt to stay connected.

"What about this one?" She held up a handcrafted mug. It was shaped like an upside-down bell. The lip was midnight blue, and the pattern turned spiral-like to the base, the faintest shade of sky blue.

"Felicia doesn't like blue things," Buck sighed.

Izabel set the mug back in its place amidst a dozen others. It was odd, looking for a gift for Buck's wife, but Izabel had insisted it was what they must do when he told her Felicia had twisted her ankle and was recuperating at her sister's house in Friday Harbor. "You can't go back empty-handed," Izabel had said.

Buck had slipped away for the day, saying he had some boat repairs to sort out. "She won't even notice I'm gone," he'd grumbled.

Again the guilt weighed on Izabel. She was a man's mistress, and not a very good one at that. Instead of spending the morning in her cozy bed, she'd insisted they come to town for coffee and browsing.

"Hey y'all. How's it shakin'?" Beth's distinctive voice rang out. "Did you see the new stack of stones we got from that artist down on Whidbey Island? She makes the most amazing designs I've ever seen."

Izabel and Buck nodded at Beth, all their words used up from small-talk and strained chitchat.

Beth continued her path along the aisle opposite them, straightening here, dusting there. "Those stones are over here in this basket if you wanna take a peek. Okay now, I'm off to make more muffins."

Izabel wished she could steal even a fraction of Beth's boundless energy right now. She was already exhausted, and Buck's surprise visit was draining her like a bilge pump working overtime on a sinking ship.

They made their way over to the basket of stones. Izabel picked them up, one by one, resting each one in the palm of her hand. Every one was unique, but Izabel's breath caught when she picked up an onyx-colored oval and turned it over to see the inscription on the back. The word was as pungent as nutmeg, and the memories even more powerful.

"What is it?" Buck asked, standing at her elbow.

Izabel turned the smooth rock over and over in the palm of her hand, as if in a daze. "It's like the small stone from the window ledge of my room, when I was a girl," she whispered. "I kept it hidden behind the pink ruffles and taffeta. It waited there like a hidden talisman." Izabel wavered on her feet as if blown by a gentle breeze.

"I remember the first time I turned it over and saw the word etched on its side. I was still too young to read. I begged my sister, 'What does it say? What does it say?'

"It was the size of a Kennedy half-dollar. It shone like the ebony keys of the piano in our cordoned-off living room; the piano that no one played once my sister was gone. But the stone, my touchstone, always held its glimmer.

"Whenever I felt scared or lonely, I would curl myself into a ball on my window seat and pull the stone out from underneath the pillows that draped over the ledge. Turn. Rub. Turn. First, I tested the smooth side with my thumb, feeling the relief of things going smoothly."

Buck watched from a foot away as Izabel's face relaxed into a peaceful expression. He started to reach over and embrace her, but stopped, as if wary of breaking the spell she was weaving. She stared into a liminal space in time as she held the small stone in her hand and worked it like rosary beads.

"And then there was the rough side that only a blind person could read. How I longed to be that unseeing girl with a finger so trained as to be able to read the etchings and release the stone's magic.

"I tried every approach. Pressing harder. Hovering my hand over the surface. Pretending to be Goldilocks in search of the perfect 'just right.' My sister used to tell me if I kept my eyes closed and wished upon the stone, then the word would appear. Try as I might, I never quite felt it. It was only a blur of bumps and dashes, nothing fluid or legible.

"Finally, I would toss the stone onto the window seat and open my eyes. The word was always there just as she promised me it would be, even long after she was gone."

Buck leaned close enough to read the inscription on the stone in Izabel's open palm: TRUTH. Then he looked at her, brow furrowed.

"Izabel, honey." His voice was low. "You told me you couldn't remember anything from when you were a kid. Or from before you came here, for that matter."

Izabel stared at the stone. "I know."

"So what does this mean?"

Izabel took a deep breath. "Maybe it means the time for the truth is coming."

— — —

Buck went home not long after darkness fell. Any longer than that this time, and his wife would start to get suspicious. Izabel pretended to be disappointed, but in reality, she was relieved to see his truck pull away. Since what she'd seen—and remembered?—in the store, she'd wanted to be alone.

She fed Lucas and sprawled on the sofa, turning the TRUTH stone over and over in her hand. She'd had to buy it, of course, even if it was a little pricey for a pretty rock with a word carved into it. She knew exactly what Miriam, and probably Sister Gabrielle, too, would have said about it: that she was meant to have it.

I hope it'll lead me to the truth. I hope I'm ready.

She wasn't even aware of closing her eyes and drifting into sleep.

DAISY

Daisy sat alone on the coral-colored beach and absentmindedly stuck a twig into the sandy soil at her feet. She dug her toes further into the grit and watched the tiny stick's shadow turn around it. *Is that what time is?* she thought. *Shadows turning? Is it true that hours pass into days and years?*

"I wonder if I'm getting older. Or maybe younger." she said to a passing beetle.

"I'd say you're perfect just as you are," replied the insect.

"Why, thank you very much. You're pretty cool yourself." Daisy smiled at the bug as he scurried on about his business. "*Je t'aime, mon petit ami.*"

Daisy had ceased to think anything was odd or out of the ordinary here in Tausi. Talking beetles, speaking French or Swahili, earthquakes and talking peacocks were all part of her life. The only thing she didn't trust was whatever Sir Albert and Chauncey were scared of.

"Did someone think of me?"

Daisy heard a crusty voice pour out of a conch shell by her feet and instinctively pulled her knees up to her chest.

"Now, now, dear Daisy. There's nothing to fear. Why do you pull back from me?"

"Go away! I hate you!"

"Oh, my dear. That simply won't do. We were born to be companions, you and I. BFFs, as they say in your world."

A blood-curdling cackle filled the air. It rang from the jungle to Daisy's right and the ocean on the left, like curling waves of evil. The earth vibrated beneath her again, and Daisy feared it might break open and swallow her up. This time Sir Albert wasn't here, and when she opened her mouth to scream for Chauncey, she croaked like a frog with laryngitis.

"Daisy. Daisy. Have you learned nothing? You can't run from me. I'm like the Truth. You can't hide from it."

Panic rose in Daisy's chest, and adrenaline launched her to her feet. She took a single step before she realized that the twig she'd planted in the sand had expanded to a two-foot diameter and was rising toward the sky like Jack's giant beanstalk.

Without thinking, she hurled herself at the trunk and grabbed on as it rose in the air.

A whirlwind formed in the sand below her and combined with swaying jungle palms and water from the ocean. It swirled chaotically and then rose, as if chasing the swiftly growing tree. Daisy screamed and jerked back when a grizzled hand with yellow nails stretched out of the funnel and grazed her bare foot.

A loud "Harrumph" followed the near miss. Daisy curled her toes around the tree trunk and held on tighter.

The tree grew until the whirlwind appeared to be the size of a child's spinning top. Daisy expanded her chest and breathed freely in the brilliant blue air high above the funnel.

A plaintive cry wailed into the sky: "You can run, but you can never hide. I will always find you!"

The whirlwind split into a million pieces and vanished.

— — —

Exhausted, Daisy rested on a pillowy white puff that floated in the otherwise cloudless sky. Out of the thin blue air, a royal blue and purple fan appeared, followed by another and then another. The fans waved in the air like belly dancers swaying to music, and Daisy lifted her hand to wave back.

"Why, hello, my dear." A snake-like neck rose above one of the fans, and Daisy realized she was watching a parade of peacocks with Sir Albert in the lead. Tucked among the royal plumages, Daisy noticed several smaller fan-less fowl. These were the peahens. While their colors were nowhere near the brilliance of the male counterparts, the hens nevertheless wore muted shades of bluish-green instead of the dreary earth-born browns she remembered seeing at the zoo.

Wherever the peacocks went, the hens were sure to follow. Daisy wasn't sure how she felt about females just following males.

"Care to join the parade, my dear?" Sir Albert called.

"Only if I can lead," Daisy called back, eyes blazing.

"I'd have it no other way," replied the wise old bird.

Daisy giggled and snapped her fingers to summon Chauncey.

"Let the parade continue," she announced, with a wave of her hand and a gentle kick of her heels into Chauncey's green and white striped haunch.

And so it did.

IZABEL

Izabel bolted awake on the sofa, sitting up with a yelp. Lucas had been curled asleep beside her. He leapt away, yowling.

The TRUTH stone had fallen from her hand while she was asleep. It lay on the floorboards, glimmering in the rapidly dimming light from outside. Slowly, she leaned over and picked it up, her brain feeling too full and her movements deadened with the cold feeling she vaguely recognized as clinical shock.

A whisper came out of her mouth, almost on its own: "I remember."

Once she could get up, she walked—slowly—into the kitchen, the stone clutched tightly in her hand. She had a laptop, but didn't use it for much of anything except looking up work-related stuff. After all, she had no one to write to. Most of the people around here weren't too keen on technology, and she didn't have any family.

Except I do.

She opened a blank document on the computer and paused, hands poised over the keyboard. Then the words started spilling out.

I was christened Lily Belle Levin, and managed to live up to my Disney princess name. That is, until I didn't. When I was a girl-woman of fourteen, my favorite throne was the center of my four-poster bed, which was decorated stem to stern with pink ruffles and polka dots. In my own pastel kingdom, I was the perfect urban princess: pink complexion, round emerald eyes, naturally wavy hair, and a perpetual look of boredom on my face.

Oh, God, what can I say? I am the second child of my parents, Darrell and June Levin, and I arrived following my mother's three miscarriages and the birth of my sister, Monica. She is four years older than I am. She was the smart one and I was the pretty one. At least that's what our mother always said.

The whole family seemed mystified by the relationship between Mom and me. Outwardly, I appeared to be the heiress extraordinaire, but anyone watching closely knew that Mom was pulling the strings. I'd heard from my aunt Claire that Mom (or June, as I rebelliously called her) had always been their household's ruling royalty, making sure every detail of life revolved around her. All those years I thought I was the princess, but it was a ruse. June was always in control, even if she did bring me breakfast in bed and cart me to ballet lessons. I was conceived to be her miracle child, and as long as I played my role, she performed hers, mixed up as it was.

I was added to the Levin roster (that is, conceived and born) because my sister had proven to be June's giant disappointment by the time she turned two. June was all about being in the spotlight, and she expected her daughters to be the same way. My sister (or, as Mom called her, "the selfish child") was far more interested in reading Go Dog Go and going to the farm with Daddy than practicing for the beauty pageants that were June's version of the Holy Grail.

Daddy always said, "You can take the beauty queen out of the South, but you can't take the South out of the beauty queen." While June was lovely in her own carefully constructed way, she wasn't a natural beauty like the women she'd grown up with in Oklahoma. In the world of her upbringing, women were born to do three things: compete in beauty pageants, become wives, and become mothers. The perfect trifecta was a woman who succeeded at all three. Since June had never made it past the Little Miss Pageant at age eleven, she had her heart set on having a daughter who triumphed where she had not. That daughter was supposed to be me.

As a little girl, I was fascinated with my older sister and wanted to be just like her. I shadowed her whenever possible and adored playing with her books and Play-Doh. We used to hide from Mother and pretend we were downtrodden peasants escaping from the evil queen. In the end, however, June was a formidable foe, and I was all too malleable to her wishes and demands.

As the years passed, my relationship with Monica became complicated and confusing. While I know she tried to love me, I didn't give her much to connect with. Our mother's influence was not easy to reckon with. I became the princess she desired, even while trying to reach Monica in my own childlike ways.

"Mo Mo, you like my dress?" (I was not yet three years old when I started asking this question.)

"It's very nice, Lily."

"You want one?"

"No thanks, Lil. I'm not much into ruffles and taffeta. Would you like to read The Cat in the Hat *with me?*"

"Ooohhhh. Yes, peas. I love dat book." Reading with Monica was one of my favorite things to do.

"Book? Did I hear book?" June swooped into the room and scooped me up like a hawk. "Oh, sweet Lily, wouldn't you rather go watch Cinderella *or* Pretty Woman *in the playroom?*"

What parent in their right mind would show a young child a movie glorifying a prostitute? June's judgment was definitely questionable, but, in her defense, she only saw the end results of being a "pretty woman"—clothes, limousines, and a handsome man bearing roses. Poor woman. She was so naïve sometimes, but she was nothing if not persistent.

"What's it going to be, missy?" June pressed, as I looked longingly between the book in my sister's hand and our mother's expectant face. "Cinderella *or* Pretty Woman?"

"How about you and I watch Cinderella *together, Lil?*" Monica was my hero.

"Yes, peas!"

"Oh, no, no, no," interjected our mother. "Monica's got chores to do. Don't you?" She lifted an eyebrow in that don't-you-dare-defy-me way. "It's the perfect time to tidy up Lily's room while she's watching the movie."

"But, Mooommm."

"Would you like me to add a few more chores to the list? You know I hate sassiness."

"No, ma'am." I can still see Monica turning her bespectacled face downward and walking away in defeat. No wonder she ended up hating me.

I remember the day I heard Monica was leaving. I'd been warned time and again about eavesdropping, but seriously, how else was I supposed to find out anything in the house that June ruled? By the time I was twelve, I'd memorized every creak in the hardwood floors and knew how to hopscotch the stairs like a three-legged fawn.

That day, I sat curled on the staircase with my knees hugged against my chest. I leaned against the wall, six steps up the passageway—out of sight of the ongoing conversation, but within earshot of all that was said. After Monica told our parents she was going to Briar Cliff, I crawled back up the stairs to my room without anyone hearing me, just before Mother burst into my room like a petulant child.

She closed the door behind her and went off on a tirade about Daddy and Monica. "Dear God, who are those losers?" she said, crossing her arms and shaking her head as if I weren't even in the room. "I can't believe I've stayed married to him all these years. But if I hadn't, I wouldn't have you, my precious Lily."

She turned her devouring gaze my way, and I felt the hair rise up the back of my neck. "Why can't Monica be more like you? Why does she always have to have her nose in a book? And a writer? Seriously? Who does she think she is? Who reads books anyway when People and Cosmopolitan tell you everything you need to know?" Mother paused and looked me over like I was a Tiffany's display case before starting up again.

"Jesus, the girl must already think she's on the East Coast, wearing khaki pants and button-down shirts. And those heavy black glasses? They make her look like Darrell when we first met. Whatever happened to a little feminine charm? That girl couldn't charm herself out of a cereal box. You, on the other hand ... " My skin crawled when I felt the weight of what she meant. "Maybe the East Coast is exactly where Monica belongs. At least she'll be out of my hair and I can splurge everything on you, my precious Lily, Oh, this idea is sounding better all the time."

She opened the door and went back downstairs. I tiptoed to my secret viewpoint and huddled against the staircase wall.

"Did you say all expenses are paid, Mo Mo?" I heard Mother ask innocently, as she arranged herself on the floral sofa.

Monica stiffened and Daddy narrowed his eyes. We could all sense trouble was on its way. Mother only called Monica "Mo Mo" when she was moving in for the sweetened kill.

"Yes, Mom. All expenses are paid except for travel, and I've got that covered." Monica fidgeted with the corner of her blouse.

I wanted to scream, Don't go!, but I knew she had no choice now that Mother had bought into the plan for her to leave.

"Well, isn't that wonderful, Darrell? Our little girl is growing up. She's gone and got herself a full scholarship to a fancy-schmancy school. Wait 'til I tell the girls at the tennis club."

Daddy rolled his eyes and glanced toward Monica to sneak a wink at her. I couldn't understand why this kind-hearted man was still with the woman he'd married more than twenty years before. She was self-centered, rude, and a mediocre mother. On the other hand, she was pretty enough and could run a household like no other. I always wondered if he stayed with her for love or out of a sense of protection for Monica and me. Even though Mother never physically harmed us, she had a quick temper and biting tongue. Her Southern upbringing had taught her to be polite and cool as ice on the outside, but anyone who crossed her could feel the simmer of spitefulness and thirst for revenge she held inside.

And now Monica was leaving. As the truth hit me, a surge of thoughts and emotions shivered through my body. Would I miss her? Yes. No. I don't know. I always felt confused when Mother criticized Monica for being book smart and praised me for my appearance.

I cherished our childhood days when we used to steal away and read together under forts made out of sheets and blankets. Monica was the counterbalance in my life, taking Mother's wrath while I soaked up her indulgence. As I sat there eavesdropping on the stairs, I had the strong sense this balance would tilt off its axis and never return when Monica left home.

When I was fourteen, Monica left for Briar Cliff College. She sent us a picture of herself sitting on the brick wall in front of the hundred-year-old library. Her hands were folded in her lap, and it looked like she was pinching the tender skin between her thumb and forefinger to make sure she was really there. She had a grin on her face that told me she finally had everything she'd dreamed of since she was a kid in pigtails making up stories and telling them to her stuffed animals.

It was New England in the fall and she was at the most esteemed women's liberal arts college in the country. Full scholarship, and best of all for her, she was three thousand miles away from our parents and me, her bratty little sister. Could she have asked for anything more?

Once, in a moment of vulnerability, she told me she wondered what to think as she sat there and watched the exclusively female student body parade across the brick sidewalk in front of her. She said she felt a slight twinge of regret that she'd insisted on an all-women establishment, but then her roommate, Jessica, introduced her to the boys at Wellington, Briar Cliff's brother school on the other side of The Commons.

Monica was never great with guys while we were growing up, and looking back, I know I wasn't much help in boosting her confidence. Still, I never could understand her insecurities, because I always thought she was the most brilliant sister in the world. She must have been really lonely, because she wrote me more than a few letters during those first few months.

Hi Lily: I'm slowly learning the ways of the Northeast, and particularly the Ivy League. Tradition is everything up here. Most of the girls I've met are at least second-generation Briar Cliff women, if not third or fourth. One girl is rumored to be related to Kathryn Clayburgh, the silent film star from the 1920s. Another's grandmother was the first female president of some big deal multi-national corporation. I feel totally out of my league. I can feel the color drain from my face when people ask where I'm from and who my parents are. Fortunately, the majority of them have never been west of Ohio and consider me a novelty for being from Seattle, so the conversation rarely gets as far as our parents. I'm also discovering that most of my classmates prefer to be the center of conversation and have a short attention span for other people's stories. Lucky me!

Your sis, Monica

I wish I'd realized when she wrote me those letters that she was looking for a friend. Instead, I sloughed them off and focused on me me me like Mother had taught me.

I didn't understand the biggest shift for me—well, for both of us really—would come when Monica met Jeremy and fell in love. Again I had those mixed feelings as I read her letters about sleepless nights dreaming of the boy she believed was her soul mate. Even though I missed her, I was jealous when she wrote about endless hours of staring at the ceiling, headphones on, and a goofy smile lighting up her face. She said music had never sounded more beautiful and poetry flowed onto the page. I nearly gagged.

She even talked about getting contact lenses and wearing lipstick. As long as I'd known her, Monica had defied everything that could be described as girly: makeup, stylish haircuts and frilly clothes. Cute shoes were her only vice. She usually just bought them, but never wore them. For the first time in her life, she said she actually felt pretty. I wondered what it would be like when she came home. After all, I had always been the pretty one.

Jeremy was Monica's dream come true. One she'd never even dared to dream. How could a few months make such a huge difference in a person? She'd always pooh-poohed the notions of love at first sight and soul mates. After all, she'd heard the stories of how our parents met. True love, they called it. Well, if that was true love, Monica always said, she wanted none of it.

Our mother was a tyrant, and Daddy spent as much time as possible out at the family farm. They'd moved from Skagit Valley to Seattle shortly after Monica was born. Mother couldn't stand the stigma of being a farmer's wife. She'd left home to escape exactly that. What irony that she'd found the one man who didn't live within an eight-hundred-mile radius of Stillwater, Oklahoma and married him, only to find herself back in the middle of farm land that wasn't so different from where she'd grown up.

As kids, our picture of love had been formed by incessant arguing and parents who got along best when they were separated by at least a hundred miles. It was weird how similar Monica meeting Jeremy and their story was. Mom had been looking for a man to take her away from her roots, and Monica wanted someone who would never make her go back.

There was another letter she sent that I remember because it was so cute:

Saturday nights on The Cliff are pandemonium. The kids look like a pageant of puffed-out peacocks strolling up and down the brick sidewalks that line the clubs and coffee shops in the center of town. Mating calls sound: "Hey baby," or "What's up, handsome?" But the body language and sexy clothes do most of the talking.

I feel like a peahen next to my girl friends. You know flashy has never been my style, but one night my roommate decided to give me a makeover and got me to wear my punk heels with tight black leggings and an oversized sweatshirt torn at the shoulder. Ooh la la, right?

I spent all afternoon practicing walking in the heels that I'd never dared to take out of the box. Jeremy called and buoyed my confidence by saying he hoped to see me, and even though we weren't going on a date, I wanted to look as good as possible just in case we ran into each other. Cindy even let me borrow a pair of disposable contact lenses. Mother would die if she could see me now.

Even though my friends boosted my spirits with their ooh-ing and ah-ing, I still felt like a big old fraud! It was still a super-fun night with kids hanging out everywhere, and then, oh my gosh, it happened.

Jeremy was driving by with a bunch of his friends. Before I knew what was happening, he lunged out the passenger window, spread his arms like a soaring eagle, and shouted, "MONICA GAYLE LEVIN, I LOOOOOVVVVE YOOOOOOUUU!"

The whole block went quiet and turned to stare at me. I just knew the heat from my blush was generating enough energy to make a spotlight around me, but I didn't care. I teetered up on those six-inch heels, flung open my arms to match his, and shouted back, "I LOVE YOU, TOO!!" just before I tipped sideways and landed in Cindy's lap.

The entire neighborhood burst into applause and hoots and hollers. Then I untangled myself, got up, kicked off my shoes and ran barefoot into the middle of the street to meet Jeremy. We stood there hugging like a modern-day version of the sailor and his girl in Times Square. You remember that picture, right?

Oh Lily, it was so cool! I think I'm in love!! Your sis, Monica

For the next two years, Jeremy and Monica were inseparable. I wanted her to come home, but she made up excuses for every holiday and break: she had to work, needed to study, or couldn't afford it. I felt left out and couldn't decide if I was madder at her or Jeremy. Still, I loved getting her letters and the occasional phone call.

Monica told me once that she and Jeremy had made a pact that they wouldn't have sex until after they were married. It was a weird decision in my eyes, but one that made sense to both of them for their own private reasons. Monica said she could always hear Mother's voice in her head: "If you give the milk away for free, why would a man buy the cow?" It was a disgusting analogy, but nonetheless one that rang in her ears whenever she thought of giving over her virginity to the boy she loved. And, boy, did she love him!

I always wondered what she believed about sex when she was truthful with herself. I got the feeling she was terrified. I wasn't in any rush either, but then I was four years younger. Our collective knowledge and experience of intimacy came from movies and hushed stories we'd heard from friends. Our parents' marriage was a poor example of love. Monica said she liked to imagine they'd only had sex about five times: one time each for her, me, and the little lost babies.

When I asked her how Jeremy handled the no sex thing, she told me that he respected her so much, he didn't even carry condoms. They'd both decided that if he did, that would increase their temptation to break the pact. If he was anything

like the guys in movies, I could only imagine he spent a lot of time taking cold showers.

I missed her, but I can't deny that I sort of liked having all the attention at home.

And then I came home from that weekend at the dance competition, and the police were waiting for me to tell me there'd been an accident, and everything—everything—changed.

MONICA

Monica shifted back and forth in the wooden chair. A deep sigh escaped her lips as she thought about the events surrounding her return to Seattle. She wasn't sure she could talk about Lily without bringing Jeremy into the story.

"It's kind of a complicated story," she said, and then paused.

"I'm all ears." Jack grinned and wiggled his eyebrows.

"Well, after the initial news of our parents' deaths, we were forced into a new kind of relationship. I hadn't been home for a couple of years. Lily and I had been writing each other letters, but the last time we'd been together, Mom was still stirring the pot between us and Daddy was our mediator.

"Lily was in that awkward stage between teen and woman, and our initial conversations were laced with both a surprisingly mature Lily *and* the wild, petulant child. She insisted she was perfectly capable of taking care of herself, and encouraged me to wrap up my classes before coming home. She said she'd be fine, but I always wondered."

"Sounds reasonable on both your parts." Jack nodded and took a sip of his coffee.

"One time I suggested she fly out to Massachusetts to stay with me, and she about took my head off. Swore she was an adult." Monica shook her head at the memory. "Huh. Some adult. Since we didn't have any living relatives and we'd agreed on cremation, there wasn't a rush for a funeral service. School was officially out for break mid-December, but I felt like I owed it to Lily and my parents to go home before then. The professors all agreed to let me take early exams or turn in late term papers. Lily ended up being home for a few days without me. Her best friend lived next door, so she promised she'd either be there or at home.

"Mom had never been a domestic goddess, and Daddy spent more days away from home than there, so they had a full range of people to take care of the house." Monica paused when she thought about the house.

"What was it like going home after so long?" Jack asked.

"It was weird. *Really* weird." Monica took a sip of her lukewarm tea. "I couldn't wrap my mind around the fact that my parents were both gone. Killed by logs. Who else could say that about their parents? 'Hi, my name is Monica. My parents were killed by logs.'" A forced laugh gurgled out of her throat. "It was absurd. My academic advisor at school had recommended I attend a grief group on campus, and I didn't have the nerve to tell her I wasn't *in* grief."

"Denial?" Jack asked quietly.

"That's exactly what my roommate, the psych major, said. 'It's one of the five stages of grief,' she told me. All I wanted to do was scream: 'It's not denial! I just don't care!'"

"Those were the thoughts that consumed my days. Who would have imagined that the people I'd thought so rarely about over the years while they were living would consume so much of my time when they were dead?"

"What about anger? You know, the second stage of grief."

"You're not going to get all psychological on me, are you?" Monica frowned at Jack.

"Sorry. It just seems like you had a lot to be angry about."

"No kidding! I about took the cabdriver's head off when he dropped me at the house." She shook her head and drifted off. "And then, when I walked in . . ."

Monica's eyes pooled with tears, and Jack squeezed her hand as the scene played out in her mind.

IZABEL

Izabel paused to flex her aching hands. She looked over at the window, where the sky had gone black. She bent over the keyboard again.

"Lily? Lily, where are you?"

I could hear Monica calling from the entryway and knew by her halting steps that she was moving cautiously through the house.

I have no doubt she was shocked by what she saw. Anyone would have been. Everywhere was chaos: furniture on its side, half-empty food containers mixed with knick-knacks, and pillows with stuffing oozing out of their seams. It looked like an intruder had ransacked the house, but anyone who knew the house like Monica did could do a quick inventory and notice that valuable things were still in the room. Silver candlesticks lay on their side. My own Walkman sat in the middle of a cup-covered coffee table, and the television rested on its stand in the corner.

The place looked more like a raucous after-party scene from a John Hughes movie than the site of a robbery.

"Lily?" Monica called again from the bottom of the stairs.

Screwing up my courage, I called out in a placid-sounding voice, "I'm up here." Her footsteps stopped at the first room along the hallway, mine. It was a total disaster, but that had always been the case.

"Where are you?"

"I'm in your room, silly. Where else would I be?"

She passed our parents' unoccupied bedroom where, looking in, she would have noticed chaos similar to what she'd seen downstairs. As she peeked into the threshold of her own room, I could tell she was prepared for the bedlam to continue.

I'd seen to it that Monica's room was exactly as she'd left it when she packed her bags and moved to Briar Cliff. Tidy and neat. Her posters of Michael Jackson and Jon Bon Jovi hung undisturbed on the walls. The bookshelves held her alphabetically arranged collection of The Baby-Sitters Club. *Nothing was amiss. Nothing, that is, expect for me sitting propped in the middle of the double bed with polka-dot-sheets, leaning against blue ticking pillow shams. I was painting my toenails. I must have looked like a slightly deranged character from* The Rocky Horror Picture Show.

"Lily! Are you all right?"

"Sure. Whaddya mean?" *I glanced up from my toes.*

"What do I mean? The house is destroyed! I was worried sick about you!"

"Oh. Yeah. That. I, um, kinda had a little meltdown, but everything's cool now."

"Cool? Are you kidding me? The house is a wreck!"

"Gosh, Monica. Don't be like Mom. It's just a little mess. No biggie."

That seemed to stop Monica's momentum. I had her number. I knew the last thing she wanted to be was controlling and bitchy like Mom. When she glanced over at me again, I made sure to appear much more child-like than rival-esque.

"Okay. I guess you're right. No biggie." *Monica let out a sigh that sounded like air leaking out of a tire.*

Score one for me.

Since Monica didn't have the heart to push me out of her bedroom, she decided to camp out in my wreckage of a room. Feathers and shredded bedding were spread from corner to corner, like a bizarre bird had been plucked and gutted on the premises. Something had been thrown at the center of the dressing table mirror; spider-web cracks splayed from the point of impact. Monica found the broken bottle of Giorgio perfume on the table, its base a perfect fit for the mirror damage. When she came to me, holding the bottle up with a questioning look on her face, I just shrugged.

Monica was a workhorse. For the next several days, she did her best to restore the previously pristine house to order. I, on the other hand, continued to act as though nothing had changed. I drifted through the house ghostlike, staring at the shrinking disarray, feeling like I was visiting from another world.

I don't know how many days went by before I finally got up one morning, took a long shower, blew dry my hair, and dressed in my cheerleading uniform.

Monica was sitting in the breakfast nook, sipping her morning tea and looking at her chore list when I came bouncing down the stairs.

"Hey. What's for breakfast?"

"What's for breakfast?" Monica stared at me, her face all scrunched up.

"Yeah. Do we have any of that lemon yogurt left? Or maybe you could scramble us up some eggs? Please, Mo Mo." I tilted my head to one side, with a slight pout.

"Mo Mo? Are you kidding me? You walk around the house like a zombie for days, that is, when you weren't screeching like a banshee, and now you call me Mo Mo and want me to scramble us up some eggs? What is going on?" She shook her head in wonder.

"Hm. I dunno. I was kinda upset. I guess I just needed to get it out of my system. It's really good to have you here, Mo Mo. Too bad about Mommy and Daddy, huh?"

Monica looked like she was about to rail and screech. Her face turned crimson red, and she clutched the side of the table until her knuckles turned white. After a few seconds of glaring at me, she suddenly let go, took a deep breath, and smoothed out her hair. "Yes, too bad about them."

She got up from her seat and busied herself with breakfast until the phone rang. I could only hear one end of the conversation, but I knew it was Jeremy on the other end of the line.

"Oh, she seems just fine. Yep, the broken creature masquerading as my sister is gone, and overnight, it seems, the original Lily has returned. She bounced downstairs this morning like nothing had happened and simply said, 'Too bad about Mom and Dad.' Weird, huh?"

Monica was quiet while Jeremy carried the conversation. Finally, she said, "I can't wait to see you. I love you, too." She placed the phone in its cradle and leaned against the kitchen counter, resting her hand over her heart like a woman in love.

I'd never felt more alone in my whole life.

MONICA

Jack squeezed Monica's hand as she finished the story about finding Lily tucked in her room behind the trail of disarray. "That must have been so tough, to go it alone." His eyes looked very soft.

"It was," Monica twisted in her chair while considering whether or not to tell him about Jeremy. She let out a deep sigh and continued. "Until—"

"Oh my gosh, look at the time," Jack interrupted. "I'm so sorry, Monica, but I have to get back to the office. I didn't realize it was so late. Rain check on the rest of the story?"

"Sure. Rain check it is." Monica put on her good girl smile and breathed a sigh of relief.

Jack stood and gave her a quick hug. "Really, I'm sorry. I'll call you soon, okay?"

Monica nodded. She watched him head out the door, then sat down again and put her face in her hands. Her heart beat rapidly as the memories cascaded to the forefront of her mind.

— — —

"I can't believe you're actually here." Monica squeezed Jeremy's arm as they walked from the baggage claim to the parking lot.

"Me, either. So where's the rain?"

"Oh, that's a myth. It doesn't really rain here. It's just what we say to keep the tourists away."

"Right. You look good, Mo."

"I'm better now that you're here."

"So when do I get to meet the infamous Lily?"

A pit formed in Monica's stomach at his question. "She's got drama club practice tonight, so she'll meet us for dinner when she's done."

"Sounds good. That means I've got you to myself for a few hours." Jeremy nuzzled into Monica's neck. "It's been too long, babe."

Monica laughed as they climbed into the car.

They had dinner reservations at Ray's Boathouse on Shilshole Bay. It had been her father's favorite spot in the city, because he could look out over the water and see the mountains in the distance. That night, however, it was approaching the shortest day of the year and the sun had set, limiting the view to reflections in the darkened windows.

"Daddy loved wide open spaces," Monica murmured, while they drank Cokes and waited for Lily to arrive. She fidgeted with the white cloth napkin in her lap, folding and unfolding it between her fingers.

"Me, too." Jeremy looked out into the dark expanse of the night. "I bet this place is great when the sun is out."

"It is." Monica nodded and sipped her Coke through a straw.

"Mind if I get a drink?" Jeremy asked, twisting his neck like there was a crick in it.

"Sure. No problem." She shifted from side to side in the cushioned seat. There was a tension between them she couldn't identify.

"Bourbon. Rocks, please," Jeremy called to the nearby waiter.

"Yes, sir, right away."

Monica impulsively reached out and touched the tail of the waiter's dark jacket as he passed. "Make that two."

Jeremy raised an eyebrow, but didn't say anything. She knew he'd never seen her drink bourbon.

Before he could say anything, a flash of red hair and gold sparkles rushed toward their table and wrapped Monica in a demonstrative hug.

"Mo Mo, I missed you," Lily said theatrically, then released the embrace as quickly as she'd entered it. The girl's voice then turned sultry as she leaned toward Jeremy, giving him a full view of her developing breasts. "And you. Wow. You must be Jeremy the Gorgeous."

Jeremy hustled to stand up, extending his hand to Lily as Monica sat silently beside him. All Monica's old insecurities about being bookish and bland rose to the forefront in the presence of her glamorous sister. Lily was playing her role as family beauty to the max. She wore a dark skirt that landed just below the spot where her long legs met in a vee and a shimmering, sleeveless, draped blouse. Dangling earrings glittered against her strawberry-colored hair, and painted red toenails peeked out of spiked heels.

"Oh, silly boy, you're family. Give me a hug." Lily pressed her body against Jeremy's and wrapped her arms around his waist in a more-than-sisterly hug. Monica watched from her seat, feeling the color rise up her chest. In her opinion, Jeremy lingered a bit too long before reaching behind his back and gently extracting himself from the embrace.

"Nice to meet you, Lily." Jeremy glanced sideways at a seething Monica.

"Indeed," Monica grumbled. "That's my little sister."

Drama club had paid off. Monica could hardly fathom all the "Lily's" who'd shown up since she arrived home: broken waif, perky cheerleader, demanding sister, and now sexy vixen. Monica wanted to either yank a handful of strawberry curls out of her sister's pretty head, or crawl under the table and die of mortification. Instead, she downed her entire bourbon as soon as the waiter set it on the table, the warm elixir burning her insides on the way down.

"Hey, Buddy. Imagine meeting you here." Lily directed her attentions toward the waiter and playfully walked her fingers up his arm. The young man's face turned from tan to crimson. "Would you mind bringing little old me a rum and coke and another of whatever my sister's having?"

Buddy glanced over his shoulder. "Lily, you know you're not twenty-one," he said, leaning his head toward her and shifting his eyes toward the maître d'.

"Shhh, honey." Lily placed her hand back on his arm. "Of course I know that, and you may know it too, but nobody else has to know, right? Pleeeeease, Buddy. I promise to make it worth your while."

"Lily!" Monica had had enough of her sister's behavior.

"Oh, shut up, Mo. You're not my mom."

Silence suffocated the table like Houston humidity in August. Buddy quietly said, "I'll be right back with those drinks."

IZABEL

Somehow we managed to make it through dinner without anything major happening. Jeremy seemed to lose track of the number of drinks we downed. He looked like a wide-eyed owl when he saw the bill Buddy laid next to his arm: $337.26 without tip. I think that was probably as much as a whole month's rent for him. I could see sweat bead on his forehead as he reached into his pocket for a credit card. Just before he placed it inside the black sleeve, Buddy scooped up the bill.

"Sorry. My mistake. It's on the house."

"What?!" all three of us said in unison.

"Your parents used to come here all the time. The manager was a big fan of your dad and said to tell you it's the least he could do. He had to leave about an hour ago, or he would've told you himself."

"Wha-what about the tip? Can I put it on my card?" Jeremy sputtered.

"No problem, man. Tip's on me." Buddy smiled at me.

"Actually, it's on me," I giggled.

Like a jack-in-the-box, Monica stood up, grabbed her bag, and zigzagged toward the door. I'd never seen her drink before, and the bourbon made her all wobbly. As she stepped into the night air and onto the wooden walkway, her pointed heel caught between the gray slats and she pitched forward, face down.

"Monica! Are you all right?" Jeremy rushed to her side.

I started laughing so hard it hurt. I couldn't contain myself.

"Shut up!" Monica screamed, her face turning red. "I'm sick of you and all your Miss High and Mighty airs! Get away from me. Now!"

To make matters worse, Jeremy tipped back to sit on his heels and burst into hysterical laughter. "Well, babe, I mean, you are lying on your face in front of a restaurant."

"Oh, you shut up, too! I hate you both! Leave me alone!"

The hostess poked her head out the door to see what was going on. "Miss, is everything all right?"

"No, everything's not all right!" Monica sniffled and glared at us. "Could you please call me a cab?"

"If you can wait five minutes, I could give you a lift myself," the hostess said, turning her nose up at Jeremy and me.

Monica was livid. "Great. Thank you, but feel free to call a cab for those two. I don't want to be anywhere near them. On second thought, maybe you should just drive yourselves. Then you could crash and die, just like Mom and Dad!"

I'd never heard her say anything so mean. Jeremy stood open-mouthed, looking at the screeching woman in front of us. Then he turned to the hostess. "No cab for me, thanks. I think I'll walk."

"I'll walk with you," I whispered.

"Perfect. You two deserve each other," Monica sneered.

Izabel stopped typing as the full memory of that visit surged into her mind's eye. She stared at the blinking cursor as Lucas wove in and out around her ankles, meowing plaintively.

Then she added:

I was awful to her.

I wish that was the most awful thing I did that night.

MONICA

Monica pulled the car into the driveway. She glanced around to see if her neighbor was anywhere in sight, then slogged her way to the front door. Thinking about Jeremy and Lily was more than she could bear.

After entering the house, she didn't pause to remove her shoes. Instead, she walked into the kitchen, pulled a wine glass out of the cupboard, and poured herself a full measure of *vino* from the bottle on the counter.

"Come on Red, we need to have some serious conversation."

Grabbing the half-empty bottle by its neck, Monica shuffled to her bedroom like an old woman in house slippers and pushed the magic button for her closet. She heard Jack's voice whisper in her mind: *Call me anytime.*

With a deep sigh, Monica let the breath go out of her body and lowered her weary limbs onto the satin pillows in the center of her closet, allowing herself to be carried backward twenty years.

— — —

It was the night after the terrible incident at the restaurant. She was exhausted as she stood at the kitchen counter, her mind as dull as the yellow onion she was chopping. The only motion in the pristine kitchen was the rhythmic lift and drop of her knife. Engrossed in the mundane task, she failed to hear Jeremy sidle up beside her.

"Oh my gosh! You scared me," she said, continuing to chop.

"Sorry, babe. Whatcha cookin'?"

The tone in his voice nudged Monica to turn and look Jeremy in the eye. "Beef stew. Why do you ask?"

"Just wondering." He placed his forehead in the space where her shoulder and neck met. *"Any chance you could leave it for a while?"*

Monica liked how his tender gesture felt. The night before was fuzzy in her mind, and she felt embarrassed that she didn't remember much of anything after they'd finished dinner.

"Sure. What did you have in mind?" she said, softening and wrapping her arms around his waist with one side of her face lifted upward.

"I thought maybe we could talk, if that's okay."

"Talk? Is that what you want to call it?" she said coquettishly.

Jeremy reached behind his back and gently uncurled her arms from his waist. Taking her left palm in his right hand, he glanced downward. *"Mo, I want nothing more than to be with you. That's why I think we should talk."*

Monica's initial instinct was to break loose and run. Her heart pounded rapidly, and the inside of her mouth filled with a sickening taste. Swallowing hard, she ignored her instincts and answered, *"Ohh . . . kay."*

Silently, Jeremy led her into the living room and settled them both on the sofa. With breath held, Monica squirmed like a kid waiting outside the principal's office. Jeremy's clammy hand held hers tightly.

"Monica, I—" He looked down and inhaled deeply.

"What? You're scaring me."

Raising his eyes, he saw her before him, young and fragile. His face looked pained. *"You know how much I love you, right?"*

"Yes," she answered softly.

"And you know I'd never intentionally do anything to hurt you, right?" Jeremy looked down, inhaled again, and then looked back into her eyes.

"Um. Yes."

"Well, I don't know." He lowered his head again. *"It was all a mistake. A big mistake. It just happened, you know? And I was so mad, and more than a little drunk, and she was so sexy and, well, she was just* there.*"*

"What the hell are you talking about? Who was where?"

"I didn't mean to do it. It didn't mean anything. I just—"

"What are you talking about?"

"I slept with Lily." He exhaled in a torrid rush. *"Last night."*

"WHAT? You slept with my sister?" Monica drew back and stared at him.

"Honey, I—"

"Don't you dare 'honey' me! You bastard! Get out of here. NOW!" She realized Jeremy was still grasping her hand. She shook it off like she was trying to snuff out a burning potholder.

"Can we at least talk?" Jeremy stared pleadingly at her.

"I can't stand to look at you. Get out."

"But where—"

"I don't give a shit where you go. Go find Lily for all I care. Just get the hell out of my house!" Monica buried her face in her palms, and her shoulders heaved up and down.

"But you can't mean that."

Monica glared at him. "Are you kidding me? You slept with my sister! My little sister. My seventeen-year-old goddamned brat of a sister."

"Ah, come on, Monica. It was a mis—"

"A mistake? A mistake? I should cut off your fucking balls! You son of a bitch. Get out of my house!"

The front door banged open, and Lily entered the room. "Hey, guys. What's going on?"

"Oh, isn't this just too rich," Monica growled. "What's going on? I'll tell you what's going on. Jeremy just announced that you two slept together. That's what's going on."

The color drained from Lily's face as she stood staring at the two of them. Jeremy's head looked like it would hit the floor if it kept moving downward. Monica felt angry enough to eviscerate the entire room, beginning with Lily.

"Um, maybe I should come back later." Lily stepped backward, toward the door.

"Sure. Fine. Run away. That's what you always do. First you tear up the entire house and leave me to clean up your mess. Then you hijack my boyfriend, and now you want to turn your little ass around so you don't have to clean up this mess either."

"I'm really sor—"

"Oh, save your sorry apologies for someone who cares. You both make me sick."

Monica turned her back and stormed up the stairs. She couldn't stand to be in the same room with the two of them and her instincts toggled between fight and flight. She half-heartedly threw a few things in a suitcase before stumbling back down to the living room with the bag and slumping onto the sofa like a deflated balloon. She needed to finish this before she lost her nerve.

Jeremy and Lily remained frozen in place; Lily, her hand on the front door, still deciding whether to stay or go, and Jeremy inert on the sofa, head hanging low. Monica's weight on the sofa seemed to be a hopeful sign, and he lifted his head and cautiously inched toward her.

"Don't you dare come near me!" Monica looked up, the fire returning to her eyes. "You son of a bitch. I hate your guts."

"Ah, Mo. You don't mean that."

"Shut the fuck up. I. Hate. Your. Guts."

"Mo Mo?" Lily edged farther into the room.

"And you! Who the fuck do you think you are, you little bitch? I trusted you. I came home to take care of you. I thought maybe we'd be okay now that Mom and Dad were gone, but hell no. It's all about Lily. It's always been all about Little Miss Perfect Lily. I shouldn't have expected anything less from you."

Lily's face crumpled in response. "Mo, please? I'm so sor—"

"Yeah, sorry. Right. I get it. No one meant for this to happen, blah, blah, blah." Monica squeezed her eyes shut and buried her face in the palms of her hands.

Jeremy and Lily glanced at each other. Lily shrugged her shoulders while Jeremy shook his head.

"What? Cat got your tongues?" Monica snapped. "Now you're afraid of me? What, did you think I wouldn't find out? That I was some stupid pushover?"

"You know that's not true, Mo—" Jeremy turned toward her, remorse in his eyes.

"Don't you dare 'Monica' me! I don't know what's true anymore. I thought it was true that you loved me. I thought it was true that we wanted to spend the rest of our lives together. I thought it was true that you were going to be my first and last. I thought. Fuck. Truth? Where the hell did that get me?"

"Or me?" Jeremy muttered under his breath.

"Oh, don't you even try to make this about you."

"I was just thinking maybe—"

"Yeah, I know exactly what you were thinking. If you hadn't opened your stupid mouth, maybe I never would've found out. Right? Is that what you were thinking?"

"Well, I didn't—"

"Want to upset me? Hurt me? Have me find out? Too late, buddy boy. If you haven't noticed, I am upset. I am furious. In fact, I'm not sure I've ever been this mad in my whole life." Monica closed her eyes and took a few deep breaths. *"But you know what? I feel pretty damn clear right now. This may be the truest moment I've ever had."*

Jeremy and Lily stood like frozen statues as Monica's words hung in the air. No one could decipher them except Monica, but the words didn't bode well for either of them.

Monica gazed into the distance, like one of the living sculptures at Pike Place Market. Without warning, she suddenly doubled over and burst into hysterical laughter.

"Truth?" She sucked in a breath between her teeth. *"I think I finally know what truth is. And it sucks!"* Crazed laughter wracked her body, and the disturbing sound filled the living room.

Neither Jeremy nor Lily had ever seen Monica like this. She'd always been the epitome of composure and grace, except the night Jeremy had found her curled up in the bushes at The Commons. Jeremy made one last move toward her.

"Stay back, you bastard!" Monica's voice turned to ice. *"I want you to pack your bags and leave this house tonight. And just to be clear, I never want to see you again. Ever."*

"But—"

"EVER. Are we clear?"

"Monica—"

"Are we clear?" she growled through clenched teeth.

Jeremy nodded.

Just when it was evident that Monica's point with Jeremy was understood, Lily made the mistake of shifting her weight. Monica whirled toward her, eyes aflame, as Jeremy backed out of the room toward the stairs.

"And you! Thank God you're almost eighteen. I never want to see you again, either. Go stay with one of your friends. Or something. I don't care."

"But—"

"Save your breath. Don't worry. I'll take care of everything before I leave, but once I'm gone, we're through!"

Lily began to sob.

"Oh, God, really? Tears? Gimme a break." Monica looked at Lily with disdain,

resisting the tiny urge to comfort her sister. Standing up, she squared her shoulders and grabbed the suitcase. "I'm going to a hotel for the night. When I come back tomorrow, you'd both better be gone."

— — —

Inside the closet, Monica's stomach growled like Pavlov's dog hearing the dinner bell. Instead of heeding the call for food, she poured another glass of wine and began rifling through her shoes. She was still looking for the perfect soles to soothe her wounded heart.

IZABEL

Jeremy took Monica at her word and left that night. I crept up the stairs like a guilty convict who'd just been sentenced to life imprisonment. When she returned, Monica managed to ignore everything by busying herself with packing up the house she'd sold when no one was looking. A cash buyer from California bid on our family home the day it went on the market, and the deal closed less than two weeks later.

She moved me into a tiny duplex on Holman Road and promised she'd check in as often as she could. I never understood how that would be possible, since she was going back to Massachusetts. It didn't really matter. All I wanted was to be left alone.

I stayed in Seattle to finish my senior year of high school, trying unsuccessfully to ignore the rumors that I had "gone off the deep end" and was turning into a recluse since my parents died. Everyone said I'd changed, which was basically true. I mean, who wouldn't? I didn't go out partying anymore and quit all my extracurricular activities like cheerleading and drama club.

In the beginning, Monica checked in every Sunday with a token how-are-things-going call that never lasted more than three minutes. I could tell she did it out of obligation. She was checking to make sure I was still alive, and that was it. No "I love you" or "see you soon." Once I turned eighteen, the phone calls stopped. That was okay with me. I was busy watching Nickelodeon on television and eating ice cream for dinner, living a teenager's dream. Daddy's lawyer sent a check every month like clockwork for my living expenses, and the accountant took care of the rest of the bills.

Things were going pretty smoothly. Then one afternoon, my friend Hannah got nosy and started asking lots of questions.

"Hey Lily, what's up with the baggy clothes?" she asked as we lounged in my bedroom.

"Huh? Whaddya mean?" I asked, flipping through a magazine.

"You know exactly what I mean. It's practically summer and I haven't seen those washboard abs of yours since you quit coming to cheerleading practice last December. You've been a hermit for months, and now you're starting to dress like a bag lady. What's up with that?"

"Nothing's up. I'm just tired of being that girl in tight jeans. Baggy clothes feel lots comfier."

"Whatever you say. I guess you're going to love our graduation robes then. Lots of room to get comfy in these goofy things." Hannah held out the royal blue gown in front of her, laughing. "Très chic. Don't you think?"

"Très!" I laughed with her. It all seemed so silly.

"Is your sister coming for graduation?" Hannah walked around my tiny room, picked up a music box, and set it back down again.

"No, I told her not to bother. It's no big deal." I shrugged.

"Yeah, I wish I could get my parents to quit making such a big fuss. You'd think I was graduating from Harvard or something."

My hand froze in mid-page turn and Hannah realized she'd made a mistake. "Oh, Lil, I'm so sorry. I shouldn't complain about my parents." She moved toward me for a hug, but I shrugged her away and zeroed back in on the magazine. She was getting too close.

"It's okay. I'm sure I'd be complaining about mine if they were here."

Hannah stood on one foot like a crane as she twirled her hair between her fingers. "You sure you don't want your sister and Jeremy to come?"

"No!" I threw the magazine across the room.

Hannah ducked. "Geez. Sorry. I thought maybe they could help you feel better."

I felt so bad. "No, I'm the one who should be sorry. I'm just not into graduation, that's all."

"Have you heard back from any colleges yet? I heard from Western. Looks like that's where I'll be going. I doubt I'll get into UW."

"I don't know. I haven't checked my mail in a while."

"Are you kidding me? Why not? Let's look now!" Hannah was like a new puppy at the dog park, bouncing from one scent to another.

"Help yourself," I nodded toward a pile of mail and papers lying on the bedroom floor.

"Hey, this looks like my letter from Western," said Hannah. "Can I open it?"

"Sure. Why not?" Again, I really didn't care.

Hannah tore into the envelope without hesitation. "You're in, Lily! This is so great! We can be roommates! Yay!" Hannah started jumping up and down on the bed, and in all her enthusiasm, failed to notice I was staring at another envelope in my shaking hand.

MONICA

Once the wine was finished, Monica staggered from the closet, leaving a trail of clothes behind her, and crawled into bed without brushing her teeth or washing her face. She remembered writing the letter as if it were yesterday.

— — —

Unopened textbooks lay scattered across the dorm room floor, alongside four or five half-empty teacups and an open bag of Doritos. Monica could hear the girls in the next room guffawing while their stereo blasted Alice Cooper's "School's Out." She resisted the urge to scream Shut up! *and remind them that the summer semester wouldn't be over for another few weeks.*

Picking up the ballpoint pen, she turned her attention back to the spiral notebook. Dear Lily: Where do I begin? The questions all seem trite given the way we ended. *Monica closed her eyes and shook her head as if that might exorcise the image of Lily waving from the window of the tiny duplex as Monica drove away for the last time. Lily had looked more like seven than seventeen: a lost waif, an orphan, a scared child. For a split moment, Monica had considered asking the cab driver to turn around, but then the heartbreaking reality of her sister's betrayal and Jeremy's confession had ricocheted through her mind, and her heart had slammed shut.*

It had remained closed for all these months, but the loneliness grew like a cancer. Last night, she'd awoken from a restless sleep and a dream that the car she was driving crashed through a barn. Her still-awake roommate, Cindy, had looked at her with concern. "What's up, Mo? You look like you've just seen a ghost."

"Oh, it was just a weird dream."

"Cool. We're studying dreams in psych class. Why don't ya tell me about it?"

Monica had hesitated before beginning. "Well, I woke up because I crashed through a barn. I swerved off the road and drove through the side of the building because I couldn't take it anymore."

"Couldn't take what?" Cindy had asked. "Oh, wait. We're not supposed to analyze it yet. Keep going."

Monica wasn't sure she liked revealing her subconscious, but the alternative was closing her eyes and being alone with her thoughts, so she'd continued. "There were other people in the car, and they got out unharmed. I sat staring at the inside of the barn, where a man sat undisturbed and playing Solitaire inches from where we'd just crashed. No one approached me, but I could hear a voice a few feet behind me saying, 'Are you okay, honey?' I was aware that someone had called the sheriff and someone else was recording the scene on a small video recorder.

"The car was like a sixties Oldsmobile or something with wings on the back. Part of me wanted to drive it all the way through the building and crash out the other side, but I had a rational moment and slammed on the brakes instead." Monica had stopped and stared out the window at the corner streetlight.

"Is that all?" Monica thought Cindy sounded disappointed.

"Pretty much." Monica hadn't told her that she was now wondering if slamming on the brakes was indeed the rational moment, or whether she should have busted through to the other side. "I think I'm good now. I'm gonna try and get some sleep."

"Okay." Cindy had shrugged her shoulders and turned back to the book she'd been reading.

Monica had tossed and turned throughout the night and woken up knowing it was time to "bust through to the other side," especially when she'd remembered another face from the dream car: Lily.

She picked up her pen again and read the last line of the letter before continuing:

Words seem futile. I want to say "I'm sorry," but the voice inside my head tells me you are the one who made the crack in both our lives. You took a jackhammer and shattered our world into jagged pieces. You did all this. But there are always the pieces, aren't there? Jeremy's piece. Yours. Mine. And in the background, but always present, Mother and Daddy's piece.

Monica shivered as she thought about her parents and the grief that had piled *up—stayed in the barn—while she simultaneously remembered they'd been the other passengers in her dream car.*

Are they why you betrayed me? Is that why I shunned you? Because they finally left? I don't know about yours, but my heart was already so jagged and threadbare, I couldn't take another tear and seeing you again after your betrayal was just too much. *Monica paused again and hugged her knees to her chest, tears leaking from the corners of her swollen eyes.*

But there they are again, those two words. I'm sorry. I think that is where we have to begin. I forgive you. Well, at least I can try. If I were to say those words out loud today, I would choke, but I don't think I would die.

They say time heals all things. I wonder if that's really true. I saw Jeremy across campus yesterday and the chasm in my heart grew wider. I turned and ran as fast as I could the other way. Time has not healed what happened between him and me.

But Lily, you are my sister and I truly want to love you again. Can I? Yes, I think that's what I'm trying to say. I need you, Baby Sis, and my hope is that you need me too. That's all I can say for now. I know it's a small flicker of light shining through the cracks, but I hope it will be enough for us to start again.

Your sis, Monica

IZABEL

I held the crumpled and tear-soaked letter in my hand, looking at my chewed fingernails and bleeding cuticles, wishing I'd been brave enough to reach out to Monica first.

Time has not healed what happened between him and me.

I sat with covers pulled around me in the middle of my unmade bed and ran a hand over my swollen belly. "It hasn't healed what happened between him and me either. Has it, baby?"

I read Monica's letter at least a dozen times. The first time through, I cried tears of relief and reached for the phone to call my sister. Then I read it again: You took a jackhammer and shattered our world into jagged pieces. You did all this. *Monica's words mirrored the shame I'd felt for the past months. The words screamed in my head. I turned away from the phone, wadded up the letter, and threw it across the room.*

Each time I retrieved and re-read the letter, I latched onto something different. I'm sorry? Can we please start over? *"Yes. Yes. Yes," I whispered to the ink on paper and hugged it to my chest.* Seeing you again after your betrayal was just too much. *I yanked at my hair and groaned as the baby kicked me in the ribs. "Too much. Too much!" I choked.*

I need you, Baby Sis, and my hope is that you need me too. *"Now more than ever, Sis." I reached for the bedside phone as a giant contraction roared through my body.*

"Oh my God!" I gasped for air.

"Lily? Are you in here?" Hannah poked her head around the corner into my bedroom. Then her gaze locked onto my bare stomach.

"Lily? What the—"

I scrambled to pull the covers up to my chin, but it was too late. Through a masquerade of baggy clothes and feigned modesty, I'd managed to keep my pregnancy a secret from everyone, including Hannah. Until then.

"Lily? I don't understand." Hannah stared at me, mouth open. "What's going on?"

"What's it look like?" I snarled. I couldn't stand the shocked expression on my friend's face. It reminded me of the night I walked in on Jeremy and Monica's fight. Fear and panic surged through me just as another contraction grabbed hold.

"Owww. Fuck. It hurts," I cried, doubling over. "I think I just wet my pants."

"Yoohoo. Hannah? Lily?" It was Hannah's mom, Mrs. Copeland. "Where are you girls?"

"What's your mom doing here?" I hissed through clenched teeth.

"We just stopped by to see if you wanted to come to dinner at Red Robin with us. She was waiting in the car. I'll go—"

"What's going on here?" Mrs. Copeland appeared in the bedroom door, her brow furrowed and head tilted as she watched Hannah bouncing nervously in place where she stood, and me with bed sheets pulled up to my chin.

"Nothing," we chimed in unison.

For a split second I thought I could continue my charade, at least with Mrs. Copeland, but the baby had another idea. What felt like a magnitude-four earthquake wracked my body, and I couldn't help but scream. "Ooowwwwwwww!"

Dropping the sheet, I doubled over and writhed on the bed before passing out.

DAISY

The outline of dark figures walked with heads held high and umbrellas in hand as they crossed the spindly bridge that looked like a sidewalk on stilts.

Ancestors, a voice whispered in Daisy's mind. *These are my ancestors.* The girl shook her head and glanced back in the direction from where she'd just turned away.

The parade continued. Women in wide-brimmed hats fell in line with men in chaps and coattails. She couldn't see their faces, only shadowed paper doll images, dark blue and eggplant purple.

These are my people, the voice whispered.

The voice sounded like her own, but she couldn't figure out what was meant by "ancestors" and "my people." She squeezed her eyes closed one more time, then opened them to see that the shadows had sprouted wings and were making their way across the sky like geese against a rising sun.

Standing on the shore of the beach, Daisy turned her face toward the growing light. The flapping of wings died away. Silence filled the remaining space, and her toes curled into a bed of broken shells.

She imagined the sound of a fragile nautilus shell crashing against the coral reef and being tossed to the shore. Would the breakage sound like shattering glass, or would it be a silent scream of a life, a home, being torn apart?

The wind rustled through the blue palm trees that stood like sentries behind her. Beside her, Chauncey chewed his cud and flipped his long blue tongue into the air. It zeroed in on a tiny bee whose mighty buzz punctuated the quiet symphony of the okapi's swish and chew.

In the distance, a mournful wail broke her trance. It sounded like a woman in distress, but Daisy recognized it as the mating call of an island peacock.

Waves crashed on the shore. For a moment, she imagined diving into the frothiness to silence the voice in her head.

Blue. Everything was still blue, from the inner curl of the shells, to Chauncey's lolling tongue, the ocean and sky, and her mood.

Without warning, Daisy's legs buckled beneath her. Her cheek lay on the broken-shelled beach. Her ear pressed against the ground, and she began to listen to the heartbeat of the earth. *Thump. Thump. Thump.*

The pace of her anxious heart slowed and began to match the beat that lay beneath her. *Thump. Thump. Thump.*

She imagined all was silent. The voices stopped, the waves stilled, the branches calmed, but even in the silence, the ground beneath her continued its rhythm. *Thump. Thump. Thump.*

She wondered if silence was an illusion; if blue was more than a color; if hearts were truly created to love. She closed her eyes and began to follow her breath.

The peacock wailed in the distance like a tortured woman. Another bee buzzed. More shells cracked. Her heart pounded. On it went, endless time like sand slipping through her fingers.

If the silence was deafening, the illusion of silence was even more so. Daisy longed for raucous laughter and racing cars. She wanted to hear her mother's nagging voice and her best friend's self-centered stories. She was exhausted by all the peace and quiet. She was tired of this island, this hell-like "paradise."

MONICA

Monica sat across from Jack, holding his hand atop the coffee-stained table, not knowing what else to say. She'd called and asked if she could see him again today, given what she'd been thinking about last night. And here they were, at Crazy Carl's.

She sighed deeply as she finished the story. She knew Jack was going to ask questions about the baby and Lily that she wasn't prepared to answer. She didn't know if she was strong enough to tell him about the remaining unspoken areas of her life.

"It was a week after I wrote Lily. I hadn't spoken to her since she'd turned eighteen. I was tired of resenting her. I couldn't forget what happened, but I could try to forgive. When the phone rang, I was hoping it was Lily, but it was the mother of one of her friends."

— — —

Monica sat staring at the illuminated green exit sign in the Northwest Hospital waiting room. Hannah's mother had called her at six o'clock in a panic, "Lily's gone into labor!"

"What?" Monica had thought she might faint, or throw up. She'd managed to refrain from yelling at Hannah's mother, who was only the messenger of this news. After the phone call, Monica had stood in her bedroom and counted to one hundred while trying to breathe without gasping. True to her good-girl nature, however, she'd pulled herself together, packed a small bag, and booked herself on a red-eye from Boston to Seattle.

She hadn't slept for more than twenty-four hours, and now the emerald light glowing over the door beckoned her to come closer. She could picture the stairwell behind it: metal and beige, standard issue handrails, cigarette butts tossed in the corner where employees and waiting visitors left evidence of their nicotine indiscretions.

Can I get out of here without anyone seeing me? Her eyes darted around the sterile waiting room. I hate hospitals! They give me the creeps.

Glancing to her left, she noticed a woman with gray-streaked hair clicking away with her knitting needles. The woman looked up over the top of the half-moon glasses that made her look closer to eighty than the fifty she more likely was. She smiled and nodded cursorily at Monica, then went back to the clickety-clack of metal on metal.

Across the room, a man in a business suit whispered loudly into his cell phone. "No, I don't know how much longer I'll be here. No, the doctors haven't been back out since we arrived. No, goddamn it, I don't know!" He pressed a button and shoved his phone into the holster on his belt like an old western gunslinger.

Run! Monica's instincts screamed. Make a break for it!

Just as she reached for her purse with her left hand and eyed the pathway between her seat and the exit, a doctor stepped through the swinging doors with a stern look on his face.

"Ms. Levin?" he said, as he walked toward Monica in his blue scrubs.

"Yes. How's my sister? And the baby?"

"They're both fine now."

Monica looked at the doctor's face and could tell something wasn't right. "What do you mean, 'now'?" she asked, rising out of the vinyl chair.

"Your sister is a feisty one. We thought for a bit that we might have to sedate her, but in the end she managed to regain her composure and deliver a healthy baby girl." The doctor looked down at his Adidas-clad feet.

"But?" Monica sensed there was more.

"But she didn't want to have anything to do with the baby. We can't get her to hold her or even look at her."

"A girl. You said she had a baby girl?" Monica felt confusion at the mix of emotions surging through her. She hadn't even known that Lily was pregnant, and now she had a baby girl. Lily was still a child herself.

"Yes. She's a feisty little thing just like her mother. Arrived with lungs bellowing and feet kicking. She's a real beauty." Monica smiled.

The doctor continued. "We told Lily that you were here, and she became quite agitated. Said she couldn't see you and started fighting with the nurse and trying to get out of bed again. We might need to give her something to calm her nerves."

"Oh." It was the only word Monica could form before lowering herself back into the waiting room chair. Mentally, she started counting nine months backward. October. Monica heaved a sigh of relief when she realized she was free of her worst suspicion. It couldn't be Jeremy's baby.

"There's one other thing," the doctor said, as he hovered over her like a blue Power Ranger. "As far as we can tell, the baby is somewhere between six and eight weeks premature. But her lungs look great and her heart is strong, so no worries there."

"Right. No worries." Monica felt her chest tighten. She knew that her new niece was her ex-boyfriend's child.

"Are you all right, Ms. Levin? Can I get you something? You're looking rather pale."

Monica shook her head and blotted her eyes with a tissue. "No, thank you. I'm fine. It's just been a long day."

"I understand." The doctor paused. "Perhaps you should go home and get some rest. You could come back in the morning when things have calmed down. That would give your sister time to recover."

IZABEL

Izabel and Miriam stood cloaked in morning fog beneath the centuries-old, weathered oak at Killebrew Lake. Draped with their hooded shawls, they could have been two witches gathered around a cauldron. No less mysterious were the circumstances that Izabel knew it was time to reveal.

"Sorry I called you on such short notice. And so early. But it's time for the whole truth, and you're the only one I can trust." Izabel's eyes filled with tears and she wrapped her arms tightly around her body, as if her insides might fall out at any moment.

Miriam placed an arm around Izabel's shoulders and nodded her silver-haired head, encouraging the young woman to continue. A great horned owl hooted in the distance.

"I guess I'll start with the basics. My name isn't really Izabel, but my guess is you've figured that for some time now."

Miriam dipped her head an inch and held steady, like a poker player unwilling to give away her hand.

"I was born Lily Belle Levin, and I'm pretty sure I have a daughter somewhere." Izabel glanced furtively around, like a fawn checking her surroundings for predators. Miriam nodded in assurance, and Izabel continued.

"You know how I couldn't remember anything from before I arrived on Shaw Island? Sister Gabrielle said I didn't seem sick or have a head injury or anything like that. I never went to a doctor. I didn't have the money at first, and then I was embarrassed. Thought, given my age, maybe I'd done too many drugs in high school or something, so I just never looked into it further." She shrugged. "Apart from not remembering anything, I felt fine. Why mess with it? But after what's happened the last few weeks, well . . ."

She took a deep breath as Miriam nodded. "According to what I've looked up, I very likely experienced a dissociative fugue. It's kind of like amnesia, except you run away and make up a new name, identity, and life. It usually happens after a tragic event. Well, you see, I'd run away from my home in Seattle after my parents died and I'd had a horrible fight with my sister. I betrayed her by sleeping with her boyfriend. I was so young and foolish back then. And, of course, our parents had just died, and it was horrible. I was such a freaking mess as a teenager—all self-centered and spiteful. But mainly I was lonely and scared and didn't know how to get attention, so I stole Jeremy. It was just that one night, but I knew it broke my sister's heart, and I never could face her again." Izabel twisted the corner of her shawl, and a shiver ran up her spine.

Miriam took Izabel's hand in her own and gestured toward a fallen log. The two women sat and huddled together side-by-side.

"From there on out, I guess I . . . became Izabel. That whole first part of my life, including the part with my sister, was gone from my mind. Until Shannon Andersons's baby was born. Something started to happen to me that day. When I was telling her to push, it was like it was happening to me. My body started having strange contractions, and my emotions were all over the place. Then you called me about the soul—"

" . . .dance," the two women said in unison.

"Would you like to tell me what happened after that night?" Miriam asked.

"Yes," Izabel said shyly.

"Go on."

"First let me say, the soul dance was pure magic. Thank you, Miriam. I am so grateful."

"You are most welcome, dear one."

"An awareness came over me that there was more to my story than simply running away. I woke up last night and vividly remembered exactly why I fled Seattle. It wasn't just that I'd had a fight with my sister. It was also about why I arrived at Shaw Island looking like I'd shrunk inside my clothes. Both problems had the same answer." She looked at Miriam with sad eyes. "I'd given birth to a baby girl. I left a note saying her name was Daisy, and I . . . "

Izabel's shoulders heaved up and down. Then she lowered her head and began to sob in fits and bursts. "Oh, Miriam. I had a baby girl and I abandoned her." Her words were interrupted with sniffs and hiccups. "But I was just a baby myself. Oh my God, what am I supposed to do? What if she needs me now?" she wailed.

Miriam cradled the young woman in her arms and let her cry it out, humming a gentle lullaby to soothe her broken friend. When Izabel had calmed and ceased to breathe in heaving sobs, Miriam spoke gently.

"You said something about your daughter needing you right now, yes?"

"Uh huh." Izabel wiped her sleeve across her upper lip to quell her lingering sniffles. "I don't know how I know, but she's in trouble and needs my help."

"So what can you do?" Miriam's steel-blue eyes looked directly into hers.

"What? What do you mean?" Izabel felt panic rise in her chest. She wasn't looking for practical answers. After all, she was just coming to terms with the lie she'd been living for two decades. However, practical answers and real-time action seemed to be what Miriam was offering.

"What can you do? What do you want to do?" the wizened woman asked again.

"I want to go to her," Izabel burst out. "I want to help my daughter."

"Well then. It sounds like you have your answer." Miriam smiled. "Let's figure out how to find her."

"How?"

"We'll start with looking up information about your sister in Seattle."

MONICA

Monica wavered slightly at the entrance of the upscale restaurant before stepping onto the pink marble floor with her spiked Louboutin shoes. She'd had a long conversation with herself before deciding to break out the luscious shoes that, up until now, had never ventured out of her closet. Straightening her shoulders, she took a breath and looked around the darkened restaurant for her date.

After that morning, Jack had insisted it was time to take their relationship somewhere other than Crazy Carl's Coffee House, and tonight was the night. La Petite Maison was known for its twenty-dollar cocktails and sexy escargot appetizers. It was a far cry from Crazy Carl's. As her eyes adjusted to the subtle lighting, she noticed twinkling votive candles arranged on intimate circular tables beside a parquet dance floor. A three-hundred-and-sixty-degree view of downtown Seattle and Puget Sound wrapped around the sky-high room with its floor-to-ceiling windows.

Standing on the threshold, she felt her chest tighten and her throat constrict as a waiter in a starched white shirt, bow tie, and dress tails approached her.

"Madame." He nodded. "How may I help you?"

Monica tugged at her black skirt and ran her right hand over her meticulously styled hair. "Um. I'm here to meet Jack Higgins?"

"Very good, Madame. Mr. Higgins is right this way."

Monica followed him and relaxed as she saw Jack stand up in a smart suit, like a penguin marching toward the South Pole. The marble beneath her feet masqueraded as ice, and she could hardly wait to slide into his open arms.

He was steadily working his way into her shielded heart with his easy conversation and quick sense of humor. She knew that with all his counselor's training, he must sense she was holding something back, but he never pressed for more information than she was ready to share. He approached her with the tenderness of a kind veterinarian treating a frightened puppy.

The food was exquisite and the view spectacular. The way Jack leaned in close and hung on to her every word made Monica feel her carefully constructed walls melting away.

"What about them over there?" Jack said, nodding toward a twenty-something couple that sat nose to nose just a few tables away. "What's their story?"

"Them?" Monica turned her gaze toward the youthful pair. "Oh, they're very much in love. He brought her here to propose. He probably gave the ring to the waiter and asked him to serve it on top of her dessert. Not very original, but totally sweet."

"And the girl?" Jack asked.

"The girl? Well, the girl looks just like my daughter." Monica clapped a hand over her mouth as soon as she realized what she'd said.

Even though Jack was a master of keeping a steady face, his eyes widened at her words and reaction. "*Daughter?*" He tilted his head in that please-tell-me-more way.

Monica let out a deep sigh as the burnished red rash crept up her chest and neck. "Oh, Jack. Let's not spoil this night." Her voice quivered, and tears filled her eyes.

"It's okay. Whatever you need." Jack covered her hand with his.

"Why are you so nice to me?" Monica sniffled as she looked into Jack's tender eyes.

"Because I love you."

Monica's shoulders leaned forward as she slumped and put both hands over her face. Watching the top of her head, Jack heard the muffled words: "If you really knew me, you couldn't love me. I'm a horrible person."

Jack reached over and put his arm around her shoulders. "Shh. It's okay. Everything's going to be all right."

Monica continued sobbing into her hands as Jack waved the waiter over with his free hand and handed him a credit card. "How about we get out of here?" he whispered to Monica.

She looked up with mascara-stained eyes and nodded her head.

— — —

They went to Jack's apartment. Looking around, Monica noticed walls lined with over-flowing bookshelves. A reclaimed-wood desk faced the large patio window, and a large sectional sofa wrapped around a glass coffee table covered with copies of *Psychology Today* and *The New York Times*.

After settling her on the couch and snuggling her into a loosely woven aqua blanket, Jack went to the kitchen and returned with two glasses of brandy.

He handed her a glass, clinked it with his own, nodded and said, "To your daughter."

"To Daisy," Monica whispered.

She closed her eyes and cringed at the innocent words that had started the maelstrom. "Her mother—Lily—fled from the hospital the night she was born. The doctor called me in the middle of the night and said Lily was gone. There was a note tucked in the baby's crib and all it said was, 'Her name is Daisy.' When we didn't find Lily after several days, there wasn't anything else for me to do but leave Briar Cliff and step in as Daisy's mother."

She'd never told this story to another living soul. Only the shoes in her closet knew the depth of her pain. She hoped Jack's professional training would allow him to be a patient witness.

"And so I did. I mean, what else was I to do? Oh, Daisy and I had our ups and downs. She was a strong-willed child just like her mother, and I battled my own resentment, which, of course, led Daisy to act out when she got older. I felt like I was turning into my own mother, and I hated it. That's when I started shoplifting shoes. I had to do something to keep me sane." Monica glanced up at Jack to gauge his reaction to the shoplifting confession. He returned her frightened look with a simple nod.

"Like I said, Daisy was strong-willed and beautiful like her mother. Her *real* mother, that is. I didn't know what to do with her when she hit the teen years. It was like I was living with Lily again, and I started to hate her. I had a dead-end job and an ungrateful teenager on my hands. Lily had stolen my one chance at happiness and then left me with the door prize: a baby."

"Your one chance at happiness?" Jack asked with a frown on his face, and Monica felt the heat rise in her chest.

"I had to leave Briar Cliff, and I blamed Lily and Daisy," she said, recovering once again. "My life was totally out of my control and I couldn't do anything about it. Whenever I felt like screaming at Daisy or telling her the truth, I found solace in shoes. Shoes I couldn't really afford, but oh, Jack, they were so delicious and made me so happy I couldn't help myself. They took away the pain and angst in a way nothing else could. And when the money got tight, I realized I could shoplift, which gave me a whole other thrill.

"My problems with Daisy felt like they lessened. I know this must sound totally ridiculous or sick or something to you, but it turned into my life. My poor, sick, pathetic life." Tears ran down Monica's face. "Mostly Daisy and I were okay, though. At least, we were until her graduation night." Monica paused and took a sip of her brandy. Jack followed her lead and took a drink, too.

"I've always wondered why I let my guard down on graduation night. There was something about the way Daisy carried herself as she crossed the stage that night to receive her diploma. Her long legs kicked out of the slit in the heavy blue robe and her wheat-colored hair hung in full ringlets down her back. She was so confident and beautiful, the spitting image of her mother. When I saw her, my mind instantly flashed back to the night Lily had strutted across that restaurant and wrecked all of our lives."

Monica spoke as if in a trance. Jack sat stock-still and listened intently. "So, when Daisy started pressing me to stay out all night after graduation, I snapped. She was headstrong and demanding like Lily had been at that age. 'Fine. Go ahead and leave,' I said. 'Just like your mother did.'"

Monica tilted her head and gazed toward the darkened patio window. Jack could tell she was no longer in the room with him. She'd drifted away to another time and space.

— — —

"What? What do you mean, 'just like your mother did'?" Daisy enunciated each word as if she were trying out a foreign language.

Monica put her hand over her mouth. She couldn't believe the words had finally escaped. She'd said them a thousand times in her head and never let them out, but this time Daisy had pushed too hard.

"But you're my mother!" Daisy shouted, confusion and rage creeping into her voice.

"Oh, honey." Monica reached toward her.

"Don't touch me!" Daisy jerked her arm away. Her eyes were filling with tears. "What do you mean, 'just like your mother did'?"

"Daisy, let's sit down and talk. You're upset."

"Upset? Of course I'm upset! Are you kidding me? I just found out my mother isn't my mother, and that's all you can say?"

"Daisy. I can explain." Monica stepped toward Daisy in an attempt to take her arm and try to settle her down.

Daisy jerked her arm away again and glared at the woman she knew as Mother. Her wild green eyes shot a venomous glance at Monica. Monica felt her heart constrict as Daisy's piercing gaze enveloped her with the force of a snake intent on squeezing the life from its prey.

She's just a little girl, Monica reminded herself. If I can just close my eyes and breathe, things will be better. But Daisy's stare refused to let her look away.

"What, Mother?" the girl said through gritted teeth. "Or should I call you Monica now?"

"Daisy, honey, could we talk about this later?"

"Oh, you mean when there aren't so many people around?" Daisy's fury-filled eyes darted over the courtyard filled with high school students in caps and gowns, laughing and posing for photos with their families and friends. Her voice escalated to a frantic pitch, and several revelers turned toward them.

Monica's voice cracked. Breathless and cautious. "Daisy, please."

— — —

Monica continued to stare out the patio door in silence for several minutes. She could feel Jack's gentle presence next to her. "She ran away from me and stepped into the street, just as a carload of celebrating teenagers careened around the corner. She didn't have a chance.

"I visited her daily for months," she told Jack. "The doctors said they'd never seen anything like it. She showed intermittent brain activity, but wasn't responding to any other stimulus. She looked like Sleeping Beauty lying there, so beautiful and serene, except she had all those wires and monitors attached to her. Day after day, I sat there with no change, until one day I just . . . didn't go back.

"It was like she disappeared, just like Lily. I began to feel history repeating itself. One day she was here and then she was gone."

"Who?" Jack asked gently.

"What?" Monica looked confused, then shook her head before answering, "Both of them. Lily first, and then Daisy. Like I said, I tried to find Lily, but she'd vanished in thin air. The police said they couldn't do anything without more evidence that there'd been foul play and that she hadn't just wanted to move on. I figured, after everything that had happened between us, that she didn't want to be found. So I decided to become Daisy's mother with all my heart and never look back. That is, until the night we fought and the accident happened."

Jack put his arm around her. "Go on."

"Well, once the doctor said Daisy would never wake up, it was like when Lily ran away. I knew I had to go on with my life, but this time I didn't have anyone else to look after. That's when I decided to turn Daisy's room into my shoe sanctuary. I don't know what else to say." Monica paused and looked off into the distance.

"Something is changing, though," she said. "I think I need to go see her."

DAISY

Blue. There it was again. Everywhere. Enveloping her eyes. Cradling her spirit. Choking her throat.

"Albert? Are you there?" Daisy coughed. "I can't see anything. Chauncey? Anybody?" Her voice escalated as the blue blindness surrounded her. "Somebody, help me! I can't see. Or move!"

The last time this had happened, she'd been tucked safely inside Sir Albert's majestic plumes. But this felt entirely different. Daisy tried to move her arms and discovered she was swaddled tightly like a newborn infant. Panic rose in her throat. When she opened her mouth to scream, nothing came out. Silence. It was hard to comprehend how silence could make such a deafening sound.

Daisy could feel the inside of her brain expanding and pressing against her skull. Looking more closely at the movie playing on the inside of her blue eyelids, she saw herself floating above the scene. Somehow she was two Daisy's in the same moment: one rising toward the ceiling, the other inert on a table below.

The floating Daisy observed the other where she rested, a swaddled young woman, on blue sheets, wrapped tightly with blue hospital bandages. The walls were painted baby blue, like one would find in a nursery. Even the ceiling with its disgusting popcorn plaster was the same shade. On the walls hung blue paintings of turquoise countrysides and cobalt-faced people. Was that Mel Gibson from *Braveheart*? Or maybe *Avatar*?

Get a grip, Daisy. What's going on? She couldn't distinguish the observer from the inert person. Were they one and the same?

She noticed that the blue-curtained windows opened out onto a steel-blue sea, with a matching cloudless sky above. Blue ferns and palm trees swayed in the blue-tinted breeze. Indigo trees wrapped in glowing turquoise lights were scattered in the distance, and bluebirds flitted among the branches. Blue poppies were scattered across fields of Kentucky bluegrass.

Her focus veered outside, searching for another color without success. Glancing at her fingers—the observer's fingers, that was—she saw rings of turquoise and aquamarine glimmering in the sky-blue light. Her fingernails were dark navy, and her skin had gone blue, too.

"Albert? Chauncey? Anybody?" Daisy couldn't see it, but she knew there was a blue lozenge stuck in her throat and speech wouldn't come. The dark-blue silence enveloped her as she gazed at the inert figure on the table below.

The young woman's chest rose and fell with the rhythm of a waltz, probably "The Blue Danube." What else could it be? Elvis's "Blue Christmas" was too peppy, even though the sentiment was correct. In fact, the trees outside appeared to be dressed for the December holiday.

Visible eighth and half notes danced across the ceiling. Daisy zeroed back in on the blue brain she could see pulsing inside her skull. It looked like a robin's egg in both color and texture. Musical quarter notes—sapphire, this time—squeezed through tiny fissures that appeared while Daisy watched.

The skull was cracking open like an eggshell. Her brain was being turned into an omelet. Fractures and openings appeared before her blue-clouded vision. As she watched raptly, the blue notes took on a slightly purplish tint and melted into an oozing substance that dripped onto the blue pillow cradling Daisy's bursting skull.

POP! WHAM! BAM!

The Daisy on the table exploded, disappeared, and reassembled itself as the ghastly creature with a sinister voice that now filled the room.

"There you are, my dear. I've been looking for you."

Frantically, Daisy opened her mouth to scream, but was met with a terrified blue silence.

DAISY - MONICA - IZABEL

The Master sat perched in his hive and felt his body quiver with something he had never known before: *weakness*. My power is slipping away. What is happening to me?

In his viewfinder, the girl, Daisy, was fading from his vision. He couldn't see her clearly anymore. It was as though a fog were enveloping her. Even though he knew she was still there, his hold on her was slipping away.

On the other side of the island, Sir Albert whispered in earnest: "Daisy? Daisy, my dear? Are you all right? I'm right here, Daisy. Mommy's here."

"What? Albert? Is that you?"

"Yes, Miss Daisy. 'Tis me."

"Oh, I had the weirdest dream." The young girl looked at him with clear eyes. "I thought I heard you say, 'Mommy's here.'"

"Oh my. That *is* strange." The peacock frowned.

— — —

Monica sat staring at the sleeping figure. She glanced at her watch and saw it was 3 a.m. Her clothes were crumpled and her hair was flattened on one side from sleeping in the reclining chair. The Louboutin shoes lay on the floor next to her purse.

"Ms. Levin, can I get you anything?" the night nurse asked.

"No. Thank you." Monica absentmindedly ran her fingers through her hair.

"You're sure everything's okay?"

"Yes. Well. It's just that it seems like something's changed."

"What do you mean?" The nurse looked at Monica quizzically.

"I don't know exactly. It's probably nothing." Monica stared at the sleeping figure and frowned.

"I can call a doctor if you like, but her monitors are all reading the same as before."

"No. It's okay. I'm probably just tired." Monica shook her head like she was trying to rouse herself. Jack had put her in a cab the night before when she'd protested about him driving her home, but Monica had gone straight to the hospital instead of going home.

"Yes, ma'am. You should try to get some rest. Would you like me to bring in a cot?" The nurse looked at her with a puzzled expression. No real surprise there. Monica had virtually quit visiting months ago, ever since the doctor's prognosis that Daisy would most likely never wake up.

"I'm okay." Monica nodded, a pinched smile on her face. "I won't stay long, but thank you anyway."

"You're welcome, ma'am. I'll be at my station if you need anything."

Monica watched the nurse leave the room and then turned her attention back to the lifeless figure in the bed.

"Oh, Daisy. Where have you gone?" she whispered to the comatose reincarnation of Lily.

—   —   —

Daisy shuddered like a cold vapor had passed through her.

"Miss Daisy? Are you all right?" asked Chauncey, flipping his long tongue to catch a fly. "We were so worried about you."

"The last thing I remember was a table exploding around me and some horrible cackling sound."

On the other side of the island, The Master watched his shell begin to peel away and drop to the ground.

—   —   —

Monica awoke to a nurse laughing in the hallway and the smell of freshly steeped English breakfast tea. It was a pleasant sensation, until she felt the crick in her neck from sleeping askew in the hospital room chair.

"Hey, Sleeping Beauty. I thought I might find you here."

"What? Where am I? What's going on?"

"You fell asleep at the hospital." It was Jack, leaning over her. He brushed a stray strand of hair from her eyes and handed her a paper cup of tea with the Crazy Carl's logo on it. "I stopped by your house on my way to work, and when you weren't there, I decided to try here. How are you this morning?"

"I'm good, other than a stiff neck. How are you?" She smiled before taking a sip of her tea.

"I'm good, too. Do you want to go home for a while or shall we stay here?"

He said we, Monica thought, and smiled again. "I think I'd like to stay here, if that's okay with you."

"Fine by me." Jack settled into the chair next to Monica and pulled a copy of *Psychology Today* out of his briefcase.

Monica closed her eyes and dozed. Then something stirred to her right and caught her attention.

"Mommy? Is that you?"

The words had drifted faintly out of Daisy's heart-shaped mouth. Monica gasped.

"Did you hear that?" She turned to Jack.

"What?" Jack looked up from the magazine. "I didn't hear anything."

— — —

"Daisy? Are you all right? It's me, Chauncey." The colorful okapi looked into the face of the sleeping girl, and then leaned toward Sir Albert. "It sounds like she's dreaming. She keeps mumbling something that sounds like 'Mommy.'"

"Mommy is a traditional word used in the English language for one who has given birth to another. It's typically used by young humans such as Miss Daisy," replied the stately peacock.

"Why would she do that?" asked Chauncey, a puzzled look on his face.

"Because it's time for her to know the truth."

— — —

Miriam called Izabel later that afternoon.

"I've been doing some research. The good news is that your sister still lives in Seattle."

"Yes? And the bad? What about Daisy?" Izabel gripped the phone tightly.

"Well, the only record I could find of Daisy was an auto accident nearly two years ago."

Izabel's eyes grew wide as she held her breath. Panic rose inside her chest. "What? Oh my God, Miriam, we're too late, aren't we?"

"Slow down, my dear."

"What happened? Where is my daughter? Is she okay?"

"That's the part I don't know much about."

"Is she—"

"She's alive. However, she's been in a coma ever since the accident. I found her by calling several hospitals in the area. Unfortunately, they won't give me a prognosis, since I'm not family."

"Where is she?"

"Northwest Hospital."

— — —

Daisy opened her eyes to find the stately peacock and the wild-eyed okapi staring at her. "What's going on?"

"You keep talking in your sleep. Much more than usual."

"It's so weird," she said. "I keep seeing these two women, and they both say they're my mother. One looks like Ariel from *The Little Mermaid,* and the other . . . I can't tell what she looks like. It's super strange. Ariel seems like the real one, but she's so far away, underwater, like. You know?"

— — —

"Look! She blinked again. Did you see it?" Monica fairly screamed at Jack.

— — —

"Did I see what?" Daisy asked Sir Albert.

"I'm sorry, Miss Daisy, but I didn't say anything."

"Oh, man, I must be losing my mind."

— — —

"Call the nurse! Or the doctor! I swear she's waking up!" Monica tugged on Jack's arm.

— — —

"I'm already awake, Albert. What are you talking about?"

Daisy looked at the peacock. His feathers started to shift from brilliant sapphire blue and his face began to morph into a feline-like expression. Then his mouth began to move.

"A cat's rage is beautiful, burning with pure cat flame, all its hair standing up and crackling blue sparks, eyes blazing and sputtering."

"What the hell are you talking about, Albert?"

— — —

"What the hell are you talking about, Jack?"

"William S. Burroughs. I just read this quote in the journal where they describe how poetic prose or detailed descriptions can cause shifts in brain activity. I thought it might be worth a try."

"Read it again!"

"'A cat's rage is beautiful, burning with pure cat flame, all its hair standing up and crackling blue sparks, eyes blazing and sputtering.'"

Daisy stirred beneath her covers and the brain-activity monitor blipped wildly on the screen.

"Jack! Look! She's moving!" Monica sprang to her feet, pointing at the monitor and the girl lying in the bed.

— — —

"Are you okay, Izabel?" Miriam asked, as she tucked her friend into the small seaplane. During the short ride to the airstrip, she had watched the young woman shift from wild frenzy into a trancelike state.

"I just had the oddest memory. I saw Monica reading my favorite quote to me. I was about seven years old, and she must have been eleven or so."

"What's the quote, my dear?"

"It's about a cat's rage. William S. Burroughs. I always loved that as a kid."

"Of course." Miriam nodded knowingly. "Godspeed, Lily."

— — —

"Lily loved that story as a child," Monica mused. Her mood was vacillating between exhilaration and disappointment, since the monitor had stopped blipping and Daisy appeared to have returned to her previous state. "I started reading it to Daisy when she was just a kid." She paused thoughtfully. "I wrote down the quote in her graduation card. She was so beautiful that night—all flame and fire. Until . . . "

— — —

"Albert, oh my God. I *loved* that story as a kid. Pure cat flame. Blue was always my favorite color. Did you know that blue is the only color that always keeps its character in all its hues? Of course you know that. You're blue, for God's sake."

"Yes, Miss Daisy." The peacock nodded, and his plumed headdress shook.

"What's happening?" whispered Chauncey.

"I believe we're losing her. Just like we've lost the others. It must be time," Albert whispered back.

— — —

As Izabel stepped into the lobby of the hospital, there was an electric energy in the air. Doctors, nurses, and technicians scurried about. Something unprecedented seemed to be happening.

Stepping up to the reception desk, she said, "What's going on? It looks very exciting."

"Oh, it is!" The receptionist grinned. "A young woman who's been in a coma for nearly two years seems to be waking up!"

"Where? Where is she?" Izabel felt her heart lift into her throat.

"I'm sorry, ma'am, but I can't give out that information."

Izabel didn't wait another second. She started running down the hallway, following the commotion. "Monica? Daisy? Monica? Daisy?"

"Ma'am? Come back here. Ma'am!" called the flustered receptionist. "Stop her!"

"*Monica? Daisy?*"

— — —

"Do you hear that?" Monica asked Jack. "Someone's yelling my name."

"I'll go see." Jack stepped out into the hallway and collided with a frantic-looking red-haired woman. "Whoa there," he said, as he caught her in his arms.

"Let go of me! I have to find my daughter!"

"Lily? Are you Lily?" He looked into her eyes of pure cat flame.

"Yes," she whispered softly, relaxing as she heard the name she hadn't used for two decades.

"She's in here," Jack said, motioning toward the open doorway.

— — —

"Mommy? Is that you?" Daisy whispered.

"Yes," the two women responded simultaneously. "Mommy's here."

— — —

Across the island of Tausi, a puff of blue smoke erupted where The Master had previously reigned from his elaborate hive.

Looking upward, Sir Albert noticed the blue billows punctuating the air. "Yes, we've lost her, my friend," he said, nodding to his multi-colored companion. "But today they have found each other."

THE END

GRATITUDE

While writing is in essence a solitary act, I cannot in good conscience end this book without offering immense gratitude and thanks for those who have walked each step of the way with me in this grand adventure.

Blue began as a tug of my heart. Like Daisy, Monica, and Izabel, I was stuck in time. Suffering with a bout of writer's block after the publication of my non-fiction work, *As I Lay Pondering: daily invitations to live a transformed life*, I needed an impetus to move forward. National Novel Writing Month (NaNoWriMo) arrived at the perfect time, so I signed up and tossed my intention into the universe. Friends from around the world cheered me on and enthusiastically helped launch the project that turned into *Blue*.

Special thanks to fellow author Peggy Sarjeant who graciously invited me to join her writing group for their annual retreat that serendipitously began on November 1, 2012. It was at her home in the Methow Valley of Eastern Washington that I awoke on the first day of NaNoWriMo with Sir Albert, Daisy, and the land of Tausi dancing through my mind.

Every woman needs a friend or two who will tell her the truth no matter what. This task fell to artist Dianna Stevens Woolley, and to my friend in all things present, Sharon Richards. The two of them took on the task of reading 50,000-plus raw, unedited words with the mission of declaring if *Blue* was a story worth pursuing. Both gave their enthusiastic approval and each continued to encourage me every step of the way.

Many thanks to *Writer's Digest* workshops and teacher Mark Spencer for helping me put worthwhile edits into action. I will always remember Mark writing to me: "I think you might just pull this off." His words offered comfort in the low times when publication seemed impossible.

I offer Sir Albert-sized gratitude to Elizabeth DiMarco for her generous support and unflagging encouragement. Her read-through of the first edited manuscript was kind and ruthless. Her excellent feedback encouraged me to pull the manuscript apart and put it back together for a third and fourth time. Elizabeth has been my "Miriam" in this process. She opened doors for me that held magic behind them.

Every writer needs a place to read aloud. Thanks to Julie Gardner and her supportive writing groups who listened, read rough drafts, and offered feedback for new and old chapters. My creativity blossomed in the safe place she created.

Special thanks to Shari Stauch at Where Writers Win for telling me I was ready to publish and introducing me to the amazing people at BQB Publishing. Terri Leidich, Alex Padalka, and my editors have made the publication process relatively painless and almost always fun. Thank you a million times over.

You would not be holding this book in your hands without the tenacious support of my wonderful tribe of friends and fellow artists—local, virtual, and imagined. They have been buoyant with their encouragement as I celebrated milestones and shared in my sadness each time I cried with rejection. You know who you are and I thank you.

Finally, I share my eternal love with my beautiful family—Bill, Jonathon, and Maryjane—who continue to put up with my whacky ideas and give me the space and time to pursue my dreams. I am a grateful woman.

Thank you, dear reader, for coming on this journey with me. May you always have a wonderful tribe of supporters and may you be true to your own colors—whatever they may be!